FLAGS (

A James Acton Thriller

By
J. Robert Kennedy

Detective Shakespeare Mysteries
Depraved Difference
Tick Tock
The Redeemer

James Acton Thrillers
The Protocol
Brass Monkey
Broken Dove
The Templar's Relic
Flags of Sin

Zander Varga, Vampire Detective
The Turned

FLAGS OF SIN

A James Acton Thriller

J. ROBERT KENNEDY

Copyright © 2013 J. Robert Kennedy

CreateSpace

All rights reserved. No part of this publication may be reproduced, stored in or introduced into a retrieval system, or transmitted in any form, or by any means (electronic. mechanical, photocopying, recording or otherwise) without the prior written permission of the publisher.

This is a work of fiction. Names, characters, places, and incidents are products of the author's imagination. Any resemblance to actual persons, living or dead, is entirely coincidental.

ISBN-10: 1481860275
ISBN-13: 978-1481860277

First Edition

10 9 8 7 6 5 4 3 2 1

For those who struggle for freedom and democracy, wherever they may be.

FLAGS OF SIN

A James Acton Thriller

PREFACE

On April 15, 1989, students began to occupy Tiananmen Square in the Chinese capital of Beijing. These gatherings were initially to mourn the death of a liberal reform politician, Hu Yaobang, but over the next seven weeks expanded into a general protest demanding freedom and democracy for the Chinese people, with several hundred thousand students and residents participating.

On June 3rd, hundreds of thousands of troops from the Chinese 27th and 38th armies were sent into Beijing with orders to clear the square by 6:00am on June 4th. They were opposed by thousands of Beijing residents and students, who erected barricades to block their progress.

At 10:30pm troops opened fire, and the tanks rolled over the barricades and their guardians.

And the rest is history.

In the West we call it the Tiananmen Square Massacre.

In China, it is known as the June Fourth Incident.

Today, China is thought to be a country with little dissent. What isn't reported in the Chinese press, and rarely in the Western press, is that in 2010, it is estimated that over 180,000 separate "Mass Incidents" occurred, ranging from flash mobs to organized protests.

Dissent is alive and well in today's China.

And dissent in today's China, is still not tolerated.

Court of the Tongzhi Emperor
The Forbidden City, Beijing, China
January 13, 1875

"Get Our son out of here, now!"

Li Mei bowed to her emperor, deeply, and rushed to the crib holding the most precious thing she had ever had in her charge. The future emperor. The future Son of Heaven, and God's ruler of all under Heaven. She was only fifteen, but already trusted with the care of the most valuable child in all the world. It had been a shock, she a mere servant in the nursery, but when the surprise announcement had been made that the Emperor had a son, she had been chosen to care for it. The newly selected wet nurse, and one of her best friends, Yu, had said it was the very fact she was so young that she had been picked.

She was too young to have yet been corrupted.

Screams from outside the door, and the sound of a blade being drawn startled her. She looked at the heavy wooden entrance, and knew the Empress Dowager's troops were just outside, pounding on the thick oak.

"Do Our bidding!"

Her eyes darted to her glaring master, and she immediately dropped them in fear. *Never look your Emperor in his eyes. It implies equality, of which there is none.* "Sorry, my Emperor." She bowed then turned back to the crib, reaching in and picking up the little bundle.

A cracking sound.

She spun toward the door, and she could see the head of an axe being worked out from the other side in preparation for another blow.

"Wait!"

She froze and a moment later the shadow of her Emperor graced her being. He rubbed his thumb over his son's forehead. She dared not look to see if the boy's last vision of his father was that of a smiling man, or a terrified man. *Smiling. He's nearly a God, what does he have to fear?*

"Take him out the tunnels, keep him hidden, and when the time is right, tell him who he is. For he is the future. Today We may lose the seat of power to Our mother, but We will never lose the divine right to rule this land. Today We die, so that Our son may live to rule another day. Tell him it is Our wish that someday he return here, return here and take his rightful place on the altar of power, to lead his people into this new, maddening world."

"My Emperor, the door!"

They both turned to see one of the Imperial Guards pointing. The sturdy wood had done its job, delaying their besiegers, but it was ready to give, it finally able to take no more.

She felt a hand on her back, and she almost dropped to her knees to beg forgiveness for touching her Emperor, but it pushed her forward. "Now go!"

She bowed, then ran, joined by a dozen guards, and another dozen servants, all who provided the daily care their future emperor required, and would provide it tomorrow, should they succeed in escaping.

But that was still in question.

Yells erupted from behind them, followed by bloody screams at the sound of the door splintering open. Then the shouts of her brave emperor cut through the din of chaos as his mother's troops broke through. Swords clashed, steel on steel, the shouts of the brave men fighting to save their Emperor, the shouts of those same brave souls falling to the superior numbers. But it was the thought of her Emperor, bravely choosing to remain behind, to delay the troops long enough for them to get away, that filled her heart with pride and sorrow. He knew if he fled with them, through the only escape route available to them, they would be pursued. But by remaining behind, he gave his son a chance to live.

One must die, for the other to carry on the family dynasty.

Then there was silence, the swords still, and a voice, saying something she couldn't hear, the only noise now their own padded feet as they rushed down the corridor as stealthily as they could.

There was a thud, as if something blunt had hit something soft. A cry of pain and the clatter of a sword hitting stone. Another thud, another cry, and she knew it was her Emperor being hacked to pieces. She gasped as her chest tightened. She felt as if she would pass out, and nearly dropped the now Emperor she clutched to her bosom.

Hands grabbed her by the arms as she collapsed, someone else reaching for the baby. She held on tighter as she took a deep breath. *Be strong for the little one.* "I'm alright," she whispered, as she regained her legs, and continued around the corner, and farther from the horror she had just heard.

They reached the end of the hall and a guard held aside a tapestry depicting the birth of the Dragon King, one of her Emperor's favorites, as another pushed aside a secret panel. Through the opening she rushed, followed by the others, then they waited as one of their guards sealed the secret passage, locking it from their side so no one could pursue, or flee, should they know where it was.

For they had been betrayed.

Betrayed by someone amongst them. It was the only explanation for the ease of entry into the Forbidden City. And it was her new, greatest fear, for she had been given the honor of raising the young emperor, this tiny creature who was the greatest threat to the future of the Empress Dowager Cixi's reign, this tiny creature who would be worshipped by millions of loyal subjects, none of whom would be pleased once they discovered how brutally, and dishonorably, their Emperor had been murdered.

She eyed each of the soldiers and servants as they rushed down the dimly lit passage, the only light from torches carried by several of the guard.

Which one of you is the traitor?

East Chang'an Street, Approaching Tiananmen Square, Beijing, China
Today

"If there's anywhere we're safe, it's Beijing."

Famous last words.

Charles Redford looked at his boss sitting across from him, Ian Davidson, the US Ambassador to China, with a frown. "You read the security assessment by the specialists, sir. You know there've been specific threats made against foreign ambassadors over the past couple of weeks. And there have been dozens of reports of foreigners being attacked and murdered. Something's happening that the Chinese don't want us to know about."

"Nothing's happening, Charlie. You worry too much."

Somebody has to.

There had been whispered reports from all across the country for weeks, mostly rumors on the Internet, nothing in the official press, which didn't mean much. The official press in China was a joke. It was the State's messenger of all that was great about the Party. It was hardly a news source for anything internal. But the Internet was so tightly controlled, that even the whispers of troubles were being quickly quashed.

It wasn't until tourists stopped showing up for their return flights, stopped arriving home, that the alarm bells began to go off. That was one week ago. The first real requests for investigations had begun to arrive two days later, then the specialists had arrived to do a security review to ensure the safety of the American contingent in Beijing.

And their preliminary report had sent shivers down his spine.

Woefully inadequate.

That's what Mr. White had said about their security. The words echoed in his head as they drove toward the official residence. The weakest part of their security. White had said the embassy itself was fine, and the residence was fine, but it was the travel to and from that was *woefully inadequate*. It was Ambassador Davidson's insistence on driving by Tiananmen Square every day on his way home. And his insistence on lowering the window while doing so.

"Are we at least going to follow Mr. White's advice?"

Ambassador Davidson chuckled.

"Mr. White." He leaned forward, lowering his voice. "You *do* realize that's an alias."

Redford nodded. "Of course. I just assumed he's CIA or something."

Davidson shook his head. "No, we wouldn't risk bringing them in so obviously. No, these are Delta Force—"

The panel separating them from the driver lowered. "Sir, we're almost there."

"Thanks, Tom."

Redford moved aside as the Ambassador changed positions so he could lower the window and get a good view.

"Are we really going to do this, even after what Mr. White said?"

Davidson smiled at him, as if he were something to be pitied. "Mr. White is paid to panic. I'm not."

The statement was matter of fact. *Even if it's true, maybe he's got reason to panic.* Redford looked out the back window, the bullet proof glass at least providing some comfort. Their escort vehicle was close behind, four armed men, in addition to the four in the lead vehicle. Plus their driver and one escort in the passenger seat up front.

Ten armed, highly trained men, all to protect one man.

FLAGS OF SIN

Redford had no illusions that he would be anything but cannon fodder if the Ambassador's life were at stake, and it didn't really bother him that much. Dying did, and of course he would try to save himself as best he could, but he was also a realist. He was a plebe compared to the Ambassador.

"Here we go, sir!" called Tom from the front.

Redford watched Davidson press the button, the window lowering as they slowed. Tiananmen Square. It was beautiful. And massive. And a tomb to hundreds if not thousands of forgotten souls, the memory of the massacre that had taken place here in 1989 washed away by the communist state, and conveniently forgotten by Western governments eager to do business with the burgeoning economy.

It was almost sickening.

But it hadn't stopped him from jumping at the job. But then again he wasn't even in high school when the massacre had happened. He remembered it vaguely, but those memories might have been mixed in with his more recent viewings of all things China when he had first heard of his assignment.

That was two years ago.

And he had to admit, he loved it here. It was a mix of ancient history, with modern day wonders. The pollution knocked your socks off some days, the crowds could be intense, the cyclists infuriating, but you couldn't go ten feet without seeing something older than anything back home.

"Something's happening."

It wasn't the words, but the tone of Tom's voice that caused him to snap from his reverie.

"What is it?" asked Redford, the Ambassador apparently not having heard it, or simply not concerned.

"Holy shit!" It was the agent in the front this time. Redford followed his gaze and saw a person flying backward, then skidding twenty or thirty feet along the concrete of the square.

"What the hell was that?" asked Ambassador Davidson as his head jerked back in the window.

They all flew forward as Tom slammed on the brakes. Redford picked himself up off the floor of their hardened limo. "What the hell happened?"

But there was no response. Tom's head had turned back, and at first Redford thought he was checking on them, but when he tumbled forward again he realized the car was now in reverse, the accelerator pressed hard as the engine protested and the car raced away from whatever was happening.

"Fuck me!" exclaimed the agent in the front, whose name Redford couldn't remember at the moment.

"What's going on?" demanded the Ambassador.

"We're under attack!" yelled Tom. "Lead vehicle has been taken out. Shit!"

Brakes squealed and the rear seat passengers tumbled again. Redford took the opportunity to shove himself into the nearest seat and strap in. The car jerked forward again, and Ambassador Davidson rolled backward, slamming into the seat. Redford reached over and grabbed him, pulling him into the seat and strapping the disoriented man into place.

"You're bleeding, sir!"

Redford leaned forward, retrieving a handkerchief from his pocket and pressed it against the gushing wound on his boss' forehead. A shattering sound from up front, then something hit Redford in the back of the head. He gasped as the Ambassador's face was smeared in a red, sticky goo.

"Holy fuck!"

It was the agent. Redford's head spun toward the front and he gagged.

There was a six inch hole in the front windshield, and Tom's head wasn't where it should be. In fact, it was completely missing.

The driverless car jerked to a halt, hitting something, but Redford's seatbelt held him in place.

"What do we do?" he yelled at the agent, who was on his radio, providing their status. Something hit the car, then the windshield was blocked slightly as someone jumped on the hood. Redford's heart slammed into his chest and he reached down to unbuckle his seatbelt.

A gun shoved through the hole and began to belch led as he dove to the floor.

The Imperial Gardens, Beijing, China
January 13, 1875

Li Mei urged the little bundle in her arms to stop crying, her heart a lump in her throat as her eyes, filled with fear, probed the gardens they now ran through. It was an area of the city she wasn't familiar with, much of the life she remembered having been spent in the service of her Emperor, confined within the walls of the Forbidden City, with little time to enjoy its treasures.

Please be quiet!

The poor creature wailed, and Li Mei knew the tiny thing was terrified. She was sure he could sense the fear they all felt. It was palpable. Shouts of anger, screams of pain, were mere hedgerows away, and if the future emperor didn't quiet himself soon, they risked being discovered.

"Give him to me," said Yu, the wet nurse and her friend. Mei immediately handed him over, and the silence that ensued when placed on Yu's breast was a relief to them all.

A twig snapped, then a branch. Mei froze, as did Yu, but the four guardsmen in the lead continued forward, their swords drawn, their pace slowed, but only slightly.

They all knew they needed to get out of the gardens and into the prearranged shelter until nightfall. Two guardsmen took up position on their left, another two on their right, horn bows drawn, arrows in position, strings drawn back tight. Mei looked at the rear where the remaining four guardsmen, swords at the ready, warily walked sideways, their heads as if on pivots, looking about as they covered their escape.

Then all hell broke loose.

Shouts from all sides were heard, and the tall hedge began to shake, the branches snapping, loud against the tranquil garden, and the baby wailed as Yu spun toward a sound, her nipple popping free of his mouth.

"We need to move, now!" hissed Fang Zen, a well-respected warrior who had fought, and survived, many of the battles his Emperor and Empress Dowager had ordered him to. And in the ultimate indication of their Emperor's faith in him, he had named the warrior personal guard to his heir, and most prized possession. His son.

They moved forward, quicker now. Mei's world narrowed to the armor of the soldier directly in front of her. The sounds became distant, her ears consumed by the adrenaline fueled panic pounding inside her. She heard curious whooshing sounds to her sides, and distant screams, along with the blurred motions of the guards at her sides as they reached behind them for another arrow from their quiver.

A cry from beside her caused her to turn. It was too close to be one of the unseen enemy fighting its way through the thick hedge, the escape route having been grown over centuries, nursed lovingly by gardeners who intentionally guided the branches amongst each other, intertwining them over the years to create an almost impenetrable barrier. A single, long alley from the secret exit in the palace, through the heart of the gardens, and outside the city walls.

A secret passage, that no one knew about, even the gardeners segregated to work on it from the outside only, then once a year, a group of peasants would be selected from a distant province, and brought in, under blindfold and threat of death, to trim the interior, then returned, never to have known they were actually in the Forbidden City.

It was a total secret, a secret that no one knew except a few of the inner circle. A secret that had been revealed to the closest of the Emperor's staff only last night, out of necessity. A secret that someone had obviously revealed, if they were now under attack.

The source of the cry became evident as Yu began to fall to the ground. Mei reached forward as a look of horror spread across Yu's face, not at her impending doom, but at the baby now falling. Mei stopped, her slippers sliding on the gravel, causing her to fall to the ground. She watched the baby slip from Yu's grasp, wailing in confusion. Mei reached forward in a desperate bid to catch the child before he hit the ground, pushing with her toes against a rut her feet had caught in their slide. She fell toward the ground, arms outstretched, and barely managed to get her fingers under the tiny bundle before it hit. She pulled the baby to her chest and felt hands on her shoulders, dragging them both to their feet, as the group continued to silently move forward, the swoosh of arrows, the cries as impacts were made, the only sounds.

She looked ahead, and could see their destination, and wondered what awaited them there. If they had been betrayed already, and their route revealed, how could they possibly assume it would be safe ahead. She glanced over her shoulder, at the palace they had just fled, and knew they had no choice. They had to move forward, there was no going back, there was no remaining.

Whatever their fate would be, it would be decided at the end of this hedgerow.

And suddenly it stopped.

The shouts, the cries of arrows finding their targets, the sound of air being shoved aside as an arrow loosed. All silent. She looked at Yu, confused, but Yu wasn't looking at her. Her eyes were red from crying, and were focused on the baby, still clutched in Mei's arms. Mei reached out and squeezed Yu's shoulder with a reassuring smile. She looked up for a moment, and was about to say something when the column stopped.

Mei looked ahead, and saw they were at a rather nondescript door, a plain, heavy wood, unpainted, but reinforced with metal on this side at least.

And secured by a simple latch.

The sword wielding guardsmen rushed forward, leaving only two at the rear, the staff still flanked by the archers. The lead, Fang Zen, looked at his men, then pulled open the door, stepping back and out of the way as the door swung open.

Mei heard footsteps, and it took a moment to realize her eyes were squeezed shut, her heart, slamming against her ribcage, refusing to settle. "Let's go!" hissed someone. She stumbled forward, then forced her eyes open for the child's sake, and breathed a sigh of relief. The room on the other side of the door was empty. They had been betrayed, but even their betrayer must not have known where the hedgerow ended.

How long they could count on not being found, was anybody's guess, but she was certain it couldn't be long. She stepped through the door, which was then secured by a large wood bar, hooked across the frame.

No one else would be able to follow, without breaking down the door.

"Quickly, everyone change!"

Mei looked about, and saw the room split in two, Fang Zen urging the women to one side, behind a large screen, his men already stripping out of their armor. She followed Yu behind the screen, and found dozens of peasant's outfits, their dull blue almost an assault on her senses, she so accustomed to the opulent designs and colors of the imperial court.

But today was a day to blend.

She handed Yu the baby, then stripped out of her clothes as Yu removed the baby from his swaddling clothes, a wrap far too opulent for the masses. It took longer to disrobe than it did to put the simple outfit on, and when she was done, the baby was ready and handed to her as Yu began to change. Mei gave the little boy a kiss, her still hammering heart thankful he had remained quiet during the entire changeover.

"Ready?"

It was Fang Zen on the other side of the screen.

Mei looked about at the women, and all nodded.

"Yes."

Fang Zen rounded the screen, followed by his men. He turned to face them all. "Beyond this door"—he pointed at a small door she hadn't noticed before—"is the city. We will leave in pairs. One guard for each woman, separated by a one-hundred-count. Turn right, and walk this street until you reach a fountain. In that square there's a butcher's shop. Enter, and say, 'Our people have stood up.' You will be taken to the back, and to safety." His hand gripped the door handle. "Try to be calm, try not to run, and for the sake of our Emperor"—he nodded toward the tiny bundle Mei held—"remember who you are pretending to be. You are now commoners, amongst commoners. Don't forget that. Don't take on airs you are accustomed to when walking amongst these people, otherwise you will be spotted instantly."

He pointed at Yu. "You and I will go first." He pointed at his second-in-command, Su Ming. "You go with the boy next. Count to one-hundred before leaving."

Su Ming nodded, and Mei stepped over to him, trying not to squeeze her charge too tight in her fear.

Suddenly there was pounding on the door to the hedgerow. Yu yelped, and someone on the other side yelled, "They're still in there!"

Fang Zen lowered his voice. "Forget the one hundred count. Make it twenty. We can't all be seen leaving in a jumble. If they break through, those who remain, leave, but go left. Try to meet us at the butcher's shop later. But if you are captured, I expect you all to do your duty, and die for your Emperor."

With that he opened the door, peeked outside, then nodded at Yu, the two disappearing. Mei counted to twenty in her head, apparently quicker than Su Ming, who waited another full ten-count by her calculations, the door behind them beginning to splinter, several of the men having gone back to try and hold it in place. Now she knew why it opened toward the gardens. It was designed to keep people out of here.

She felt Su Ming's hand on her arm, and the door opened as he dragged her into the dusk. He gripped her arm tight as she tried to run, then as she looked about, she realized why his grip continued to tighten. They were surrounded by hundreds if not thousands of people. Her heart leapt into her throat, and she was about to scream when she felt herself being pulled to the right. She looked at Su Ming, who had his head down, his eyes looking at the ground, a sad look on his face.

She looked around again, and realized they weren't surrounded, they were merely amongst the regular throngs of people that inhabited the city. It had been so long since she'd been outside the palace walls, she had forgotten how crowded the city actually was. Her heart began to calm, and she dropped her head, falling in beside Su Ming as he established a steady pace that went with the flow of the crowd, rather than trying to push ahead.

His grip eased as he apparently realized she was okay, and eventually he released her. Mei, her head still bowed, tried to look up, to see if she could spot Fang Zen and Yu, but she couldn't, and she took that to be a good thing. She risked a quick glance over her shoulder, and saw a door open where she thought they had just come from, and two people exit.

She wondered who they might be.

And how many more would escape.

A scream rang out, and she looked back to see the same door thrown open and several women run out, a couple to the right, the rest having the presence of mind to go to the left, followed by a group of men, the guardsmen in disguise. She felt the hand grip her arm again, urging her forward, as she felt herself begin to become faint.

"Don't look," hissed Su Ming.

But she couldn't help it. The Empress Dowager's men were now appearing through the door, spreading out in all directions, and chasing after anyone that was running away.

She felt a hand on her chin redirect her head away from the scene.

"You must remain calm, or you will get us all killed!" he whispered.

She nodded, and they continued moving forward. Footsteps pounded by them, and she recognized two of the servants from the court, ignoring their instructions to flee in the opposite direction.

More shouting, more foot falls, then someone grabbed her by the shoulder, twisting her around and pushing her into Su Ming. She nearly dropped the baby, but Su Ming reached out and caught him, pushing him back into her arms, as he put his other arm over her shoulders and pulled her to the side of the road as the Empress Dowager's troops rushed by. They stood and watched, heads low, much like the rest of the throng caught in this moment of history.

A cry, a voice she recognized immediately as Yu's, tore through the narrow road. A shout from Fang Zen, the sounds of blades clashing, then a groan as someone's blade successfully penetrated. More clashing, and Mei swore she saw sparks fly into the air as if fireworks were spewing from their blades, then Yu rushed by them, two of the Empress' guards chasing her. Yu gave Mei a quick glance, the terror in her eyes causing a pit in Mei's stomach to open up and swallow any courage she might have had.

Su Ming's hand rose slightly off her shoulders and pushed her chin away from the pursuit of Yu. And he was right. If she paid too much attention, it might make them a target. Another groan from the right, and her head darted to where Fang Zen had been fighting. Swords continued to clash, grunts of exertion, moans of pain filled her ears, but the fact the fight continued gave her hope that Fang Zen might still prevail. He was the most skilled fighter she knew, and if anyone stood a chance against the Empress Dowager's guardsmen, he did.

Even if it was six to one.

Su Ming pulled her toward the fighting, but continued to hug the edge of the street. As they moved past the scene, she could see four of the guardsmen on the ground, either dead or writhing in pain. Blood flowed freely from Fang Zen's left shoulder, but his sword, wielded from the right, continued to swing smoothly, and a fifth man went down. Su Ming urged her forward, and for a split second she saw Fang Zen make eye contact with her, as he plunged his sword behind him, burying it into the belly of his final opponent. With a twist, he yanked it out, then fled down the street, ducking into an alleyway.

Mei wondered if she would ever see him again.

Meridian Gate, The Forbidden City, Beijing, China
Two weeks ago

Deniz stared up at the doors, his mouth agape. He reached forward and found his hand resting on one of the dozens of golden door nails, arranged in a nine by nine array, that adorned the massive entrance to the Forbidden City. Just the name had always sent a chill down his spine, and now that he was here, he couldn't believe his good fortune. It had been a trying time. His wife, Alex, had lost her job during the follow-on to the Great Recession, and he had barely scraped by, having to take a pay cut just so the company could stay afloat.

But they had managed. They had made it through. He still had his house, albeit the price they could get for it was scarcely higher than what he owed the bank, but he had never missed a payment. Some days it had meant Kraft Dinner and tuna for supper, but since they didn't have kids at home to try and explain the tough times to, they simply made do. Cable had been cut, cellphones cut, home phone features scaled back, car sold and downsized to a tiny Mazda 2, and public transport used whenever possible.

Life had been tough.

He held out an arm and he felt Alex tuck herself under, the warmth of her touch bringing him all the comfort he had ever needed in those hard times. He squeezed her against him and sighed, still staring up at the massive doors.

"Amazing, isn't it."

She pressed her head harder against his chest.

"It's beautiful."

He looked down and kissed the top of her head, inhaling her scent, so familiar after almost thirty years of marriage. She looked up at him and smiled. Her eyes were starting to show her age, and her golden blonde hair was a little more dull, but to him, she was still the beauty he had married, and all he saw was her brilliant smile that conveyed the love they still shared, and the golden curls he had so desperately wanted to run his fingers through when he first met her in college.

"I can't believe how lucky we are," she whispered.

He leaned in and gave her a peck.

"Incredibly lucky."

And they had been. There was no way in hell they could afford this vacation, but on a whim she had entered a radio contest, and six months later, here they were. An all-expense paid ten day trip to China. They had debated trying to sell the trip to someone else, but in the end had decided they should take it themselves. They hadn't been able to afford to travel for years, and had no idea when they'd be able to travel again. This might be their last chance, so they were treating it like a second honeymoon, their first, back when they were dirt poor, searching the cushions on the couch for change to go grab an ice cream, was a trip to Atlantic City for the weekend.

They hadn't gambled, except for a dollar in the slots. And once that had been eaten sixty seconds later, Deniz had said 'Never again' and left the casino. Instead, they spent their time on the boardwalk, hand in hand, stealing kisses whenever they could, and in their room, stealing a lot more.

His heart raced slightly at the memory.

God, to be young and in love again.

"Shall we?" he asked, holding his arm out toward the interior of the Forbidden City.

"Absolutely."

They stepped across the threshold, and into the massive, ancient city. It was stunning. The bright reds, oranges and golds, the ancient structures, painfully preserved, impressive in their detail, left him breathless. He looked down at Alex, and was about to say something when she was torn from his arms. His head spun to follow her as she was dragged away from him, outside of the city, the expression on her face one of shock.

Then a loud cracking sound, as if the end of a whip had snapped inches from his face, echoed through the walls of the mighty palace, sending a chill through him that rippled goose bumps up his arms, his hairs standing on end. He turned to run toward her, his mouth opening to cry out her name, when he felt something shove against his back. He jerked forward, his body picked up from the ground, and he found himself racing toward his wife, now prone, with, to his horror, a gaping red hole, grapefruit sized, in her stomach.

He collapsed unceremoniously beside her, and tried to reach for her, only inches away, but couldn't move his arms.

Then the pain hit.

Excruciating, all-consuming pain, radiating from his back. He lay, unable to move, the only fortunate thing he could find in the situation the fact his head was facing his beloved Alex. Her head turned toward him, the pain and fear in her eyes evident. Her mouth moved, but no sound came, then he gasped as he watched the last of the life drain from her face, her eyes dimming, the golden locks he had loved so much, seeming to tarnish before his eyes.

Alex!

But he couldn't move his own lips. The pain was gone now, as if drained away from him, along with any energy he might have once had. He heard voices yelling, footsteps pounding, and his own heart, beating in his ears, a dull remnant of what it should be, a pace so slow, he knew he was dying.

With one last effort, he willed his arm to move, and his last vision, his last sensation of any kind, was the feeling of his hand on his wife's face, as everything went black, his heart taking one final beat, sending a burst of blood toward his outstretched hand, so he could feel her soft cheek one last time.

Outside the Forbidden City, Beijing, China
January 13, 1875

Li Mei, her priceless bundle, and Su Ming, the second-in-command of the Imperial Guard, and her sole protector, stood at the mouth of an alleyway, staring at the fountain gently gurgling not twenty feet away. And beyond that, their sanctuary.

"Why don't we go?" she asked quietly.

"Wait," was the whispered, abrupt reply.

Mei chanced a look up at him, and saw his eyes darting back and forth, as if he were examining every corner of the square, every face that occupied it. She looked at the fountain, and realized that she had looked at nothing but since they arrived.

She decided to help.

She started on her left, her eyes peering in every window, every doorway, any place a guardsman might hide, and found nobody who appeared to be hiding, simply the residents of this area going about their business.

Then she turned her attention to those residents. She figured if they were moving, then they were probably not watching the butcher's shop, they were merely innocent bystanders.

Instead, she focused on those not moving. Those standing. Sitting. Lying in wait. To her left, a man squatted on the curb, his ratty blue pants all he wore, no shirt in sight to conceal a weapon. She dismissed him. Next candidate. A younger man, standing with a woman, both with their heads held low. The woman fidgeted, her sandaled foot kicking at a stray rock. She looked up.

And Mei gasped.

"It's Xiao!" she hissed.

"I know. And Zhu, one of my men."

She felt butterflies in her stomach as she realized they had been behind them, and had fled away from the butcher shop. If they had been able to make it, then perhaps there was a chance others had as well.

"Stop smiling."

She immediately frowned. Perhaps a little too much. She tried to relax, but she couldn't. Her heart was pounding harder and harder, and she felt her legs and feet twitching, wanting to make the desperate race across the square and into the safety of the butcher's shop themselves, her brain be damned. She leant forward, and felt the grip on her arm tighten slightly.

"They're moving."

"Yes, I ordered them to."

"How?"

"With a nod of my head."

Mei was impressed. Zhu's eyesight must be much better than hers, as she wasn't certain she would be able to see someone nod their head slightly from that distance, with so little light left. She watched, her mouth agape for a moment before she realized and snapped it shut, as Xiao, led by Zhu, strolled across the square, and into the butcher's shop, as if with a purpose. No hesitation, no looking about, simply a husband and wife going to the butcher's.

And no one followed.

Her twitching increased ten-fold.

The grip on her arm only tightened slightly.

It was as if Su Ming could read her thoughts. His mere hand on her arm was enough for him to read her entire body, to know how desperately she wanted to flee across the square and into the arms of whoever stood on the other side of that door.

"Look." She glanced up at Su Ming, then followed his stare to watch a robed figure enter the square opposite them, glance around, then limp to the entrance of the butcher's shop, and finally disappear inside.

"Who was that?"

"Fang Zen, my captain."

Her face erupted with a smile that she quickly wiped away by clamping down on her cheek with her teeth.

"It's time," said Su Ming. "Keep control of yourself. Head down, dutiful wife, no talking or looking at anyone, especially once we get inside. We don't know who we can trust in there."

She nodded, her head already down, her chin on her chest.

He tugged slightly on her arm, and they stepped into the square, crossing it at a reasonable pace. Though her head was lowered, and her teeth clamped shut, her eyes were flitting from side to side, looking for anything out of the ordinary, and she willed her ears to listen harder than they ever had before, and prayed that her little majesty would remain quiet.

As they approached the door, they heard voices, raised. She immediately recognized Fang Zen's, and felt her heart leap into her throat as the words "Unhand me!" escaped the darkened entrance. The grip on her arm tightened. More than slightly. But they continued to approach. She felt herself tug away, desperate to go in any direction but the butcher's shop, but Su Ming kept leading them directly there.

He's the traitor!

It made sense. It would have to be someone high ranking in the guard or among the servants in order for them to have known of the escape route. And now, here they were, among a small group to have survived, and he was leading her, with an iron grip, directly toward their capture.

She wanted to cry out, to scream for help, but who would help her? Clearly there were soldiers on the other side of that door, and probably hidden throughout the square, concealed far better than her untrained eye could detect.

They were less than twenty paces from the door. Her heart hammered in her chest, the baby stirred, perhaps detecting her discomfort. A tear rolled down her cheek, the grip tightened further as she pulled away again.

Then, gradually, to her amazement, they turned to the left, past the door, and into an alleyway to the side of the shop. They continued walking, and her heart began to settle. They stopped, about one hundred paces further on, in another square bustling with activity, it apparently a farmer's market of some type.

"Wait here. I'm going back to try and stop anyone else from going inside. I'll send them this way if I can."

She nodded, her head bowed low in the shame of what she had thought he might be. She felt Su Ming's hand on her shoulder. She looked up. He smiled at her.

"You thought I was a traitor."

It was a statement, not a question.

She nodded.

"As I would have," he said, his voice gentle. He lowered it further. "If I'm not back in one hour, it will be up to you to hide the baby, and raise him. Do you have family?"

She nodded.

"Then go to them if I do not return."

She nodded again.

He squeezed her shoulder then turned around, walking casually back to the square, and the danger it contained. She watched him disappear into the shadows, only to reappear as some sliver of sunlight revealed him once more. Then finally, with the turn of a corner, he was gone.

And she waited.

Forbidden City, Beijing, China
Two weeks ago

Inspector Li Meng absentmindedly scratched behind his ear as he took in the scene in front of him. It was something he would imagine in a war movie, or some Hollywood blockbuster, meant to shock and titillate an American audience long ago desensitized to violence.

But as a thirty year veteran of what was now called the Public Security Bureau, he had never seen anything like it. To Li it was something out of a horror novel, and he had a hard time looking at it.

Two bodies, gaping holes in their torsos, as if they had been impaled by a large tree, lay side by side, the male's hand resting on the cheek of the female.

Touching.

But it was the blood pattern that had him shaken. It began with a massive spray at the gates to the Forbidden City, where the initial impact had obviously taken place, an impact that had blown them away from the doors a good ten meters at least.

What kind of weapon can do this?

He squatted at the entrance, putting his head at about the height he estimated the victims were hit, then, taking a bead on where their bodies now lay, he tried to determine where the shooter might have been. He found himself looking at the roof of the Gate of Supreme Harmony.

"Don't you know squatting is frowned upon in modern Beijing?"

He looked over his shoulder and up at his partner, Inspector Hu Ping. She smiled and held out a large Starbucks coffee. He pushed himself to his feet and took the steaming brew.

"Thanks," he said, taking a sip. He looked at her. "And I'll have you know I wasn't squatting. I was trying to figure out where our shooter may have been."

Ping looked at the victims. "Are you sure we're not looking for a tank?"

Li chuckled then immediately cut himself off. "We must be serious. There are too many eyes here," he muttered.

Ping nodded, sipping her coffee. "Sorry," she mumbled into the cup.

Li gave her a half wink, just for her benefit. She was young, only twenty-five, and the first of her cohort to begin taking real jobs in society, and the first cohort to have been corrupted by the modern influences of the Western decadent lifestyle. He was of another generation, a little simpler perhaps, much more conservative, but he had to admit the new freedoms and prosperity that had come to his country over the past decade were welcome.

And he took a sip of one of those new freedoms.

Li beckoned one of the officers and he jumped it seemed several centimeters straight up then rushed over.

"Yes, sir?"

"Have someone look at the top of that roof"—he pointed through the gates—"and see if they find anything. Bullet casings, anything. Be careful not to destroy any evidence—everyone wears gloves."

The man bowed, then rushed off to carry out his orders with one of his fellow officers. Li turned back to the blood splatter.

"So what *do* we have here?" asked Ping.

"It looks like two tourists were shot with a *very* high-powered rifle from—I would guess—the top of that roof." Again he pointed.

"Motive?"

"None of the traditional motives, I would think. Obviously not robbery, I doubt it was jealousy or some love-triangle. Not with a weapon like that."

He rubbed his chin then scratched behind his ear. "No, I'm guessing they were specifically targeted—some sort of assassination—or randomly targeted, perhaps for being tourists, for some political statement."

"I think we can operate under the assumption that the latter is not true."

Li jumped at the voice behind him and Ping almost spit her coffee. He instantly recognized the voice of Superintendent Hong Zhi-kai, their boss.

"Practicing your stealth techniques again, sir?" asked Li with a smile as he turned to face the man five years his junior—at least. With good family contacts, Hong had risen up the ladder far faster than Li could ever dream, and would continue rising so long as his family was in favor with the Party apparatchik. Li, on the other hand, came from a poor family, and was lucky to have risen as far as he had.

That was one difference in Chinese society compared to Western. At least he thought it was if he was to believe the limited Western propaganda he'd been exposed to. In the West, you could advance on merit and hard work, all the way to the top. A black president with a Muslim name was proof of that, or so he had heard. But in China? You only advanced to the upper levels if you were connected.

Or had something on someone who was.

But he didn't care. It was a good life. A life of service, a life he could be proud of, and it afforded him a salary sufficient enough to take care of his beloved Xiao, and their daughter Juan. And if things kept going the way they were going, he could only see things getting better.

"I hardly think humor is appropriate at a time like this," scolded Superintendent Hong.

Li gave a bow. "Of course, sorry, sir. It is just my way of relieving the tension such a gruesome scene inevitably produces."

Hong seemed satisfied with the explanation, and pointed to the roof inside the Forbidden City that now had several officers on top.

"What are they doing?"

"Looking for shell casings. I believe the shooter may have been on top of that roof."

"Based upon what?"

"Just a guess at the trajectory."

"We don't guess when it comes to homicides."

Li bowed, getting a little pissed off. "Of course not, sir. It was simply an hypothesis based upon my nearly thirty years of experience, sir."

There was a yell from the roof, and one of the men stood, waving.

"That appears to have paid off," interjected Ping, who quickly looked away from the glare Hong gave her.

"I see your insubordination has rubbed off on your partner."

Li wasn't sure what to say.

"Relax, both of you, I'm just keeping you on your toes." He sighed. "Sometimes I wonder if I'm cut out for this type of life."

Now Li definitely wasn't sure what to say. He scratched behind his ear.

Hong dismissed the statement with a wave of his hand. "Don't worry yourselves. My mother-in-law is visiting. This is about the only opportunity I get to feel like I'm in control of some part of my life. For two weeks I definitely haven't been in control at home." He smiled and slapped Li on the back. "We choose our wives, but not their families!"

Li smiled politely, and bowed.

Hong leaned in, lowering his voice.

"But I was serious about one thing. Keep this quiet. No press, no leaks. We can't have people finding out that tourists are being killed by some crazed sniper."

Li nodded, his alarm bells immediately going off as Hong walked away to glad-hand with an official who had just arrived.

"Did you hear that?" hissed Ping.

Li nodded.

"Do you think he means that these aren't the first?"

Li frowned. "I hesitate to guess what he means."

But if these aren't the first, then what we have here is far bigger.

And far more terrifying.

FLAGS OF SIN

Outside the Forbidden City, Beijing, China
January 13, 1875

Li Mei stepped deeper into the shadows. It had been far longer than an hour, perhaps two or three. She had lost track of time, and could only guess by how low the sun was on the horizon, the long shadows cast across the now quiet farmers' market speaking volumes to the hour.

And a woman, alone, with a baby, standing in the street, was bound to draw the attention of anyone looking for exactly that.

She knew what Su Ming had said. Go to her family if he wasn't back in an hour. But she hadn't lost hope yet. She had edged much of the way back down the alley on several occasions, and peered around the corner where she had lost sight of him, and she was certain she had seen him on at least one of those occasions, though it was hard to tell in his peasant outfit.

A sandal scraped on stone, and her head whipped around to find two people half walking, half running, down the alley. Her heart leapt. It was Yu and one of the soldiers from the court whose name she did not know.

"Over here," she whispered.

They stopped and looked, then smiled as they walked casually over.

"Are you okay?" Mei asked.

Yu nodded, and peeked at the baby. "And you?"

"Terrified. Have you seen anyone else?"

Yu shook her head. "Only Su Ming and you. I found Jun just minutes ago near the fountain."

Mei looked at Jun and nodded, now that she had a name to go with the face. "We saw Xiao, one of the maids, and Zhu, one of the soldiers, enter the butcher's shop, then Commander Fang went in. There was a struggle inside when Su Ming and I walked by, so we kept going."

"We've been betrayed," said Jun, his face grim, his eyes flaring with anger.

"What are we to do?" asked Yu, biting her finger.

"We can't leave without Su Ming," said Mei.

Yu nodded. "I told him I have a brother not far from here. I gave him directions and told him to meet us there. He's going to pass the word to anyone else who may show up. He didn't mention you, so I suspect he thinks you've already left."

Mei nodded. "I was supposed to leave two hours ago, but I just couldn't bring myself to."

Jun put a hand on her shoulder. "You'll come with us." He looked about. "We'll go on ahead, you follow us, no closer than twenty paces."

Mei nodded, and Jun took Yu by the arm, and they walked purposefully across the mess of the market. Mei counted to twenty, then followed, praying the little one would remain quiet now that they were moving again.

Jun and Yu disappeared around a corner, and she found herself wanting to rush forward to regain sight of them, but she resisted, maintaining her pace, despite the hammering of her heart in her ears. She rounded the corner and nearly peed, as four of the Empress Dowager's personal guard ran toward her. Her eyes darted to the left, then the right, desperate to find a hiding place, but none was to be had. And besides, it was too late. They were only paces from her when she first saw them, and now were almost upon her.

She dropped to her knees and bowed, dropping one hand to the filthy stone and rubbing it in the mud. She raised the hand and rubbed the dirt on the little one's face, then she smeared the rest across her own as they came to a halt and surrounded her.

"Get up!" ordered one of them.

She stood slowly, keeping her head bowed.

"What is your business here?" demanded the man directly in front of her.

Her mouth was dry, her tongue like withered reeds. She mumbled.

"Speak up, woman!"

"Do you have any food for a poor woman and her child?" she asked, her voice barely a whisper.

The man reached forward and grabbed her by the chin, pushing her head up. She caught a glimpse of Yu further down the street, stopped, but not facing her. The man's eyes looked at her in disgust, then down at the baby.

"You're both filthy! As a mother you should be ashamed!"

She dropped her head as soon as he let go, and bowed profusely. "Your words are too true, too true," she repeated, again in the hoarse whisper.

"You disgust me," he said, spitting at her feet, then stepping around her. "Let's go, these aren't the ones we're looking for."

She began to breathe a sigh of relief when a hand tapped her on the shoulder and she nearly screamed. She spun her head around and saw an outstretched hand. It contained several scarred coins.

"Take them, you need them more than I do."

She stretched out her hand, and her heart nearly stopped as she saw how much it shook. The coins were deposited in her palm, then the soldier closed her hand around them lest they should fall onto the road.

"Now go."

She stood frozen, unable to move. She felt his hand on her shoulder. It squeezed gently. She looked up. Her jaw dropped as she recognized the young man in front of her as a soldier she had seen many times in the Empress Dowager's court.

He smiled at her.

"Go, Mei, and save our future emperor."

National Stadium, Beijing, China
One Week Ago

Chris looked up at the massive structure, his mouth agape. "It's incredible!" he exclaimed. He looked down at his much shorter wife, who too was staring at the combination of glass and metal towering above them. "You can see why they called it the Bird Cage."

Anne-Marie nodded. "Reminds me of that nest above our door that bird kept trying to build last year."

Chris chuckled at the memory. "I think I had to clean that out every day for almost a month. Persistent little bugger." His experienced eye took in every square inch of the structure it could manage. An architect himself, he had just finished his involvement with the Freedom Tower in New York City, and as a reward, he and his wife decided to fulfill a lifelong dream—visit China.

It was a blowout, four week vacation, where he wasn't skimping on anything. The downturn hadn't hit them at all, his work secure due to the project he was on, and though he felt some sympathy for those actually losing their jobs, he felt little sympathy for those losing their homes due to having taken on ridiculous mortgages.

Think people! How can you earn forty-k a year and expect to afford a four-hundred-k home?

As an architect, he was always floored at how much square-footage the average American thought they needed to live comfortably. Every year the average seemed to go up, the footprint getting larger and larger as each new-home season began. He thought of the homes he had seen last year in

Europe when travelling on business. These were well-off people, living in half of what an American would find acceptable, yet perfectly content.

And we wonder why it all collapsed.

A massive Ponzi-scheme, funded by the average person, who trusted the experts advising them. *Don't worry, just pay the interest now, and when the balloon comes due, your house value will have risen so much, you can just flip it and double your money.*

Chris frowned. *Yeah, and what happens when someone wises up?* But he knew the answer. The bubble bursts, and the very people who gave the bad advice, not out of the desire to improve their customers' lives, but to line their own pockets, get bailed out by the very taxpayers they bilked.

He understood the anger of the Occupy protestors, but their anger was directed at the wrong people, at least it was after the first couple of weeks. Once the unions and politicos got involved, the protesters were merely pawns, their message manipulated by experts without them even knowing it.

One thing the kids protesting didn't get was that they were most likely part of the one percent. This was the fault of a society so successful until the Great Recession the kids had no way of knowing how good they have it compared to most of the world's population. There are almost two hundred countries in the world, and less than a couple of dozen actually have any significant immigration.

It's so bad out there, despite all of our problems, they still want to come here.

When the daily wage for eighty percent of the world is under ten dollars, food is a constant struggle and personal safety is a daily concern. The average American salary of over $30k per year is an unimaginable dream that the Occupy protesters apparently feel isn't enough for the common man. Laughable.

Protesting against bailouts, he agreed with. You never throw good money after bad. Auto bailouts? Never should have happened. He firmly believed that those that couldn't survive, should have been allowed to fail. The proof was Ford. A rock solid American company now, but not always. It had had its difficult days, but made the proper decisions years before the recession hit, reducing costs, improving their product, and when the buckets of cash were offered, they were able to turn them down.

And the naïve notion that if they weren't bailed out, hundreds of thousands of jobs would be lost, was ridiculous. He knew enough about supply and demand to know that for one thing, the millions of cars produced by GM and Chrysler would still be needed. It wasn't like millions of Americans were ready to just stop driving because there were no cars to buy, and second, other companies would have swooped in to fill the demand, and the only way to quickly fill the demand, is to keep those factories open, with the existing workers. Would those workers have been forced to accept a more reasonable wage and benefits package? Absolutely, but when your workers are getting free weekly Viagra handouts, perhaps your union has run out of reasonable things to demand.

He understood the need for unions years ago. It was the unions who helped bring in decent salaries, five day workweeks, forty hour workweeks, benefit packages. But now they had lost their way. The laws were now in place to protect workers from the very things they had formed unions to gain protection from. It is now against the law to force someone to work more than forty hours, to put them in dangerous situations, to not give them time off. Would some employers take advantage of workers if there was no union? Absolutely. But with the vast majority of Americans not unionized, if this were a real concern, wouldn't they all be up in arms?

Unions helped make America great, but now some were destroying it by becoming politicized and forgetting their real role. Manufacturers were fleeing the country to build the wares Americans demanded, fleeing to countries with far cheaper labor. Did he agree with the ridiculously low wages paid to these workers? Of course not, but it was an economic reality that America had to wake up to. A unionized bus driver shouldn't be getting nearly six figures with overtime, when a researcher in a lab, working on the cure for cancer, who spent seven years in university, but isn't unionized, makes less.

And is perfectly happy with what he makes.

He stared at the incredible feat of engineering in front of them and wondered how much it cost to build, and how much it would have been in America. What he had seen in his first two weeks in China had been breathtaking. The progress they were making was incredible. This was where the unions were needed. He wasn't blind to the fact the population was poor, and those building the infrastructure were paid a pittance, but he also wasn't blind to the fact that this economic progress had created a burgeoning middleclass that would soon rival that of America.

And if we don't get our act together, it will be a Chinese flag planted on the moon or Mars, orbiting in space, or on the soil of the very countries we have vowed to protect.

He shuddered to think of what would happen when China had a blue water navy that could rival our own. Their first aircraft carrier was in testing, a second was being built. Their first stealth fighters were already flying, and with no qualms of stealing any and all industrial and state secrets, with no repercussions because we needed them to buy our treasury bonds due to our massive deficit, there was little we could do to stop them.

And the next Bird Cage would continue to be built.

I just hope democracy catches on here before it's too late.

He felt a tug on his hand and he looked down at Anne-Marie. "Sorry, Hon, lost in thought."

She smiled. "I recognized that distant stare. Let me guess, wondering about how much this would have cost to build back home?"

A smile stretched across his face as he laughed. "My God, you know me waaay too well."

She motioned with her head. "Let's go. There's lots more I want to s—"

It was as if she had been grabbed by the back and torn from his hand. Her arms and legs seemed to remain in place for a split second, then her entire body was shoved thirty feet from where he stood as a snapping sound he didn't recognize echoed through the park.

"Anne-Marie!"

He turned, pushing his legs as hard as he could, trying to close the distance between them. A moment later he saw the prone figure of his wife jerk, and shoot back another ten feet, but this time something was different. As he closed the distance, it took a few seconds for his mind to comprehend the horror it was witnessing.

His wife's body had been torn in two pieces.

Her waist and legs were nearest, her upper torso, including arms and head, were another ten feet distant. His realization of this sent bile spewing from his mouth as he felt a terrific force slam into his back, then heard another snapping sound as he was sent sprawling forward. He hit the ground hard, then rolled several times before coming to rest beside the upper half of his wife's body.

There was no pain. No feeling whatsoever. No sensations. Just the dead stare he saw on his beloved's face, the same stare all he too could manage as he felt the life drain from him.

His last sensation was that of a single tear rolling across the bridge of his nose, then dripping onto the ground.

I love you.

Outside the Forbidden City, Beijing, China
January 13, 1875

Li Mei rubbed at the mud that had now hardened on her face. Then she stopped herself. It was a disguise that had worked once, and she may not have a chance to replace it should it be necessary.

But the little one.

If the Emperor saw his son, how his face was soiled with common street grime, he would most definitely be horrified, and whoever had let his son get in such a state would most definitely be put to death. Or at least cast out of the palace with nothing but shame on their family name.

But he was dead. She was sure of it. She was certain she had heard his cries as he was murdered by the traitorous troops loyal to the Emperor's "doting" mother, the Empress Dowager Cixi.

Mei had been in the next room when they had fought. It was plain to everyone from the beginning that there was no love shared between the eighteen year old emperor, and his mother. Her child being a boy meant continued power. Having usurped the regents appointed to rule in his stead until he was old enough, she was the true power until he had come of age, and even then, had continued to be the iron fist behind the young man.

But when he had a son, it had all changed. He had begun to assert himself, to overturn some of her rulings, to push back against some of her mad philosophies.

And she would have none of it.

Mei had cowered in the next room when the Empress Dowager had her final fight with the Emperor. But her style wasn't to yell. It was to talk at a near murmur, barely audible to those not close to her. Her voice, old, gravelly, to the point she almost sounded like her late husband should, sent fear through those around her. And that fateful evening, when Mei was in the side chamber washing the baby in preparation for a visit with his father, she had heard the Emperor's side of the conversation, increasingly agitated and angry, but consistently answered by the low, sotto voce of the Empress Dowager.

Until her final line, delivered louder than Mei had ever heard her speak. It wasn't a yell by any means, merely a line spoken at a volume most would consider normal, but from her, it was chillingly ominous.

"Never doubt, my son, that you can be replaced."

He had yelled after her, demanding she explain herself, but she had left. When Mei had entered the room with the baby shortly thereafter, she found the Emperor perched on the edge of his favorite chair, his head held in his hands with a distant, vacant stare that bore through time as he apparently recalled the conversation.

He held a hand up at her as she approached, and she stopped, bowing low. He snapped his fingers at one of the aides. The man jumped several inches, running to his Emperor, bowing deeply.

"Get Us the Captain of the Guard."

The man bowed even deeper, and backed away, not turning until he had reached the door. His footfalls could be heard tapping down the stone hallway as the Emperor waved Mei over.

"Let Us see Our boy," he said with a smile, his hands held out. She handed the child over, herself still in a deep bow, then began to back away when something that had never happened in her entire time at the palace sent her heart racing.

"Sit with Us, Mei."

Mei felt the blood rush to her ears, suddenly becoming lightheaded. As if under the control of some conjurer, she found her feet shuffling her to a seat indicated by the Emperor. She sat, her head so low her chin threatened to push a hole into her ribcage.

"We are certain as a true loyal servant you would never dare to overhear a conversation between your Emperor and his mother, however We are also not a fool, and are fully aware that the ears cannot be made to ignore what they are exposed to, nor the mind feeble enough to not listen to what the ears present. But let us pretend that your ears are weak, for We know your mind is not in any fashion feeble."

He paused and she wondered if he expected a response. She bowed in her seat even lower than she already was.

He continued. "You of course will repeat none of this, and if We trust you with our son, and your future Emperor, then We must trust you in this matter, as it concerns the very life our Little One." She heard the baby gurgle as the Emperor did something to amuse him. "We fully believe Our mother intends to have Us killed, perhaps as early as tomorrow."

Mei nearly passed out, her head spinning, her heart slamming against her chest. *How could this be? Weren't her words simply an idle threat?*

"We can see you are shocked. You shouldn't be. Our mother is a wicked woman, who will stop at nothing to maintain power. Her forces are strong, stronger than Ours, as Ours do not fear Us as they fear her."

He sighed.

"You need not worry yourself over this. But there is one thing you need to do, and you need to do it very quietly. You must, tonight, prepare to take Our son away from here. Inform whatever staff you may feel are essential that We will be departing tomorrow morning, and to have all of the provisions required for a two day journey packaged so they can be carried on one's back. Have everyone, and everything, assembled outside this room when the sun rises."

She felt a hand on her shoulder and she jumped in her seat.

The hand remained.

"Do you understand Us, Mei?"

She nodded and bowed several times, a confused, scattered mess of acknowledgement.

The hand left her shoulder.

"Very well, take Our son, and make the preparations."

She stood and took the baby, hurrying out of the room as the Captain of the Guard, Fang Zen, entered the room at a bow. They exchanged a short, curious glance, and he gave her a quick smile from the half of his mouth facing her, and a slight wink. He had always been sweet on her, and she had to admit, she too was attracted to him. He was incredibly handsome, very well respected, and would make a fine husband to any woman.

But that was forbidden amongst palace staff. Families meant your loyalty couldn't be relied upon, lest they be threatened in some way, an otherwise loyal servant blackmailed into performing some vile act in exchange for not harming his family.

It made sense to her, but like anyone, she had her fantasies, and at night, she sometimes found herself hugging her pillow, dreaming of what it might be like to walk through the gardens, hand-in-hand with Fang Zen.

Somebody hissed nearby, and her reverie was broken, snapping her back to the reality of her current situation. A situation in which she would never see Fang Zen again. One where the precious package she carried was covered in common mud, and her own face smeared with the combination of dirt and dung.

She looked and saw Jun motioning with his head from a doorway and she walked over as naturally as she could manage. She stepped across the threshold, and the door closed quietly behind her.

She collapsed on a nearby chair, her shoulders slumping, her head dropping forward as she lost all strength. Yu rushed over and took the baby from her arms, and with her final responsibility addressed, she gave in, and let the darkness take over.

St. Paul's University, Maryland
One week ago

Professor James Acton pressed the button on the remote control he gripped in his left hand, and glanced to make sure the image he was expecting appeared. He looked out at the class of several hundred students. His Introduction to Archaeology was one of the university's most popular courses since he had become big news after recent events. He hoped the attention would die down sooner rather than later. It wasn't that he didn't love teaching these young, fresh minds, but he feared many of them were here for the wrong reasons.

But it was out of his control, the past couple of years being more eventful than the first forty years of his life combined, a life that had included serving in the First Gulf War, and traipsing around the globe on one archaeological expedition after another, doomed to the single, lonely life that necessitated.

Until two years ago, when everything had changed, and his life hadn't slowed down since, the most recent events at the Vatican probably his most harrowing experience yet.

And because of this new, sometimes public, life, far too many times a camera flash went off, or a hand was raised with a question about the Pope or some other thing related to one of his misfortunes over the past couple of years. It usually lasted the first week, and once people realized he wasn't going to respond, it settled down. A few dropped the course, but most stuck around, which he took as a hopeful sign that he might actually teach some much needed history, our high schools doing a dismal job of it.

He pointed at the flag emblazoned on the screen behind him.

"Easy one. Who can name it?"

A bunch of students yelled out, "Germany!"

"Correct. Now, who can tell me what the colors represent?"

Silence.

He expected that. Unlike some modern day creations, flags of old actually meant something.

"Nobody?"

Again silence.

"Very well. Black, Red and Gold. The colors were chosen from the uniforms of German soldiers during the Napoleonic wars—our topic after the break!—and were described with this phrase: 'Out of the *black*ness of servitude through *blood*y—as in *red*—battles to the *golden* light of freedom'."

He clicked the button.

"Union Jack!" yelled a voice.

"England!" yelled another.

Acton smiled. "Union Jack, yes. England, no."

"Aw, come on, Professor, we all saw the Olympics."

"Yes, which were held in the *United Kingdom*. A *united* kingdom implies more than one, doesn't it?"

Murmurs.

"The *United* Kingdom was actually the union of two kingdoms, in eighteen-oh-one. Can anyone name them?"

"Great Britain and Ireland," yelled a voice with a Cockney accent.

"Hey, that's cheating!"

The class laughed.

"Yes, Chuck, you're right. It's since been renamed to the United Kingdom of Great Britain and Northern Ireland, and is actually made up of four countries: *England*, Wales, Scotland and Northern Ireland. It happened so long ago that they are effectively one country—although there are some

Scots who'd like something to say about that—but when the flag was adopted, it represented the merging of two symbols. That of the red cross of Saint George, the Patron Saint of England, and the diagonal red cross of Saint Patrick, the Patron Saint of—"

"Beer lovers everywhere!"

"—*Ireland.*"

The students roared with laughter as Acton lost control momentarily. He clicked the button and took a glance over his shoulder, the shimmering gold background with the distinct blue dragon emblazoned across it brought a smile to his face as he thought of the vacation he and his fiancée were about to take.

He calmed the still snickering class with his hands.

"So, who can name this one?"

"Looks Chinese," piped up a voice.

"And you'd be right. This was the flag of the Qing Dynasty, the last dynasty to rule China before political reforms effectively removed the idea of an emperor. Then the Japanese kind of moved in uninvited, and after they were defeated, another brief stint at political reform, then the communists took over under Mao Zedong, and have ruled ever since."

"It's beautiful," whispered one of his students closest to him. He looked over his shoulder then back at her.

"It is, isn't it?"

"Aren't these all just flags of sin?"

Acton looked at the student who had just made the comment. All eyes were on him and he shrank a little in his chair.

"I mean, not ours of course."

"And not the UK!" piped up the Cockney accent.

"Yeah, I'm from Canada. No way you can call ours that!"

Acton held up his hand before the poor kid sunk to the floor.

"I assume you mean because killing has been done in the name of the flag of every country in the world?"

The boy nodded.

"Then, yes, these are flags of sin, as you call them. But only if you take things out of context and ignore the broader meaning of a flag. Are flags used at the head of armies, proudly displayed on our uniforms, draped over the coffins of our fallen? Absolutely. But flags are also held high at sports events to instill pride in a nation, as beacons in foreign lands to symbolize our embassies and a refuge for our diaspora, as symbols of who we are, and what we believe in. I think the vast majority of people think of their country's flag as something that symbolizes them as a people—their beliefs and values, as opposed to the wars they have fought, or acts carried out by their governments that they might not agree with.

"Most countries, if not all, have committed atrocious acts against their own populations, or the populations of others, through history. Unfortunately that's the way the world was, and still is in some cases. Are some of these acts sinful? Absolutely. Has the United States committed sinful acts in the name of the flag? In some people's minds, absolutely. Some people think any war is unjustified, which is why we had a pacifist movement before and during World War Two. Should we not have fought? I doubt there are many people who know their history who would think we shouldn't have fought that war. Were sinful deeds committed during that war by individuals—absolutely. Did our country do sinful things—absolutely. But one thing that needs to be asked is, were they considered sinful at the time?

"Carpet bombing civilian populations to try and destroy the will of the people, to destroy the factories they worked at, today we would consider horrifying. At the time, it was part of war. Today we have options, back then we didn't. Today we have smart bombs, cruise missiles, and other advanced weaponry, where we can be very precise in our targeting, but back then? No. You needed to drop a hundred bombs in the hopes that one of them would hit your target."

"But some are definitely flags of sin, aren't they, Professor? I mean, the Soviet Union, for example. Or China?"

"You'd be hard pressed to get me to disagree on the Soviet Union, having grown up during the Cold War, that's for sure. I wonder however if you were to ask a Russian how they felt about that flag, without fear of repercussions, what they would say? And as to China, if we look at the history of that country under the Communists, especially the early days, I'd have to agree as well. Mao killed millions, by his own admission, *after* he had won the civil war. Mao is blamed for as many as eighty-million deaths in his time, a number even Hitler and Stalin can't measure up to."

"What about China today?"

Acton shrugged his shoulders. "Do they do things there that we wouldn't? Absolutely. Is it as bad as it used to be? Absolutely not. I think the question for China is where are they headed? Where will they be in ten, twenty, fifty years? Right now I think China is in a race with itself. Their burgeoning middleclass are demanding more freedoms, thus weakening the regime. But the economy fueling that middleclass, is also fueling the growth and modernization of their military to the point where we, the United States, can no longer be guaranteed to stop them. So, where's it all heading?"

"What do you think, Professor?"

Acton smiled.

"Luckily for me, I'm an archeologist, so don't need to answer questions about the future." He held up a finger. "But, I'll be there in a few days for a two week vacation, and I'll give you my opinion when I get back."

"Hey, China's about to get Actoned!"

Acton's eyebrows shot up.

"Huh?"

There were snickers and a few bouts of laughter cut off abruptly.

"Actoned?"

Chuck raised his hand. "It means when you go on vacation, and like everything gets bolloxed up, you know, mate?"

Acton chuckled and shook his head.

"*Please* tell me *you* guys made that up, and didn't find it somewhere on the Internet."

Shrugged shoulders.

"Oh well, hopefully my fifteen minutes of fame will soon be forgotten." He pointed at the Qing Dynasty flag. "Now, for when I return in two weeks, I want a paper on who the true power was in China during the end of the reign of the Qing Dynasty, and whether or not it may have continued had it been someone else."

He turned off the screen and slapped his hands together.

"That's it. I'll see you all in a couple of weeks."

The class jumped from their chairs as if their seats were suddenly hot, and filed out.

And Acton sat on the edge of his desk wondering about his upcoming trip.

And whether or not China was about to get 'Actoned'.

Yu's Brother's Residence, Beijing, China
January 13, 1875

Li Mei stirred, the world slowly coming back into focus. She found herself lying on a bed, a blanket covering her, Yu sitting nearby.

"Good, you're awake."

Mei sat up and pushed herself toward the wall the bed sat against, and leaned on the cool plaster. She looked about. It was a simple home. A humble home. A poor home. It was nothing like what she had become accustomed to.

But it reminded her painfully of where she had grown up.

Her parents had been poor, extremely poor. But they had given birth to a daughter, which in itself was a great disappointment to her father she was sure, as she could only help so much on the farm, but thankfully she had had many brothers to take care of that. As she grew up, it quickly became clear she would be remarkably beautiful. Her teeth were perfect, her eyes clear, her hair healthy and straight, and with brothers to do the hard work, her skin remained unblemished with scars.

And she had a mother who wasn't at all disappointed with having finally had a daughter. Someone she could dote on and have help her with the household chores.

It was while performing one of those chores, fetching something in the local market, what, she could no longer remember, when she was spotted by one of the Emperor's consorts. It took less than an hour, and she had been selected as a palace servant. Her parents were paid, her father overjoyed to receive the money, her mother, ever the dutiful wife, not objecting, but as Mei, barely ten at the time, looked out the rear of the carriage, she saw her mother crying, and her father with a long, sad face.

And she had never seen them again.

Perhaps that is where I need to go.

She looked at Yu.

"What news?"

Yu smiled. "Jun has gone to see if he can find Su Ming, and any others. So far nothing."

"How long has he been gone?"

"He left immediately after you passed out, and the sun has now set."

Mei's eyebrows shot up.

"That long?"

Yu nodded.

"And the Little Emperor?"

"He is fine. My brother's mother-in-law is taking care of him in the next room."

Mei sighed and closed her eyes, still exhausted. A commotion at the door sent her heart into her throat and Yu jumping for the entranceway. Mei grabbed the blanket, sinking slowly under it as her heart slammed into her ribcage. She felt herself blacking out again as her eyes slowly rolled up into her head.

The little one!

The thought of her precious charge in danger forced her back to reality. She threw off the covers and jumped out of the bed, steadying herself with a hand on the closest wall, then quietly approached the door, peering through the crack Yu had left. She heard harsh whispers, and she could see Yu's back, but none of the others. Yu glanced over her shoulder, causing Mei to duck away from the door.

Mei held her ear to the crack.

"—suspects nothing—gave the neighborhood—location—any minute—"

Her eyes burned with tears, her heart broke, and a pit formed in her stomach as she finally found the answer to the question that had been gnawing at her all day.

Yu was the traitor. Yu, her friend, her confidante for most of her life at the palace, was their betrayer. The revelation left her numb, and the question that gnawed at her even more so.

Did she act alone?

What about Jun? The two of them had gone in the opposite direction, chased by the Empress' guards, yet had managed to escape. And appeared to be the only ones who had managed such a feat. And she found it hard to believe that they would let both Yu *and* Jun go, if Jun were not in on it from the beginning.

Regardless, if he wasn't in on it from the beginning, he must be now.

She peeked through the crack and saw Yu move toward the entrance, and out of sight.

This was her chance.

She opened the door, thankful its old hinges didn't creak, and tiptoed deeper into the house, peering into the next room where she had been told the little one was being cared for.

She sighed.

Inside.

There was the baby, lying on a bed, completely unattended. She stepped into the room, tightened his swaddling blanket in the hopes it would keep him quiet, then lifted him gently. Returning to the door, she stuck her head out, and, seeing she was still alone, crept deeper into the house in search of another exit.

The house was small, poor, cramped, and at the moment, appeared empty, save those gathered at the entrance. She stepped into another room that appeared to be the kitchen, and nearly gasped. Staring at her from the far corner was an impossibly old man, sitting on a stool, pipe in hand, a cloud of smoke enveloping his head, circling into a fog of sweet tobacco that seemed to fill the upper half of the room.

She looked at him, her eyes, filled with fear, beseeching him for a way out, and to not betray her to the others. She dared not speak, lest she be heard, or worse, disturb the baby and guarantee she would be heard.

The old man stared at her, then pulled the long pipe from his mouth, twisting it around and jabbing at the far wall. Mei looked and saw a door. She smiled at him and bowed. He nodded, returning the pipe to his mouth, never saying a word.

Mei opened the door and stepped into an alley, gently closing the door behind her. She looked both ways, trying to decide which way to go, when she heard a yell from inside.

"She's gone!"

Mei bolted in the direction she happened to be facing, her sandaled feet making little noise as she rushed forward, toward what, she did not know, she only knew she needed to get out of sight, to turn some corner that would lead her somewhere else, rather than to a dead end.

She heard a shout behind her, a voice she recognized as Yu's, but still muffled. It didn't sound as if she was outside yet.

Mei didn't look back.

An alley opened to her right, and she ducked into it. Staring down the dark passage and seeing the street torches at the end, she nodded to herself, and continued to run, a little slower this time, this particular alley not benefiting from the light the moon was providing.

Someone coughed to her left and she yelped.

The baby woke.

Mei stuck her finger in the baby's mouth, and felt him immediately begin to suck on it. She came to a stop at the mouth of the alley, looking onto the nearly deserted street. She knew she had to get out of the area, out of the city in fact. She had no one here she could trust. Her life had been at the palace; she knew no one beyond its gates.

Except her parents.

She barely remembered the name of the village where they lived, and certainly had no idea how to get there. But even if she knew, she had no money to travel with, and nothing to sell or trade in exchange.

Shouts behind her sent her into the street, turning to her left and continuing her zigzag pattern away from her betrayers, and deeper into the unknown labyrinth that was Beijing.

"Mei!"

She froze.

Her blood rushed, her ears pounded, and she turned toward the voice she recognized only too well.

It was Jun.

Hidden in an alleyway to her left, he was waving to her.

"Come here," he whispered.

She shook her head, but her feet wouldn't move. Either to obey his call, or to flee it.

He waved at her again, and when she didn't move, he darted from the alley and was immediately at her side, taking her arm, and directing her into the darkness from where he had just came.

"We've been betrayed," he whispered.

What?

She didn't reply, confused.

"Thank God you escaped. When did you realize it?"

Mei shook her head, backing away. "No, you were with her. You're working for her."

Jun held up his hands, shaking his head. "No, Mei, I didn't realize Yu had betrayed us all until I returned a few minutes ago and saw her cousin talking to the local magistrate. I went to the back of the house, to see if I could get you and the baby out, but saw you already leaving. I'm just grateful I was able to find you."

Mei held the baby protectively, tight against her chest, unsure of whether or not to believe him. She looked into his eyes. They flickered from the flame of a torch nearby, but to her, they appeared earnest. Honest. Concerned.

She nodded.

"What do we do now?" she asked.

"We need to get out of the city. Clearly we can't trust anyone here."

"Where?"

He shook his head. "I don't know. Let's just get out of here as quickly as possible."

"We could go to my parents' farm."

"Where is it?"

"Shaoshan, in Hunan Province."

Jun frowned. "That will take weeks—months—if we can't find transportation." A yell erupted from the alley she had just come. Jun's expression revealed what she already knew.

It was Yu.

"We must get out of here. Now."

Mei nodded, and they began to hurry down the street, and away from their betrayers.

And despite the horror of that day, Mei found herself thinking of her mother and father.

FLAGS OF SIN

Then something hit her causing her to stop in her tracks.

"What's wrong?"

She looked at Jun.

"I don't even know if my parents are alive."

National Stadium, Beijing, China
One week ago

Inspector Li Meng scratched behind his ear then massaged the back of his neck. It had been a frustrating week, and he knew from the horror he was now facing, it would be an even more frustrating week to come. They had two new victims, killed in exactly the same way as the first two.

But that was the problem.

Were *they the first two?*

He had used every contact his thirty years on the force had provided him, and no one was willing to talk. But from the hasty hang-ups, and the abrupt denials, he knew something was going on. If he was a betting man, which of course he was, he would bet everything he had that there were other killings, and it was being covered up.

Ping slid another scorpion off her kabob with her teeth, the bamboo skewer she held sporting another three. He heard the crunch as she chewed. His stomach rumbled. She held the stick out.

"Want some?"

"You heard that?"

"The dead heard that, sir."

Li frowned and patted his stomach. "I missed lunch."

"I told you to eat when you had the chance. Instead you decided to make phone calls." Ping pulled off another of the fried snacks.

"*Important* phone calls."

"That told us nothing," she mumbled in mid-chew.

"Actually, I think they told us a lot, without telling us anything."

Ping stopped chewing. "Huh?"

"As I said to you earlier, it's my opinion that there are other murders happening."

"Well that's obvious. What I want to know is how long they think they can cover this up? The thing about tourists is that somebody is always expecting them to come back home. When they don't show up…" She shrugged her shoulders and grabbed the last of her snack off the skewer.

"People start to ask questions," finished Li. And that was what puzzled him. He could understand why they would keep this from the press. The last thing the government wanted was to have panic amongst the foreign tourists—they stood to lose billions of yuans in revenue. But what did they hope to gain? Eventually it would have to come out.

Ping walked over to a nearby garbage can and tossed her skewer inside, then wiped her mouth with the back of her hand. "Maybe they hope we'll solve it before they have to tell anyone?"

Li nodded. "That's my guess as well. But how do they expect us to solve it?"

"With hard, honest police work, of course."

Li jumped as did Ping.

"Sir, I'm getting old. If you keep sneaking up on me like that, Ping will be looking for a new partner."

Superintendent Hong laughed.

"A good shock to the heart is healthy for you. Think of it as a workout squeezed into a tiny space of time. Your heart beat harder than a moment before, therefore I have just made you exercise!" He laughed hard at his own joke.

Li and Ping chuckled politely.

"So, what have we got?"

"Same as last week. Looks like the same or similar weapon. Two foreign tourists, husband and wife. We're looking for the casings now."

"Any other clues?"

"Nothing yet. Just like last week, I don't expect to find anything. They probably policed their brass, and left no fingerprints or fiber evidence."

"But we do have the shooter on camera."

Li nodded. "Yes, we do, but we can't see their face, and we lost them once they got on a bus."

Ping pulled out her notebook. "All we know is that they are most likely male, one hundred-forty-five centimeters tall, approximately fifty-five to sixty-five kilograms."

"So is half of Beijing," said Li.

"Such pessimism. It is beneath you, Li."

Li raised his eyebrows and scratched behind his ear. "I call it realism."

"Perhaps today we will get lucky," smiled Superintendent Hong, and with a swat on Li's back, he walked away.

"Lucky? How does he expect us to get lucky?"

Li shook his head. "Our only hope is to comb the cameras, and see what we find. The story will eventually go public, and then we'll be able to begin coordinating our efforts with the other investigations. Hopefully then we'll find something."

But for now we're fighting not only a murderer, but a government more concerned with appearances, than safety.

Shaoshan, Hunan Province, China
March 28, 1875

Li Mei stirred as the cart they were in stopped and the baby made a noise. She felt a hand on her shoulder. A now familiar hand. Jun. It had been almost three months of travel. She was exhausted. He was exhausted. And the baby was exhausted. But thankfully healthy, and visibly bigger than when they had started the ordeal.

The journey had been long, and slow, far slower than the news that had spread out before them. It was scant at first, and terrifying. The few particulars that made it into each town and village before them were incomplete, and mostly incorrect. As they fled farther away from Beijing, the news firmed up, became more complete, more certain in the minds of those who delivered it.

But it was all lies.

The claim was that the Emperor had died from smallpox after a two week battle with the horrendous disease. No mention was made of the son they now ferried to safety. It was as if he had never existed. Jun had even inquired on several occasions, "What of the son?" to which the reply was always some variation of, "What son? The Emperor had no son!"

After weeks of this being repeated, the news reached them that a new Emperor had been appointed, and once more the Empress Dowager Cixi was essentially in control again. It had been devastating news, but there was a blessing hidden amongst the lies.

Nobody was looking for them.

At least not publicly.

But they couldn't rely on that. If the Empress Dowager feared the true heir to the throne, she would send out her spies to seek them out, which is what had led to their fateful decision, one that had sent her heart aflutter. Last week they had married in secret, and decided to claim the baby as their own, so they might have some chance of surviving.

She squeezed the hand that now rested on her shoulder, then tilted her head so she could feel his skin on hers. "What is it, my love?"

His hand left her shoulder.

"Look, I think we're here."

Large lettering filled a sign at the entrance to a town she had long forgotten.

Shaoshan.

Her heart began to pound a little faster as the cart they were on resumed its journey, taking them deeper into the town. She recognized nothing, it having been almost five years since she left, and when she had, she had only been ten.

But then she saw the farmers' market, in the center square, and her heart leapt. It was something she recognized. She elbowed Jun.

"What is it?"

"See that man, selling the cabbage?"

Jun nodded.

"I remember him. Ask him if he knows where my family's farm is."

Jun jumped down and ran over to the man as the driver continued through the market, toward his own destination. The vendor pointed to their left and Jun bowed, running back to the cart.

"We must get off now," he said to the driver.

The cart and its lumbering oxen stopped and Jun helped Mei to the ground.

"Thank you!" called Jun as the man flicked the reigns and the decrepit vehicle moved on.

Jun took Mei by the arm and they hurried through the various stalls, and eventually into a wide boulevard she immediately recognized.

"What of my parents?"

Jun turned and smiled at her. "They are well, and still on your farm."

Tears welled in Mei's eyes as she looked down at the baby who was now awake and examining his surroundings.

"This will be your home, little one. What do you think?"

The baby looked up at her, eyes wide in wonder.

"I think he likes it," said Jun.

Mei wiped her eyes dry with the back of her hand and nodded.

"I think so too."

"The man in the market said the farm was—"

Mei cut him off.

"I know exactly where it is."

And she did. With each step forward, the memories flooded back. Her childhood of running up and down these streets as she performed chores for her parents replayed themselves in her mind, like a favorite dream remembered.

They soon left the town, and were on an old dirt road, well-worn, the ruts of generations of carts etched down the center. She found herself almost running, Jun carrying their meager possessions behind him as he followed, continually begging her to slow down for the baby's sake.

She couldn't, but when she rounded a hedge of trees, she stopped, Jun nearly running into her. Tears poured freely down her cheeks, the smile spread across them interrupting the flow, as she saw the home she had grown up in, still standing there, still as humble as she remembered, perhaps a little more so.

A figure brushed snow off the porch with an old broom, a broom she had held a hundred times before, a figure whose stooped form she could never forget.

"Mama!" she cried, handing the baby over to Jun then rushing headlong across the field in front of the house, the snow soaking the cloths that wrapped her sandals to keep the cold out.

But she didn't care.

The stooped form straightened, looking in her direction, then began to cry out herself, yelling for everyone to come outside.

"My baby is home!" cried the now unmistakable form of her mother as she hobbled down the steps and rushed toward her, arms stretched out wide.

Mei pushed through the last of the snow and onto the cleared path and rushed into the arms of her mother, sobbing in happiness like she had never before. They both held each other tight, crying and saying things in between gasps that neither could understand. She looked over her mother's shoulder and saw her father standing on the porch, his face as unemotional as ever, his embarrassment over his poor teeth having stopped him from smiling years ago.

But the tears that poured down his cheeks at the sight of her told her all she needed.

She broke free of her mother and ran up the steps, hugging her father as hard as she could, and her heart melted as she felt the arms she had thought she'd never feel again, envelope her in their protective barrier, and for the first time in months, she finally felt safe.

Other excited voices surrounded her, and she felt hands slapping her back in welcome, as her brothers joined them.

She pushed gently away from her father and began hugging the rest of the family, when she gasped.

"Oh no! I forgot!"

She looked at the road for Jun and found him walking up the path, baby in hand, a smile on his face.

Mei rushed down the steps and escorted Jun forward.

"Mother, Father. I would like you to meet my husband, Mao Jun." Her mother gasped, the smile on her face threatening to crack her worn façade. Mei took a deep breath, hating to lie to the ones she loved. "And this is our son, Mao Shun-sheng."

Jun bowed deeply, as did her parents and siblings. Finally, the introductions complete, her mother urged them inside to examine the baby, her daughter, and her new son-in-law.

And once inside amongst the familiar surroundings, Mei knew they would be safe.

Beijing National Stadium, Beijing, China
One week ago

Inspector Hu Ping jumped forward with one foot, stomping it on the ground. Li Meng looked at his junior partner with a smile as this was her third attempt to trap the elusive piece of paper. Why she wanted it, he had no clue, but doubted it was her strong belief in civic duty and a requirement to pick up litter.

Finally successful, she reached down and picked up the paper, smiling in triumph at Li as she waved it in the air.

Then he saw the words emblazoned on the paper and realized why she had picked it up.

"Foreigners Out!" it screamed in bold red characters.

"Let me see that," he said, holding out his hand as she quickly read the contents. Finished, she handed it over.

"I think we have our first break," she said, her smile now gone.

Li took the paper and read the brief diatribe.

Foreigners Out!

Foreigners are destroying the purity of China, destroying our heritage. Our leaders are consumed by greed, hungrily devouring foreign money to feed their decadent ways. It is time to take our country back. It is time to take it back from the foreigners.

Remember the Boxer Rebellion!

Remember the Revolution!

Remember The June Fourth Incident!

Li's eyebrows shot up at the last line. He of course understood the first two references. The Boxer Rebellion of 1898 to 1901 had been an attempt to force the foreigners of the Eight-Nation Alliance out of the country, to free China from their influence, and restore the true power of the Emperor.

But it had failed.

Tens of thousands had died on both sides, and it had been a humiliation that the country never recovered from.

Until the revolution.

When Mao Zedong fought the regime of old, its complicity with foreign powers before, during and after the war, had threatened the Chinese way of life. He and the communists had won, and established a new country under a new flag, and forced the foreigners out so the country could be rebuilt in the Chinese image, with everyone prospering as equally as possible, through state ownership and control.

Yes, through communism.

It had been a glorious time, though it was before Li's generation. But as with all things, good or bad, they must evolve, or die. And China had evolved. The Party was as strong as ever, but it was slowly giving the people rights.

Li was the first to admit that the new found freedoms were most likely not for the people's benefit. No, they were most likely for the benefit of the Party loyalists so they could legally enjoy the new Western ways made available to them with the lowering of barriers previously foisted against anything foreign. The people of his parents' generation were having a hard time adjusting to the new ways. His generation had adapted, though at times he wondered how far things would go, and if they would be for the best.

It was Ping's generation that he feared for the most. They never knew the old times, and as they clamored for more and more freedoms, they might just get what they wanted.

And that was the one thing Li feared.

If China's new freedoms went too far, too fast, someone, somewhere, would decide things had indeed gone too far.

And hit the Reset button.

And that could be disastrous for all. He feared the day when the Party turned hardline and decided the Western capitalist values that had been embraced over the past decades must be suppressed. A population of over one billion, hundreds of millions of whom were born into a society far freer than he had been, would suddenly find themselves back in the dark ages of communism, where there was no freedom, no Western movies, music, television. No Internet, controlled or otherwise. No cellphone networks or text messaging, as those could be used to subvert the State.

He feared what would happen.

Civil war.

It was the only logical outcome.

Who would win?

Of that, he had no clue. He tended to lean toward the adage that no one would be a winner.

But what would trigger it? What would cause China to spiral back in time?

He looked at the paper.

This.

Had a nationalist movement begun again? Were these shootings actually not hate crimes, but targeted killings designed to trigger an end-goal? Start killing foreigners randomly, heinously, and Westerners would stop coming.

Eventually businesses might pull out, and worse, the Western populations begin to boycott Chinese made goods.

Economic collapse.

The West would label China a communist pariah, and push for democratic reforms. The population would demand these reforms in order to get the way of life they were accustomed to, back. There would be protests. Tiananmen would be repeated but on an even bolder scale, since this generation had actually tasted some of the freedom the previous had fought for.

And the Party would fight back.

He looked at Ping, and he felt his chest tighten as he pictured her crushed under the treads of a tank, fighting for a cause he knew she would support.

And he wondered just what side he would take.

"What have you got there?"

It was his boss, Hong, only inches away.

Li sometimes wondered if the new Chinese stealth fighter he had been hearing about was simply an old Shenyang J-8 fighter with Hong strapped to the nosecone.

"We found it on the ground," replied Ping.

Hong snatched it from Li's hand and crumpled it into a ball.

"What are you doing?" exclaimed Li, immediately regretting his tone. He lowered his voice, bowing slightly. "I beg forgiveness, sir, but isn't that evidence?"

"Evidence of what?"

"Perhaps if you read it?" suggested Li.

Hong leaned in even closer, lowering his voice.

"Forget you ever saw this."

He spun around and marched off, leaving Li and Ping agape.

"What the hell was that all about?" hissed Ping.

But Li knew what it was about.

It was what he had feared.

These killings are organized, with a political purpose, and the State knows. And they're covering it up.

FLAGS OF SIN

Shaoshan, Hunan Province, China
December 26, 1893

Li Mei held her adopted son's hand as they waited outside the bedroom. Screams sliced through the calm every minute or so, each time sending her son, her Little Emperor, Shun-sheng, to his feet. And each time Mei would take him by the hand and pull him back into his seat.

She was about to be a grandmother.

She smiled at the thought, but a pang of regret shot through her chest as she thought of her beloved Jun, and how he was missing the birth of their first grandchild.

Oh Jun!

He had died of a fever just last winter, and she knew this winter would be hard without him. Her son, Shun-sheng, whom she silently still called Little Emperor, had taken it hard. He had been close to his father, and it was a regret she had always carried that she had never told him the truth.

He had had such a happy childhood, surrounded by her family, and by his own siblings as they had been born, seven in all, for his own safety, her and Jun had agreed the secret must die with them. There was no hope of him ever regaining the throne, therefore there was no need for him to know the truth about his past.

Another cry from behind the door, another jump from the chair, Shun-sheng pacing far enough away now that she would have to get up to settle him. She began to push herself from her seat when he waved her off and returned on his own.

A smack and a cry, and they both looked at each other with smiles on their faces.

The door opened, and the mid-wife appeared, holding the baby, swaddled tightly. She handed him to Shun-sheng and bowed.

"It's a boy, sir."

Shun-sheng took the tiny infant and carefully cradled him in his arms, as Mei had done so many years before. "And my wife?"

"She is fine. Resting. You may see her."

The mid-wife bowed, then went back into the room, followed by Shun-sheng and Mei. Her daughter-in-law, Lin, lay exhausted on the bed, but with a glow that only mother's understood. She stretched her arms out, and Shun-sheng handed her the baby. Lin placed a gentle kiss on his forehead.

"So, what will you name him?" asked Mei.

Shun-sheng held Lin's hand and smiled at her, then looked at Mei.

"We shall name him after my uncle, Zedong. Mao Zedong."

Mei leaned over the bed and stroked little Zedong's cheek.

"I think he is destined for great things."

Detroit Metropolitan Wayne County Airport, Detroit, Michigan
Six days ago

"Welcome back. For those of you just tuning in, we're at Detroit Metro Airport, awaiting the arrival of our Dream Vacation winners, husband and wife Deniz and Alex Berkin, who should be coming through those gates any moment now, returning from their *dream* vacation, an all-expenses paid trip to China. People have been streaming out the doors for a few minutes now, so we should see them any moment and we'll find out how their vacation went. While we wait, here's a reminder of how it all started."

Steve Madely pulled the headphones off as a recording of the phone call he had made to the winning household was played. He turned to his partner in crime, Shelley McLean.

"Have we heard anything?"

She shook her head and beckoned one of their colleagues over. Rob Snow left a small gaggle of VIPs, including the station manager, several sponsors, and a representative from the airline.

"Anything?" asked Madely.

Snow shook his head. "Nothing. And the airline isn't being too helpful. They won't confirm if they even got on the plane. They're citing privacy laws."

"What are we going to do?" asked Madely. "I can't drag this out much longer."

"Let's just go with the next segment, and we'll come back to this—"

"Rob!"

The station manager was waving and Madely turned to see that another airline representative had arrived, a frown on her face.

"This doesn't look good," he muttered to Shelley.

"Look at the kids."

Madely turned his head slightly and saw the Berkin's two adult children standing, their own tots clearly restless, talking to an airline representative.

"But that's impossible!" exclaimed the son, whose name escaped Madely at the moment.

Rob Snow rushed up to them.

"They weren't on the plane!" he hissed as he took a knee between the two hosts.

"You're kidding me!" Shelley shook her head. "How the hell do you miss your flight in this day and age?"

"Has anybody reached them? Are we sure they're okay?" asked Madely, his mind immediately putting on his reporter hat, rather than host hat.

Snow shook his head. "No, that's just the thing. They haven't been heard from in several days. I just spoke to the tour organizer, and she said they didn't show up for a planned event yesterday, and they confirmed they never boarded the plane."

"And the hotel?" asked Madely.

"Hasn't seen them in over a week."

Madely had a sinking feeling. *They're dead.* He made eye contact with Shelley, and could tell she was thinking the same thing.

"What do we tell our audience?" she asked.

"We tell them the truth," said Madely. "But only what we know for sure, which is that they aren't here, and apparently missed their flight, to which we'll chalk it up to having too good a time, and move on with the show. There's no point speculating right now, and this entire thing is a co-sponsor event—we have a responsibility to not have this turn into a PR nightmare for them, before we know all the facts."

Snow nodded and their producer stepped in front of the table they were sitting at, the station's call-sign emblazoned across the front.

"We're back in five, four, three..." He finished with hand signals, and Madely took a deep breath.

"Well folks, you're not going to believe what's going on here. It looks like they missed their flight!" He chuckled, giving Shelley a look, his eyes widening slightly as if searching for something else to say.

"That's live radio for you, Steve," said Shelley, jumping to the rescue. "You don't get this type of stuff happening on reality TV. Only here on the radio can you have the stars of your show just not show up."

"Well, it was one fabulous package Middle Earth Vacations put together for them, so I guess they just didn't want it to end," laughed Madely. "Let's run through once again what they've been doing, then we'll hand it over to our news department at the top of the hour."

Shelley began running down the list of vacation features as Madely leaned back in his chair, a pit forming in his stomach.

They're definitely dead.

He looked over at the kids and could tell by the expressions on their faces they were worried.

Madely looked at the floor, his chin resting in his hands as he tried to get a hold of the situation. He had picked the name out of the proverbial hat, had made the phone call, had rejoiced with them, had met them personally before they had left, and seen them off at the airport. The excited couple, down on their luck, had been in his mind two of the most deserving winners he had ever seen in his nearly fifty years of broadcasting.

And he felt responsible for whatever might have happened to them.

Shaoshan, Hunan Province, China
October 2, 1908

"So, mother, what do you think?"

Mei stood beside her adopted son, her Little Emperor, Shun-sheng, and smiled as she looked out over the vast fields he now owned. He had ambition, of that there was no doubt. *And what did you expect, the son of an emperor?* Through his boldness, and lack of fear, he had built the largest farm in the region by purchasing the produce of the local farmers too intimidated to sell it in the cities, then doing just that. And he was now very wealthy compared to his counterparts.

"You have done well, your father would have been proud."

But your true father would have demanded more.

With her beloved Jun gone over fifteen years now, she had been forced to keep the secret herself, and it was getting more and more difficult as she felt herself aging. But it was something her and her dear husband had decided was for the best, and she agreed, but the promise she had made to her late Emperor still gnawed at her from time to time, especially when she would hear news of the Empress Dowager Cixi and the puppets she used to replace the true heir to the throne.

"Mother, may I ask you something?"

"When have you ever needed my permission?"

He pointed at one of the chairs that occupied the porch of his estate. Mei lowered her tiny, creaking frame into the chair. Shun-sheng sat beside her, but didn't look at her.

"I need you to tell me the truth, no matter how painful. Do not worry, it won't affect how I feel about you or Dad, but I need to know."

Her stomach suddenly felt hollowed out, and her heart beat a little faster.

"Very well."

He gave her a quick glance, then looked away again, across the fields.

"I heard you talking in your sleep last night."

The pit in her stomach got a little deeper.

She said nothing.

"Who are my real parents?"

She knew if she could see herself, she'd be ghostly pale, as she felt herself almost become faint. She gripped the arms of the chair she sat in, and steeled herself.

And she said nothing.

His head turned toward her, and she looked into his eyes, eyes filled with questions, eyes filled with pain. And she knew he had to know. The secret that had become almost too much to bear, the unkept promise of over thirty years, the guilt in lying to her son, to her family, to herself, every day.

And she said nothing.

"Please, mother. I need to know."

She sighed, then reached out and took his hand.

"Are you sure you want the truth?"

His head bobbed, but she could tell he was several shades paler, as he realized there was indeed a truth he knew nothing about.

"Very well. Please realize, first, that to me you are my son, the same as any of my other sons. I feel no differently about you, than I do them."

He nodded, and paled some more.

"Your father and I, are not your real parents."

His hand began to slip from hers, but she held onto it tighter, not letting him draw away.

"Then—"

She leaned closer, lowering her voice.

"We had to pretend to be your parents, because you were in danger."

His eyebrows rose slightly.

"Danger?"

She nodded, then took a deep breath. "You are the son of the Tongzhi Emperor, the last true Emperor to hold the throne, and *you* are the rightful heir to that throne as his first and only son."

He dropped back in his chair, his eyes darting between her and various objects on the porch or in the yard. They finally settled on the gold and blue flag fluttering at the entrance to the town in the distance.

"How is this possible?"

"Your father had a son, and he kept it hidden from his mother—"

"The Empress Dowager Cixi?"

"Yes." Mei paused then looked at her son, her expression curious. "What is your opinion of her?"

He looked at her, startled, the question apparently catching him off guard.

"I-I don't know. I've heard bad things, and good things. She's the Empress Dowager, the most powerful person in China. I just assumed, I guess, that she's good, and that the stories were spread by her enemies."

Mei shook her head. "She's an evil, evil woman, who will do anything to keep power, including kill her own son. And grandson."

Shun-sheng's jaw dropped, and Mei nodded, affirming her last statement.

"How do you think your father, your *real* father, died?"

Shun-sheng looked at her, then the floor, turning a shade redder than usual. "The official story is smallpox, but I heard from some friends it was syphilis, caught from one of the whorehouses he frequented outside the walls of the Forbidden City."

"And now that you know the truth of who you are?"

He frowned.

"I don't know. I guess the syphilis story was spread to destroy his legacy?"

"Exactly. And the smallpox story wasn't true either."

"What do you mean?"

"What I mean, my son, is that your father died, with sword in hand, saving your life, by delaying the soldiers sent by your grandmother, his mother, to kill you."

Shun-sheng's eyes narrowed, and his face flushed.

"He was murdered?"

"Yes, and I and many others fled with you, but we were betrayed. Only your father—your adopted father—and I survived, and while trying to get you to safety, fell in love, married, and swore to raise you as our own." She patted his knee. "And we couldn't be more proud of what you've become."

"But I would have been emperor," he whispered.

Mei shook her head. "Your grandmother would never have allowed it. You would be dead now, of that there is no doubt."

He shoved himself from his chair and stood. Mei did the same, only slower, and by the time she was on her feet, he had already gone into the house, returning moments later with a money belt, and a small bag.

He marched off the porch without a word, and Mei called after him. "Where are you going?"

But he never replied.

She watched as he stormed off the property, then turned toward the village. And with horror, she gasped as he walked up to the pole holding the fluttering flag of the Qing Dynasty, the symbol of his true family, and hacked the cord with a knife, sending the flag quivering to the ground.

What have I done?

Fort Bragg, North Carolina
Three days ago

Command Sergeant Major Burt "Big Dog" Dawson, BD for short, leader of Delta Team Bravo, peered through his scope, eyeing Niner's target. Five dead center, one off by an inch.

"You're slipping, Sergeant."

Niner, his parents South Korean immigrants from the war, his self-chosen nickname a variation on "nine iron", a racist insult spat at him during a bar fight, gave Dawson the "Is that a second head growing out of your shoulder" look.

"If putting five in the right testicle, and one in the left, is slipping, I'll take slipping any day."

Dawson chuckled.

"Or, five in the HT, one in the hostage."

"Wind shift," piped in Jimmy, Niner's customary spotter, his own nickname given after the unit had found out he was editor of his school paper, Jimmy Olsen apparently sticking in someone's mind.

"Yeah, Jimmy broke wind, caused me to shift."

Dawson shook his head, Niner's crude, constant humor, legendary.

"Lucky you're the best shot in the unit, otherwise I'd put you on the bench for your sense of humor."

"You know you love me."

Dawson's eyebrow shot up, as did Spock's who had just walked up.

"BD, the Colonel wants to see you, ASAP."

Dawson nodded and handed Spock the clipboard.

"You take over. Everyone requalifies today."

"Hey, what about you?" asked Niner with a teenage whine.

"Check the first page," said Dawson as he walked off the outdoor range.

"Holy shit, I thought he said I was the best shot in the unit!" exclaimed Niner in the distance. Dawson smiled and climbed into his 1964½ Mustang convertible, in original poppy red, and fired up the engine. Several minutes later he was in front of HQ, and in Colonel Thomas Clancy's office.

"Have a seat, Sergeant."

"Thank you, sir," said Dawson as he sat down in front of the Colonel's desk. Clancy was a man he respected, a man he even admired. If Dawson had gone the officer route, he hoped he would have turned out to be a man like Clancy—no nonsense, respected by his men, and loyal to them as well. When Clancy was Control on a mission, Dawson always knew his back was covered from home.

And Clancy would stop at nothing to get him out of whatever shit he had managed to get himself into.

London was a prime example of that.

For those of his men that had survived, at least.

Dawson eyeballed the desk.

Something's different.

Clancy seemed to pick up on it, waving at a prominently empty section.

"Humidor. Promised my wife I'd try to quit smoking cigars, or at least cut back. With them calling out to me from two feet away I knew I'd surrender like a Frenchman when he hears a German, so I declared my office Vichy France and banned the cigars, rather than admit complicity with my wife's desires."

Dawson grinned, enjoying Clancy's sometimes unique take on history. Dawson had loved history as a kid, and with his recent escapades with two archaeology professors, his interest had been rekindled, and he spent many a night sitting in front of the TV with a beer and his iPad, browsing

Wikipedia, reading about long dead people, and events too many had forgotten about.

"Well, sir, unlike the French, I'm sure you won't need Ike to come in here and save your ass."

"Funny you should mention him. Just watched a great movie about him the other day with Magnum PI. If any Frenchman wonders why half the world thinks they're arrogant, they should watch that movie. The actor playing that de Gaulle fucker portrays the stereotype perfectly."

Dawson leaned forward, nodding. "Ike with Tom Selleck. I watched that too. Wanted to put a few rounds through my plasma when de Gaulle was on screen. Fortunately that's frowned upon on base, so I'm not in the market for a new TV."

Clancy chuckled, then became all business.

"I have a mission for you."

Dawson leaned back in his chair, the smile gone.

"Yes, sir."

"We've got a situation developing in China that we're concerned about."

Dawson's eyebrows shot up.

"China?" He'd been all over the world on missions, but hadn't expected China to be one of them.

"Yup." Clancy pushed a file across his desk and Dawson took it, flipping it open. "Tourists, American tourists, are turning up dead, shot by a sniper using a high-powered rifle. Very professional. It appears to be politically motivated, at least that's what our sources tell us. The Chinese were denying everything, and only yesterday finally acknowledged they have the bodies of over three dozen foreigners in their morgues across the country."

"What's the motive?"

"It seems to be one of those China for the Chinese type things."

"Has this gone public?"

"Sort of, just not the extent of it. A couple from Michigan failed to return from a radio contest vacation earlier in the week. That's what set off the alarms. A bunch of disparate stories from around the world started to be reported, and now the Chinese have been forced to acknowledge, privately, that they have a problem. Shit's going to hit our news any minute now."

"And what do you want us to do?"

"We're concerned about our diplomatic assets over there. I want you to take a team of four, unarmed, on diplomatic passports, to Beijing and review our security arrangements for the embassy and our other key assets over there, especially the Ambassador. Apparently that idiot drives by Tiananmen every day on his way home. Identify the holes, recommend how they can be plugged before that moron gets himself, or more likely one of his security staff, killed, then get your asses out. We don't want another Benghazi."

"Why us? Why not Secret Service? Isn't this their job?"

"Oh, they're doing their own review, but ever since Columbia, the President hasn't exactly been in a mood to put all his eggs in one basket. Especially when the basket tends to turn out to be a whorehouse."

Dawson grinned from half his mouth.

"You can count on us, sir."

"I can count on you not to get caught," said Clancy, returning the grin. He waved at the door. "Now get out of here."

Dawson stood up and paid his respects with a brief moment at attention, then strode out of the Colonel's office.

China! He had always wanted to go there, to see the incredible history, but as long as he was active, it was an impossibility. But on an op? He had never thought that would happen. But here he was, on his way to arguably

America's biggest military threat that everyone loved to buy from, essentially as a spy.

And he knew what could happen if they were identified.

Shaoshan, Hunan Province, China
November 16, 1908

Li Mei sat on the porch of her son's estate, waiting as she had done for over a month. There had been no word from him since the day he had stormed away and sliced the flag from its poll, an act that had not gone unnoticed. She had been questioned. They all had. And the story she gave them was that she had had a fight with him over him having more children, and he had left, angry, and had lashed out at the flag in anger at her, not the Emperor.

The story had been believed, but they still wanted to question him when he returned.

And they wanted an apology.

And it wasn't something she was certain he would give.

His return terrified her, as she knew what was expected of him. She found herself torn between desperately wanting her son to return, regardless of whether or not he was her son by blood, or love, and between wanting him to stay away, safe from the authorities who demanded answers.

But the mother in her wanted him back.

And so her vigil. Every day she sat on the porch, waiting for his return, and every day she went inside disappointed. And as the temperature got colder, she found she could stand fewer and fewer hours outside, and would instead warm up inside, in front of the fire, with a view out the window, at the path that led to their door.

And so it had been for six weeks. Six long weeks of waiting, six long weeks of worrying. And as she warmed her hands over the fire, she thought of whether or not she should have told him the truth, but she knew she was right. It was a promise made to her Emperor, a man she barely knew, but all these years later, was still intensely loyal to. A man who in the end had treated her with honor by bestowing his greatest treasure to her care, and had saved her life, by standing his ground and refusing to tell where they had gone.

A man who would have been a wonderful leader, had he ever been given the chance.

She realized she had romanticized the idea of him. For all she knew he might have been the same tyrant his mother was, but in her heart she felt that he was different. And when he had stood up to his mother, yelled at her, demanding the respect of his position, Mei had felt both a surge of fear and pride.

And as she sat back in her chair and looked out the window once again, she saw him walking up the walkway, haggard and old, and for a moment thought she was dreaming, until she realized it wasn't her Emperor at all, but his son, her son, returning.

Her eyes immediately burned with tears as she leapt from her chair and rushed to the doorway. She threw it open and ran down the steps and through the light dusting of snow, closing the final few feet between her and her boy with her arms outstretched.

She buried her head in his chest and hugged him hard, and she felt his arms envelope her, and she knew everything was going to be alright. She looked up at him, and frowned.

"You look so old, my son."

He sighed, then looked at the house.

"I feel old, mother."

"Where have you been?"

She drew him toward the house and up the steps. The rest of the family stood respectfully on the porch, and when he had stepped onto it, he stopped and looked at them.

"I've been gone too long."

He was immediately smothered in hugs and pats from the huge family. Tears and laughter spilled off the porch and down the path, so loud she was certain it could be heard in the nearby village. She looked up and saw the gold and blue flag rustle in the wind, flying high above the town entrance, as if snubbing its nose at her son in defiance.

She looked away from the flag she once adored, and now feared.

She looked up at her son, and she saw that he too was looking at the flag. When he looked away, his eyes came to rest on her face, and her expression of concern. He shook his head at her questioning look, then urged the family and servants inside the house, soon leaving the two of them alone together.

"The town magistrate wants to meet with you."

"I'm sure he does."

"What will you tell him?"

"That the flag of Qing reigns over us no more."

She shuddered. "What do you mean?" she asked, her voice barely a whisper.

"I mean the Empress Dowager Cixi will never haunt this family again."

He patted her on the back, then stepped into the house.

Mei looked over her shoulder, and saw the flag suddenly jerk, then drop several feet, then stop. Another few feet, and another stop. She squinted, trying to make out what was happening, when she noticed several people gathered at the base of the pole, lowering the flag. More began to gather, and stand, staring up, agape.

And Mei's heart sank. She turned back toward her son, who stood in the doorway, looking at the flag, then at her, a curious smile on his face. Not one of happiness, but of satisfaction.

And he looked even older than when he had walked up the steps only minutes before.

She felt her chest tighten, and she grabbed the railing to steady herself.

"What have you done?"

He looked back at the flag, then her, and turned away, entering the house. Mei looked back, and saw dozens were gathered around the pole now, the flag having halted its descent halfway.

And she had to know.

She found her feet carrying her down the steps, along the path to the road, then rushing as fast as she could in her slippered feet toward the growing crowd.

She rushed into the midst, trying to calm the thundering that filled her ears as she listened for some explanation.

"What's wrong, what's happened?" she demanded of her neighbor when she saw him.

"The Emperor and the Empress Dowager are dead!" he cried, tears flowing freely down his cheeks.

Her own tears burst forth, burning paths of fear, relief and pride down her own.

She had no proof of it, but she knew it to be true.

Her son had taken his first step to regaining the throne.

Delta 173, JFK Airport, New York City
Two Days Ago

Burt Dawson took point as he led his team onto the airplane, pocketing his passport showing that one Mr. Virgil White, State Department, was heading on official business to China. It was a well-worn, well-travelled document. That had been generated yesterday. He mentally began to tally how many countries' stamps he would have in his passport if he actually had one, losing count after thirty.

He exited the jetway and stepped onto the plane, showing the smiling stewardess—flight attendant!—his boarding pass. He looked for the hooks in her cheeks and the string drawing them back toward her ears, the smile so painfully artificial it had to have assistance from something. He stepped by and eyed the first class passengers and stopped in his tracks.

Niner bumped into him from behind.

"What's up, boss?"

He nodded toward two first class passengers, already enjoying a glass of champagne.

"Jesus," whispered Niner, "what are the chances of that?"

Dawson didn't know, but couldn't afford to find out what would happen if these two passengers saw him first.

"You guys go on ahead."

Niner, Jimmy and Spock moved past him, careful to turn their heads in the opposite direction, away from the two passengers. Dawson stepped over to them and extended his hand.

"Excuse me, Professors. I'm not sure if you remember me, I'm Virgil White from the State Department. I helped you with some permits for a dig of yours a few months ago."

Professor James Acton's jaw began to drop, then it tightened up as their eyes met. His fiancée however, Professor Laura Palmer, had less control over her jaw, it dropping completely open, but when their eyes met, she quickly snapped it shut with an audible click of her teeth, and extended her hand.

"Mr. White, of course, so good to see you again!"

They shook hands, then Acton offered his own. As Dawson shook Acton's hand, he smiled.

"You folks going to Beijing?"

They both nodded.

"And where will you be staying?"

"The Hilton."

"Nice?" asked Dawson, not having any doubts, Laura Palmer rich nearly to the point of obscenity.

She gave a modest smile.

"Then that's not where I'll be staying," said Dawson with a grin.

"You should come by and see us if you have a chance."

It was Laura who made the suggestion, and Dawson nodded.

"I think that would be a *very* good idea. I'll contact you as soon as I can, but it might be a couple of days." He leaned forward and put a hand on Acton's shoulder. "You two be *very* careful."

He slapped Acton on the shoulder, beaming a smile at both of them. "Have a great flight, Professors."

And walked away before they could say anything else, taking his seat beside Spock in the much tighter confines of coach.

I need to warn those two. They're magnets for trouble.

Shaoshan, Hunan Province, China
January 23, 1920

Li Mei cursed the heavens and earth, and all realms in between. For weeks she had tried to strike bargains with the deities she believed in, those she didn't, and some she even created herself. To no avail. Her offer of her own soul hadn't been accepted, and now it was over.

He's too young!

She sat at the bedside of her ailing son, a son, fifteen years her junior, who should outlive her. Shun-Sheng was dying. Some sort of ailment of the lungs, according to the local doctors.

"Nothing to be done," they had said.

Nothing?

Shun-Sheng's children surrounded him. All but one. Zedong. He had left home at sixteen, and had been driven to fighting the government, mostly through his writings, but Mei feared he would soon be taking up arms.

She feared for his life, felt pride he had spoken out against the sham of an emperor that had replaced the Empress Dowager upon her death, and felt a mix of pride and shame that he wanted China to stand on its own, but not with an Emperor at its head.

They had barely heard from him in over ten years, the odd letter, the occasional word from a friend, or a mention in a newspaper, but word had been sent as soon as it was clear his father, her adopted son, her little emperor, would be dying.

And they had heard nothing since.

"Father?"

The call came from the front of the house. It was a little deeper than she remembered, a little hoarser, but she recognized it instantly.

My Grandson.

Zedong appeared in the doorway to the bedroom where they had gathered, his face that of the concerned son, his face that of one who had never lost his love for his father, despite his years away. It was that of a son who had expected decades more to enjoy with his father, once he had found his own way in life.

But it wasn't to be, and the anguish on his face at the first site of his impossibly frail father revealed the heartache that filled him. He rushed to his father's side and dropped to his knees, grabbing his father's hand in his.

"Oh father, I'm so sorry it took me so long," he cried.

Shun-sheng, so weakened by his condition, barely opened his eyes, but the smile that spread across his cheeks, told Mei all she needed to know.

He had been waiting for Zedong.

Zedong had always been his favorite, and had always been his greatest annoyance. Zedong's insistence on schooling, of reading until all hours of the night, wasting the oil for his reading lamp, and his dismissal of the family farm as a bother, the success of it through Shun-sheng's hard work apparently unimportant to the ambitious, curious young man.

When he had left at sixteen to go to school, never to return, Shun-sheng had been crushed. But he had never let Zedong know how much he hurt inside when he had hugged him goodbye, wishing him well. He knew he had driven him away. He had arranged a marriage, and Zedong had been furious, refusing to acknowledge the woman as his wife. She stood in this very room now, and Mei looked at her, the poor woman's eyes on the floor in shame at the sight of the husband that had refused her.

"Father, are you okay?" His father didn't answer, merely continuing to smile. Zedong looked at Mei, and her heart broke at the sight of his tear filled, desperate eyes, eyes she recognized as those of the little child that she had helped raise.

"I'm afraid not, little one," she said. "He's been waiting for you to return, to say goodbye." Her voice cracked, and she bit her cheek, squeezing her son's hand she had clasped for what seemed like days. "He doesn't have much time."

Shun-sheng's head turned toward her, and he whispered something that she couldn't hear. She leaned forward, putting her ear over his mouth.

"Tell him."

Her heart slammed against her chest as she darted away from the words. Shun-sheng's eyes opened slightly wider, and he stared at her, then nodded. She sighed, and nodded in return, then looked about the room.

"Everybody out. These words are for Zedong only."

She was met with curious stares, but her stern look soon forced them into movement, and they shuffled out reluctantly. Mei and Shun-sheng had never discussed what had happened, had never said a word about who he truly was after he had returned, and she never knew for certain if he had been responsible for the deaths of the Emperor and the Empress Dowager, the official stories never to be trusted when it came to these things.

But now he wanted his son to know.

Zedong looked at her, his red eyes filled with curiosity.

"What is it, Grandmother?"

Mei smiled and reached across his father with her spare hand, and took his. She looked at her grandson, then her son, as she held both their hands, and they held each other's. It was a moment of truth. A moment that could change things forever.

It was a moment she feared Zedong may never be able to reconcile, what with his political beliefs. She had heard rumors he was pushing for democracy, for those in power to be elected by the common man, and for the adoption of Western ways, but not Western leadership.

Mei smiled at the young man in front of her, then squeezed both hands she held. "You know that this is my home."

"Of course, you grew up just down the road."

"But it wasn't always my home."

Zedong's eyes narrowed. "No?"

Mei shook her head. "When I was ten I was taken to the Forbidden City, to serve the Emperor. When I was fifteen, I was given charge of his newborn son."

Zedong smiled. "Grandmother, for this to have happened when you say it happened, you must be speaking of the Tongzhi Emperor, and I know for a fact he had no sons."

Mei looked at the boy with pride. "You know your history well, little one, but history is written by those who control the pen, and when my emperor, whose name I am forbidden to say, yet you say so boldly, died, I was there. And I was in charge of his son."

Zedong sunk to the floor slightly, still holding his father's hand, and hers. Mei gripped him a little tighter.

"My emperor's mother, the Empress Dowager Cixi, had him murdered, because an heir had been born, and my emperor dared to challenge her power. He was dead within a day, and horrible rumors spread to discredit his memory."

Zedong looked at his father.

"Is he—" He didn't finish the sentence.

Mei nodded. "Your father is that baby. Your grandfather, who was in the Emperor's Guard, and I, were the only ones to survive the betrayal that took place that day. In fear for your father's safety, we married, and told everyone, including my parents, that he was our son. Your father did not know the truth until he was much older—after you were born in fact—and now *you* know the truth. No one else alive today knows what I have just told you."

Zedong suddenly stood, letting go both their hands.

"You mean to tell me that I am imperial blood?"

She nodded.

"That if my grandfather hadn't been murdered, I would be Emperor after my father died?"

Again, Mei nodded.

Zedong paced the room, his chin in his hand, and a bearing that she recognized from her Emperor. His shoulders were more squared than usual, his posture, near perfect, his stride, long and confident, though confined to three steps before he would be forced to spin on his heel and again cover the territory crossed moments before.

And there was a look in his eye that she recognized as well.

It was a lust for power, for control. It was an overwhelming will to seize what was rightfully his, and to command his people, and rule his country, like he deserved to, like he was always meant to.

But she feared it was the ambition of a young man told the girl he had lusted over, but was now married, had secretly lusted over him as well. She was no longer available; she was now out of reach.

Her son gasped, and she turned her attention back to him as Zedong rushed to his side once again.

"Does he know?" asked Shun-sheng.

Mei put her lips to his ear.

"He knows, my son."

Shun-sheng nodded, then looked at his son.

"Now you know who you are. Never let anyone hold you back due to your perceived station."

FLAGS OF SIN

It was the strongest he had sounded in days, and they were to be his last words. He collapsed into his pillow, and immediately his hand went limp in Mei's. She cried out, and the room immediately filled with those who had been banished to the hall.

Wails of grief filled the room, and Mei looked at Zedong across the body of his father. He met her gaze, with eyes never more focused or determined in their resolve.

He looked like his father did, the day he left to exact revenge.

Delta 173, Crossing the International Date Line
Yesterday

"I'm telling you, Jimmy, never get married."

Burt Dawson turned his head slightly, looking forward to hearing Niner's advice for his friend.

"Why not?" asked Jimmy, taking the bait.

"My brother got married and divorced in the same year."

"Really?"

"Yup. I asked him about it, and you know what he told me?"

"What?"

"He said, 'Girls are like a brochure. They let you run your fingers over their words, drool over the pictures, and when you finally take the plunge and sign up for that cruise to marriage-land, the brochure is snapped shut, never to be spread again.'"

Dawson shook his head, stifling a groan. Jimmy didn't, his plain and aloud. Dawson glanced at Spock who sat next to him, his eyebrow halfway up his forehead, a smile on his face.

"Look out, Dr. Phil."

Dawson grinned then climbed out of his seat, heading forward toward the first class cabin. He stepped around a flight attendant coming his way, then entered the bathroom, peering out the door, waiting for the lady collecting drinks to pass by his position. She finally did and he exited, walking with purpose into first class. He pulled his phone from his pocket, then dropped it on the floor, the slight push he gave it sending it between the feet of one of the passengers. He bent down, then looked up at a surprised Professor Acton.

"Sorry, I'm all thumbs at thirty thousand feet."

"Don't worry about it," said the Professor, bending down and picking up the phone. Dawson took it, and palmed a piece of paper into the man's hand, shaking it.

"Thanks for the help."

He turned around and walked past a flight attendant, returning to coach. He sat down beside Spock, and fastened his lap belt.

"Problem?"

Dawson shook his head.

"I hope not."

Shaoshan, Hunan Province, China
November 14, 1934

Li Mei sat on her porch as column after column of soldiers marched by the family farm, soldiers of the Kuomintang, or Chinese Nationalist Party, who she prayed would simply walk on by, without realizing whose farm they actually crossed.

For they were the enemy. Yes, they were the army of the official government in this area, but not of her grandson, Mao Zedong. He, the founder of the local communist chapter, who had quickly risen to prominence, and for a short time, successfully established the Hunan Soviet after leading the Autumn Harvest Uprising in 1927. He who dared to defy the official leadership of the Chinese Communist effort, his peasant army frowned upon by the urban leadership, some brought in from the Soviet Union itself.

She knew from his letters that Zedong opposed this. Though he valued the assistance of the Soviet Union, he never wanted their leadership. The entire point of the revolution was to remove foreign control of China, not to hand it over to another. Mei knew the time of the emperors was over, but Zedong's newfound determination after his father's death, and after learning the truth of his heritage, had been remarkable. Within two years of learning the truth, he was the leader of the local communist party, and now led an army numbering in the thousands.

But things weren't going well, and she knew the army that marched past her farm was in pursuit of a desperately retreating Red Army, which would include her grandson.

She didn't worry, however, as she knew his destiny was to lead his country, and destiny would not allow him to perish this day. She knew from his writings to her that he was determined to lead the land of his ancestors, to claim his rightful place as leader, and to forever remove any opposition to his family's dynasty over China.

Whether his title was Emperor made no difference, though she would have preferred if it were. To see the proud flag of the Qing Dynasty fly over Beijing once again, under a leader worthy of its history, was a dream too much to ask for. But if her grandson were to become leader, and call himself Emperor, Dictator, or Chairman, she would care not. For he would have fulfilled his destiny, and she would be able to finally die in peace, with the knowledge she had fulfilled her word to her Emperor.

The door creaked behind her. She looked over her shoulder, and at the darkness within.

"Grandmother."

She smiled as she recognized the voice. Pushing herself from her chair, she took one final glance at the soldiers, then went inside. Her eyes quickly adjusted and she held out her arms, hugging the rugged warrior that now stood before her.

"Zedong, my little one, what are you doing here?"

He returned her hug, hard, then pushed her back gently, looking into her eyes.

"I have come to say goodbye."

She wagged a finger at him. "Don't you dare lose faith."

He smiled at her and laughed. "Grandmother, I shall never lose faith. Never have I been closer to my goal, despite what might appear as setbacks. The leaders the Soviet Union sent us are failing, and once they have shown their inability to lead our glorious Chinese men and women, I shall be there, waiting in the wings, to lead once again.

"But today, we must leave this area. It will be a long, arduous journey, but if—when—we escape the imperialist hordes, we will be able to reunite, stronger than ever before, and once and for all unite our country under the flag of communism, and with that, a single leader at its helm."

"You."

He nodded, still holding her by the shoulders.

"Yes, me."

Mei took him by the hand and led him to the fire, where she took a seat, and he knelt at her feet.

"This long march of yours, where will it take you?"

He shook his head. "That, I'm not sure. For now, we must break the encirclement the Kuomintang are attempting. Once free of that, we will need to try and put as much distance as we can between them and us, and return to the North where we are strongest. It could take a year or more."

"You will send word when you can?"

"Every chance I can, but it may take a long time. Do not worry should you not hear from me. You will hear *of* me, of that I have no doubt."

Mei beamed with pride. "I hear of you every day, and must be careful that I do not burst from my clothes when my chest swells with the pride I feel at your deeds." She looked over her shoulder and out the window as the soldiers continued to march by. "But you must go now. We tempt fate with you being here, and your enemy so close." She struggled to her feet, and Zedong assisted her with a steadying arm.

She led him to the back door, then hugged him hard. Staring into his eyes, she smiled.

"Do not worry about me on your long march. For at the end, you shall find victory, and I shall be here, waiting for word of your destiny fulfilled."

FLAGS OF SIN

Zedong smiled, kissed her forehead, then stepped out the back door, closing it behind him. She watched through the small window as he ran along a hedgerow, away from the house and away from his enemy.

Be strong on your long march, my little one, for your country cries out for its rightful leader.

Hilton Beijing Hotel, Beijing, China
Today

"What do you think it means?"

Professor James Acton lay on the bed, hands behind his neck, eyes closed, relaxing in the buff after a long, hot shower that had succeeded in only removing *some* of the kinks from twenty hours on a plane. He raised his head and looked at his fiancée. She was staring at the napkin that Burt Dawson, their Delta Force "friend", had palmed him on the airplane.

"Tomorrow, fourteen-hundred," she read. She looked up at him, her auburn hair spilling over her bare, porcelain shoulders. "Obviously he wants to meet us this afternoon at two p.m., but where?"

Acton eyed the towel wrapped around her, tucked under her armpits, and pictured the wonderland it concealed. Something stirred and she stared at it, then him.

"Are you kidding me? Haven't you had enough?"

He shrugged his shoulders.

"Apparently I'm insatiable in China."

"My recollection has you insatiable in pretty much every country we've been in."

"Except the Vatican!"

His defense was weak.

"Not for a lack of trying."

He pushed himself up on his elbows. "Hey, I seem to remember it was *you* who was pushing that secret agenda, not me."

She gave him half a grin and a wink.

"Seems your memory is better than I assumed." She waved the napkin at him. "So, where? It's a plain Delta Airlines napkin, no address or anything, so *it* can't be a clue."

"Here, I guess. He asked where we were staying, so that's the only thing that makes sense."

She nodded and put the napkin on the nightstand, then pulled off her towel, turning around to grab some clothes from her suitcase. Acton eyed her backside, then reached over and pulled her into the bed. She yelped as she fell backward, then moaned as he rolled on top of her and kissed her hard.

"Batter up?" she asked as she tilted her head back, exposing her neck.

"I don't know, is baseball popular in China?"

He continued to shower her with kisses as he worked toward her breasts.

"Chopstick up?"

He stopped and looked at her.

"I think I was just insulted."

She shoved against his shoulder, spinning him on his back, then straddled him before he realized what was happening. Sometimes he forgot that their special forces training they were receiving had benefits off the battlefield as well.

He groaned as she bit his neck.

"I'm sorry, Dear, I didn't mean to hurt your feelings," she cooed, kissing his chest. "Let me make it up to you."

Acton tossed his head back and sighed, looking over at the clock.

Burt Dawson, you better not be early.

Shaoshan, Hunan Province, China
May 17, 1935

Li Mei eyed the peasant walking up her path. It wasn't unusual for beggars to ask for food or drink, or for work to earn their victuals. She preferred those. There was constantly work to do in the fields, and those who came, offering their services in exchange for food and shelter were always welcome for as long as they desired to stay. But those who outright asked for food or water, in exchange for nothing, were provided with provisions, then sent on, with a firm suggestion they not return in the morn.

But this one seemed odd. This one had pride. This one seemed to not be a peasant at all, and when he stopped at the steps leading to the porch and bowed, she saw a little bundle tied to his back, and gasped.

"What have we here?" she exclaimed, leaning forward in her chair. The man rose, the bundle on his back disappearing.

"Do I have the honor of addressing Mao Mei, grandmother to the great Mao Zedong?"

Her eyes widened slightly.

"You do."

The man breathed a sigh of relief.

"Grandmother, I bring you both sad and glad tidings. I regret to inform you that your grandson, Zetan, was captured while defending the withdrawal of our forces, including your grandson Zedong. He died honorably, executed by the Kuomintang forces, revealing nothing to them."

Mei's chest was tight. Another grandson dead. Her son Shun-sheng and his wife had had seven children. Two of their sons, and both their daughters, had died young, a pain that had still not gone away to this day.

They had an adopted daughter, Zejian, who had been executed by the Kuomintang six years ago, the word reaching them two years later. And now Zetan was dead at their hands as well. Three sons, two daughters, and an adopted daughter, all gone before their time. It left only Zemin and Zedong. She closed her eyes and said a silent prayer for her grandchildren, especially Zemin, for she felt deep in her heart that her Emperor was watching over Zedong, and her prayers were unnecessary.

She motioned toward the man's back.

"What have you there?"

The man smiled. "I said I brought you good news as well. Your grandson, Zedong, is safe, and sends his respects. And he also sends you his son, Anhong, who has just turned three, for safekeeping."

She motioned at him impatiently.

"Well, release the poor child, let me see him!"

The man bowed, and removed the straps from around his shoulders, gently lowering the boy to the worn wood of the porch. He carefully unwrapped the bundle, then handed him to his great-grandmother.

She smiled and held the boy up in front of her, inspecting him in every way, as he inspected her with wide, curious eyes. They looked at each other and she made a face that elicited a giggle. She rested him on her knee then looked at the man who had brought her great-grandson all this way.

"And who are you?"

"I am an officer in your grandson Zetan's unit. When he was captured, I knew he would want the boy brought to you. His father, Zedong, was too far away, and too close to the front lines to risk keeping the boy."

Mei nodded.

"You did the right thing by bringing him here." She stood up, placing the boy on his feet beside her. "Now, you must come inside and rest after your long journey, and tell me of my grandsons."

"It will be my honor, grandmother, to tell you all I know."

She led the two newcomers inside, her aged but spry mind wondering if this was a sign from her long passed emperor. A second chance, should something go wrong.

She vowed to raise the boy, from that point on, in secret, until she could be certain he would be safe from Zedong's enemies. How long that would be, she had no idea. But with the Japanese harassing her country, and all-out war threatened, she feared it could be decades before they would all be safe.

Watch over us, my Emperor, for your enemies still abound.

Tiananmen Square, Beijing, China
Today

Professor James Acton smiled at the camera, staring not at the lens, but at the woman he loved, Professor Laura Palmer. They had been engaged now for less than a month, and after unwinding at his house for a few days following the horrific events at the Vatican, Laura had announced they should get away from it all.

And with her nearly unlimited source of funds from her late brother's hi-tech legacy, first class tickets to China were purchased, and as soon as their class schedules permitted it, they were here.

He had been to China twice before, both times on archaeological visits, and those visits had been fairly tightly controlled, so he had never had time to actually play tourist in one of the oldest cultures in the world. Everywhere he looked were thousand year old structures, traditionally clothed residents going about a daily routine that could have fit into a completely different era without question.

Clashing quite comfortably it seemed, against the ultramodern, with daring glass and steel architecture that America seemed embarrassed to build, but its citizens would ooh and aah over when they saw such structures in movies, usually not realizing that they actually existed, just not in the greatest nation on Earth.

Why are we so afraid to be bold?

He loved the look of the new Freedom Tower in New York City, and hoped it would reignite the passion of architects and city planners to dare once again. America would never have a Great Wall or a Forbidden City, but why should it be the countries that we buy our oil from that have the jaw dropping skylines like Dubai?

He placed both hands on his hips, shoved his shoulders back, and raised his chin, turning slightly away from the camera.

"Ooh, I like that one!" laughed Laura as she snapped a shot of his superhero pose.

A cracking sound, like thunder, ripped across the square, causing everyone to stop.

"What was that?" asked Laura.

But Acton knew exactly what it was, and it filled him with dread, for he had heard it repeatedly only weeks before.

Sniper fire.

He rushed over to Laura and grabbed her by the arm, pulling her toward a concrete planter containing several ornamental trees. She followed him without resistance or protest, their experiences together having taught both of them to never question the other's actions, to simply comply, and ask later.

"What is it?" she asked when they were both safely behind the barrier.

"That's a sniper rifle."

Another crack, quickly followed by a third.

"That's too quick," said Acton, poking his head up. The rest of the crowd didn't seem to be reacting, some even looked curiously at the pair as they continued about their business. "There must be at least two of them."

"Where's it coming from?"

Screams answered her question, and suddenly those occupying the square began to run.

"We need to get out of here."

A body flew past their position just as another shot thundered over the square, a hole big enough to see through, gaping in the target's back, as it skidded past them, coming to a stop ten feet farther on. Another shot, this time with no obvious victim, kept the crowds surging past them. Acton turned around and raised his head slightly.

"Are you daft?" exclaimed Laura.

He smiled to himself at her unique British colloquialisms, and ducked. "I need to see where it's coming from. We might be safer just staying put."

Laura motioned at the body that had skidded past them, the distance it had travelled indicating an extremely high powered sniper rifle. "If he went past us, doesn't that mean the shooter is over there?" She pointed toward the far end of the square without actually seeing it.

Acton nodded. "Yes, but there's more than one." Two more shots snapped through the screams, then a burst of automatic gunfire. A flood of bodies rushed past them and Acton took the chance to pop up and examine their surroundings. The crowd had thinned enough that he could now see clear across the square. Bodies riddled the concrete, its gray stone stained with bright crimson, a sickening complement to the harsh red of the Chinese flags that ringed the park.

More automatic gunfire.

He turned slightly and could see three vehicles, one a limousine, stopped. Someone was on the hood of the limo, holding some type of machine gun against the windshield, firing.

Then he noticed the flapping flags on the front corners of the hood. Stars and stripes, fluttering in the gentle breeze.

"They're American!" whispered Acton.

"What?"

Acton pointed toward the small convoy. "That's a diplomatic vehicle."

Laura ventured a quick look then ducked as another shot rang out.

"Stay here!" he said, then jumped up and sprinted along a row of trees housed in concrete planters, most hiding cowering tourists and locals.

"James!" he heard Laura yell as he dove to the ground behind one of the planters, the trunk of the tree he had just passed exploding. He yelped in pain as something jabbed him in the forearm. He felt a pair of hands grab his shirt and pants, then haul him closer to the planter. He looked up to see a white man in his sixties staring down at him.

"You okay?"

Acton looked at his arm and saw a splinter from the exploding tree, several inches long, embedded in the skin, a trickle of blood rolling toward his elbow as he held the arm up. He reached to pull it out when the man slapped his hand away.

"Let me look at that, I was a medic in 'Nam." The man took Acton's arm and examined the wound, then gently pulled the sliver out. "Not even half an inch in. You'll live."

Acton smiled his thanks. "Stay down," he said, then sprinted several more planters until he was near the road, less than thirty feet from the rear vehicle in the convoy. The opposite side of the planter exploded into a cloud of dust, the clap of the shot following close on its heels. Hugging the ground, he peeked around the planter at the black SUV behind the limo. Two men were huddled near the rear bumper, weapons drawn, taking occasional glances at the limo, with apparently no idea where the snipers were located.

Another hit to his planter, and the tree it contained collapsed, the entire root system shattered. *What the hell am I doing?* It had been instinct to run toward the gunfire, to help his fellow Americans, but it was also idiocy. He had no body armor, no weapons, nothing. What did he expect to do? Give the snipers a good stern look with a wagging finger through their scopes?

Peering around the planter he watched as one of the men hiding behind the rear vehicle took a bead on something in the distance, and opened fire, rapidly emptying his clip. Acton took the opportunity to stick his head out a little further to see what he was aiming at. It was a van, parked at the far end of the square, perpendicular to the road where the targeted vehicles were. Its side door was opened, revealing nothing but a dark interior from this distance. A muzzle flash briefly illuminated the interior and a moment later the security agent blew past Acton's position, a gaping hole in his chest.

And his weapon clattered within reaching distance of Acton's position.

But completely in the open.

His hand darted out but another crack of the sniper rifle and he jumped back. He peered around the corner, and found the remaining agent behind the rear SUV had taken up his now dead partner's position. The gunman that had been standing on the hood of the limo was down, apparently shot by one of the security personnel, which meant there was still hope for those inside.

He heard the pounding of boots closing in from behind him, and turned to look. Five Chinese soldiers, in their winter gear, Type 80 machine pistols at the ready. *They're going to get themselves killed!*

"Get down!" he yelled, waving his hand toward the ground. But they kept coming, at a crouch. Acton looked into the eyes of one, determination on his face, the dedicated soldier rushing toward the danger, not away from it, to try and save his fellow citizens. Then the eyes widened, their expression turning to fear, and pain, as a hole blasted through his chest and sent him flying away from Acton's position, as if a cable had yanked him back to where he had just come.

His comrades continued their charge as the crack from the first shot was heard, then a second of the small unit was hit, splitting him in two, sending the top half of his body tumbling away. Acton didn't want to look, but he couldn't help it. He continued to yell for them to get down, but they kept charging, as if automatons following an order regardless of the consequences.

Two finally heeded his warning, dropping to the ground, the third began, but was hit in mid-fall, his head seeming to disappear into his torso for a moment, before he dropped like a sack of potatoes in a heap. Acton tore his eyes away from the sickening site, and urged the two soldiers forward, waving to them as they lay frozen on the ground, the fear the situation accorded showing in their eyes.

"Come on!" he yelled, and one of them finally looked at him, then started to crawl toward his position, soon followed by his partner. Two more shots ripped across the square, one hitting his planter, the other impacting directly in front of one of the soldiers, the concrete exploding in his face, his cry revealing the pain he was now in.

He stopped, grabbing his face.

Something in Chinese was yelled by his uninjured partner, who turned back and grabbed him by the jacket, pulling him forward. The man began moving forward again, his eyes squeezed shut, his face covered in blood.

As they neared, Acton scrambled out the few remaining feet and grabbed the other shoulder of the wounded man, and pulled him to safety. All three of them lay gasping for breath, their heads against the concrete of the planter, their legs curled to the side, trying to keep as little as they could exposed.

Something moved out of the corner of Acton's eye and his head whipped around to see the old medic crawling toward their position.

"Stop!" yelled Acton. "We're pinned down here!"

The old man shook his head. "Covering fire!"

Acton looked at the wounded man, gasping in pain, shards of concrete protruding from his face. If the vet was determined to help, he knew there was nothing he could do to stop him. But how to help him?

"Do you speak English?" he asked the soldier beside him.

"No."

Well, you obviously speak some.

Acton pointed at the vet, jabbing the air with each syllable. "Doc-tor. Do you understand? Doc-tor."

The young man, who couldn't have been more than twenty, raised himself slightly to look over Acton's chest then dropped back down.

"Doc-tor," he repeated. "Understand."

"Good. We need covering fire"—Acton made hand motions indicating machine gun fire—"over that way"—he jerked his thumb over their heads, toward the van he had spotted earlier—"so doc-tor can come"—fingers walking on palm.

The man nodded and rolled over onto his stomach. Acton patted him on the back to get his attention.

"Shoot"—machine gun motions—"the van"—steering wheel motions, then finger jabs in the direction.

The young soldier poked his head up, then dropped down again, nodding. "Understand."

Acton turned his head toward the vet. "Ready?"

The vet was hiding behind an untouched planter. "Ready!"

Acton slapped the soldier on the back and he rose to one knee, squeezing the trigger. The distinct sound of the Type 80, so different from the American made weapons he was used to firing, rattled in his ear. He flipped over to his side as the old man struggled to his feet then stumbled toward their position. In his attempt to keep low, he never succeeded in gaining his balance, and tumbled to the ground several feet away, completely in the open.

"Shit!" Acton jumped up and rushed over to the man and grabbed him by the collar, hauling his heavy frame to cover, as the last of the young soldier's clip was emptied.

They all dropped to the ground, Acton gasping from the exhaustion of hauling the two-hundred-plus-pound man, the soldier reloading, and the sack of heroism that had just been hauled to safety rolled beside the wounded soldier, lying at his side, expertly extracting the shrapnel from the poor kid's face, the vet's obvious experience shining through.

"Get me his weapon," said Acton.

"Paul."

"Huh?"

"Paul Burns," said the vet as he removed the weapon from the young man's hands, whispering to him reassuringly. "Here."

Acton took the weapon. "James Acton."

"Why does that sound familiar?"

"No idea," lied Acton. With the shit he and Laura had been through the past couple of years, they now had followers on the Internet. They were part of conspiracy theories, fan clubs, Facebook pages, Twitter feeds. He was now his own verb amongst his students, and if what was going on right now wasn't being "Actoned", he didn't know what would qualify. He and Laura tried to ignore it the best they could, but apparently more than just their classes were popular.

He rolled over onto his stomach and looked at the other soldier as two shots slammed into their planter.

"We can't stay here!" yelled Acton, pointing at the ground and shaking his head. "We have to move!" Finger walking.

The man nodded.

Acton raised a finger. "Wait!" He rolled over the surprised Chinese soldier, and poked his head out so he could see the security agent.

"Hey! You!" he yelled.

The man looked for the voice.

"Behind the tree!"

The man made eye contact with Acton.

"Where's the second shooter?" yelled Acton.

"One's in the van!" yelled the man, "end of the square. Scope glare from that roof!" he yelled, pointing at the top of Mao Zedong's tomb to the south of their position.

Acton looked at the soldier. "Two shooters"—he held up two fingers—"one in the van"—he pointed—"one on the roof over there!" The young man's eyes opened wide at that, it obvious he didn't want to fire on the revered man's tomb.

The young soldier flipped on his back and seemed to think for a moment, then his eyes shot open and he smiled. He reached down and pulled a radio off his partner's belt, and rapid fired some Chinese into it. A few moments later there was a reply, then a quick exchange. He dropped the radio and looked at Acton.

"Help coming."

Acton patted him on the shoulder. "Your English is just fine," he said, smiling.

The young man nodded with a grin, then pointed.

"Look!"

Acton's eyes followed where the soldier was pointing, and he could see an armored vehicle racing down the street south of their position, between the square and the tomb. Suddenly the hood blew off and steam billowed from the now exposed engine. The vehicle careened to a halt as a platoon of soldiers jumped out, racing toward the second shooter's position, pouring fire on the roof. Acton and the soldier jumped up and began firing on the van across the square. Their shots were true, as dark gray pockmarks appeared in the white van's paint job.

Suddenly the door to the van slammed shut, and it sped away. Acton rushed toward the rear SUV as the Chinese platoon continued to advance, and much to Acton's relief, were joined by several more vehicles filled with soldiers. He slammed into the side of the SUV, along with his companion.

"Are you okay?" asked Acton.

"Yeah. Who the hell are you?"

"Just a tourist."

"Buddy, you can travel with me any day."

Acton chuckled. "Let's check on your limo."

The three of them rushed forward, their eyes fixed on the roof of the building they hoped contained the only remaining shooter, and reached the side of the limo. The rear passenger side window was down.

"Anybody alive in there?" yelled the agent.

There was silence.

"We're American!" yelled Acton. "Are you okay?"

"Yes! Yes! Jesus Christ, yes!" yelled a voice, shaking but sounding relieved.

"Is that you, Mr. Redford?"

"Yes."

"This is Special Agent Danson. Is the Ambassador okay?"

There was a pause and Danson was about to repeat the question when the terrified voice inside finally replied. "N-no, he's—he's gone!"

Danson's eyes narrowed. "Gone? As in dead?"

"No, gone as in they took him!"

Danson frowned. "Okay, sit tight. You're safe where you are. Once the situation is secure, we'll get you out of there. What about the driver and agent—"

"Dead!" The voice was almost a scream.

"Okay, keep it together, Mr. Redford. It's almost over. The gunfire you hear is Chinese soldiers getting the last of the gunmen." As he said the words the gunfire stopped. Acton looked up from the side of the car toward the roof across the street, and saw several Chinese soldiers waving to their comrades below.

Their companion yelled at a new batch of soldiers, who came running toward their position, guns raised, and within seconds Acton and Special Agent Danson were surrounded by at least a dozen men, their weapons dangerously close. The soldier with Acton waved them down, rapid firing something in Chinese, and Acton swore he would learn the language the first chance he got.

Weapons lowered, Acton flashed as friendly a smile as he could as he placed his own weapon to the ground, Danson doing the same.

"I tell them you help me." The words were slow, halting; the accent thick. Acton held out his hand to his new friend.

"James Acton. Call me 'James'."

The man smiled. "Tau Jié."

The weapons at their feet were retrieved and the soldiers took up covering positions as Acton began to breathe a bit easier.

"James!"

Acton looked toward the unmistakable voice and his heart leapt into his throat as several weapons were pointed at the approaching Laura.

"She's with me," said Acton quickly, and his new friend Tau said something to his fellow soldiers that calmed them.

Somebody yelled from their former hiding place, and Acton looked over to find several guns pointed at their medic. Tau immediately ran over, yelling, and the weapons were lowered.

Laura reached the limo and threw her arms around Acton. "Thank God you're okay!" she exclaimed, then, pushing him away, admonished, "What in blazes were you thinking?"

Acton pulled her back into his arms, holding her tight, his chin resting on the top of her head.

"I have no idea."

FLAGS OF SIN

Gate of Eternal Peace, The Forbidden City, Beijing, China
October 1, 1949

Li Mei sat, hands clasped in her lap, smiling, her chest swelling with pride. The voice booming from the tiny radio at her side, the distinct, thick, Hunan accent of her grandson boldly proclaiming to a crowd of nearly one million, to a nation of seven hundred million, and to a world that would eventually tremble at the feet of her glorious nation, that China was back. No longer subjugated by the imperial powers of Europe, Japan, Russia or America.

The Chinese people have stood up.

"The Chinese people have rich experience in overcoming difficulties. If our forefathers, and we also, could weather long years of extreme difficulty and defeat powerful domestic and foreign reactionaries, why can't we now, after victory, build a prosperous and flourishing country? As long as we keep to our style of plain living and hard struggle, as long as we stand united and as long as we persist in the people's democratic dictatorship and unite with our foreign friends, we shall be able to win speedy victory on the economic front."

She smiled. Though uneducated, even she understood the irony of a democratic dictatorship. But only she knew the truth of what had really happened. Though China now had a new flag, five stars on a sea of red, its true flag, its secret flag, remained gold, with a blue dragon.

For today, the Emperor's grandson had taken his rightful place on the throne.

"An upsurge in economic construction is bound to be followed by an upsurge of construction in the cultural sphere. The era in which the Chinese people were regarded as

uncivilized is now ended. We shall emerge in the world as a nation with an advanced culture."

She could feel herself grow tired. It had been a heady day. She had been whisked from her farm several days ago by government troops, and brought to this room near the Forbidden City, and left to wait, with no word as to why she had been brought here, or by whom.

But the view from her small room filled her with conflicting emotions. The memories of her childhood in the Forbidden City, that fateful day when they had been betrayed, the promise made, the promise finally kept. A lifelong mission was over, a mission she had thought impossible to fulfill at one time, but for the single-mindedness of a grandson she never thought had it in him.

She closed her eyes as she listened to his voice, hollowed out by the poor quality of the speaker in her radio, but nevertheless, distinctly his. And with each pause, the shouts of a million voices, their fists raised in joy, their hands pumping the air with the knowledge that once again they were led by one man, one dictator, one Emperor, who would ensure they remained on the right path, a path to greatness.

"Our national defense will be consolidated and no imperialists will ever again be allowed to invade our land. Our people's armed forces must be maintained and developed with the heroic and steeled People's Liberation Army as the foundation. We will have not only a powerful army but also a powerful air force and a powerful navy."

China had been invaded far too often for a country with history that extended beyond what most of their conquerors could claim. It had lost its way, but once it had rebuilt, even if it took a century, the world would tremble in fear, for the dragon had reawakened, freed from the boot of imperialist oppression, and eager to reclaim its rightful place of dominance in the world.

One quarter of the world's population was no longer willing to be ignored.

"Let the domestic and foreign reactionaries tremble before us! Let them say we are no good at this and no good at that. By our own indomitable efforts we the Chinese people will unswervingly reach our goal. The heroes of the people who laid down their lives in the People's War of Liberation and the people's revolution shall live forever in our memory!"

She thought of her grandsons, Zetan, tortured and murdered by the Kuomintang, then his brother, Zemin, killed five years ago by a warlord for supporting the Communist cause. And her adopted granddaughter, Zejian, the first to be murdered for the cause by the Kuomintang.

And she thought of her Emperor. Murdered almost seventy-five years ago.

"Hail the victory of the People's War of Liberation and the people's revolution! Hail the founding of the People's Republic of China! Hail the triumph of the Chinese People's Political Consultative Conference!"

The roar of the crowd turned the radio transmission into static, and she turned it off, the crowd's jubilation rolling in through the open window. It lasted it seemed an eternity, and she soon dozed off, only to be awoken by the sound of a door opening. She raised her head off her shoulder, and straightened her dress before looking to see who had entered.

She smiled and tried to get up, her old legs failing her from having sat so long.

But she needn't bother. Zedong, a smile spread across his face, closed the door and quickly strode to her chair, then dropped to his knees, taking her hands in his.

"Grandmother!"

She squeezed his hands, her smile beaming as tears filled her eyes.

"Did you hear my speech?"

She nodded.

"You made this old woman very proud."

He flushed slightly, and looked at the floor separating them, then back at her.

"Victory has come at a heavy price."

She nodded. "Indeed it has, but victory can be fleeting. Do not rest now, thinking your victory is permanent, founded in a base of solid concrete. You have merely poured the mixture of stone and water, and it has yet to set. Now more than ever you must do whatever it takes to protect your foundation while it solidifies, otherwise you may quickly find your enemies attacking that foundation while it remains weak in its infancy. Consolidate your power now, eliminate your enemies, and your foundation will have time to strengthen, and eventually, be built upon."

Zedong shook his head slightly from side to side. "Grandmother, you are the wisest person I know. You understand me so well, and you understand what is necessary so well. I will not rest until my enemies are eliminated, and my family's legacy is restored." He raised his hands, still holding hers, to his lips. "I swear to you, to father, and to my grandfather, that China will be great again, and our family will be great again."

Mei smiled, freeing a hand and patting his cheek.

"I saw the gold in the flag, and I was pleased."

He smiled. "It is subtle, and its significance certainly missed to all but you and I."

She took a deep breath, and shivered, the cold October air making its presence known. Zedong immediately rose and closed the windows, returning with a blanket.

"You may stay here as long as you wish, Grandmother. I will visit you every day, if I can."

"No," she replied, shaking her head. "Return me to my farm. My work is done, and it is time for this old woman to find peace at last."

Zedong frowned. "It saddens my heart to hear you talk like that, Grandmother. You have many good years left in you."

Mei laughed.

"Oh, my little one, you have no idea how old these bones are, and even less idea how old they feel. I am ready to move on, and rejoin my Emperor, your grandfather, and your father, in the afterlife, and watch our creation blossom under your guidance, with my fallen children and grandchildren at my side."

A single tear rolled down Zedong's cheek, and she wiped it away tenderly. He buried his face in her chest, and sobbed as she hadn't seen him do since he was a little boy.

And she hugged him, as hard as she had hugged his father the day she had saved him from his enemies.

"It will be okay, little one."

Tiananmen Square, Beijing, China
Today

"What is your business in China?"

"Pleasure," repeated James Acton for at least the fifth time. He realized he was being interrogated, and repetition was merely a technique, but this was getting ridiculous. He was tired, he was sore, and he was fed up. He had tried to save lives, and in fact was pretty sure he had saved some, and now he was being treated like a criminal.

"So you claim to be a tourist."

"I don't *claim* to be anything, officer, I *am* a tourist."

The man frowned. "You may address me as Inspector Li." He shook his notepad at him. "I suggest you cooperate. This is not America. We do not tolerate ignorance or belligerence here."

Acton's heart pounded a little harder. In his encounters with authorities lately, he had usually been in countries where he could at least count on the system generally being on his side.

Except for that bit in Iran. And half the Middle East.

And that's what he had to keep in mind. This was *Communist* China. This was not a friendly country. By all outward appearances they tried to look friendly and welcoming, but behind the scenes, it was graft and corruption, ruthlessness in the face of crime, and right now, he had been involved in a horrific crime.

As far as he could tell, it was the United States Ambassador to China's motorcade that had been ambushed. Four in the lead vehicle were dead, two in the limousine, and three in the rear. As well, a large number of Chinese police were dead, along with a handful of bystanders.

He was lucky to be alive.

His instinct to help nearly got him killed, but it was his nature to not just standby. His training as a soldier in the Gulf War, his position as an archeological professor and father figure to many of his students when they went on remote dig sites, and now as someone training in martial arts and weaponry, all lead him to rush into the action to help, rather than just run in the opposite direction when someone was in distress.

And it would get him killed one day.

He looked at Laura who was being interrogated by a female officer. He caught her eye and gave her a slight smile. He didn't wink just in case it might be misinterpreted by his interrogator.

He looked at the man and realized he was just doing his job. If he were back home, would he expect anything less? A massacre had essentially just taken place, and he was a key player.

"I'm sorry, Inspector Lee, but I'm tired, sore, and just want to get back to my hotel room."

"Where are you staying?"

"The Hilton. Room eight-thirteen."

"Very nice hotel. How can you afford such a thing on a teacher's salary."

Acton smiled slightly, knowing he had to keep calm.

"*I* can't, but my fiancée can. She inherited a large sum of money from her brother when he died."

"And her name?"

"Like I said before, Professor Laura Palmer, Head of Archaeology at the British Museum, and a tenured professor at University College London."

"Ah yes, so you did," said Inspector Li, flipping through his notes. He looked up at Acton. "And when you heard the gunshots, you chose to run toward them, instead of away."

It wasn't a question, so Acton said nothing.

Inspector Li continued to eyeball him, and when that didn't elicit a response, he looked back at his page. "I suppose I might have done the same." He looked at Acton. "But then again, I'm a police officer."

Again Acton said nothing. But his mind raced. If he offered up that he was an ex-soldier, that might cause problems, since China was technically an enemy. He certainly couldn't mention any of his recent involvement in London, Italy or Iran. And he definitely couldn't mention the special ops training he and Laura were receiving from her ex-SAS security personnel.

But he had to say something.

"I don't know what I was thinking. I guess I just reacted."

Li looked at him, steadily, to the point it made Acton uncomfortable. But he refused to look away.

He was saved by another officer running up and handing the Inspector a sheaf of papers. Li thumbed through them, and looked up.

"I don't think you are being entirely truthful with me, Professor Acton."

Acton felt his chest tighten. He knew a lot of what he had been involved in had been covered up as best as could be expected in the press and on the Internet, but intelligence communities were another story. And the Chinese had an extensive intelligence network. They could infiltrate anywhere, and not stand out, simply by claiming to be an immigrant. Try sending a white man into China to spy.

Far more difficult.

He sometimes wondered if the Chinese military had a fifth column of troops and agitators disguised as immigrants spread throughout the Western world, just waiting to be activated, much like the Soviet sleeper agents of the Cold War.

"I'm not sure what you mean."

"You were a soldier. You failed to mention it."

"Ex-reservist, twenty years ago."

"You fought in the Gulf War. Not exactly what I would call typical reservist activities."

Acton shrugged. "Pretty much every reservist has seen combat in the past five years in my country."

"Ah yes, America's penchant for invading foreign countries. You should be more like us Chinese and respect people's borders."

"Korea and Tibet come to mind," blurted Acton, immediately regretting it.

Li smiled. "We were invited into both those countries."

Yes, much like Hitler was invited into Austria and Czechoslovakia.

He wanted to bring up the land disputes over islands and oil rights in the South China Sea with Japan and the Philippines among others, but this time he bit his tongue.

"You want to say something?"

Acton shook his head. "I think it's best I shut up now."

Li chuckled. "Very wise." He paused, then tapped his pad on his chin. "I wonder about you. You have been very busy of late." He shook the papers he had been handed. "You are fortunate I am a Catholic, as I am a little more trusting than some of my associates. From what I have read here, I believe you are a good man, with a penchant for being in the wrong place at the wrong time, but seem to always be on the right side of whatever is going on. My supervisor"—he nodded toward a man standing a few dozen yards away—"would insist I take you downtown, but I think you are what you say you are. A tourist." He flipped his notebook shut and stuffed it in his shirt pocket. "You are free to go, Professor Acton. I suggest that for the remainder of your trip in China, you run away from trouble, as opposed to toward it."

Acton smiled slightly and nodded.

"Good advice in any country, Inspector."

Li yelled something in Chinese, and the female officer interrogating Laura nodded, then motioned for Laura to leave. She walked quickly toward Acton, who held his arm out and took her under his wing.

"What was that all about?" she asked. "I got the sense there's something else going on here."

"You too?"

"Definitely. When you were off doing your hero bit, I picked up a couple of papers that were blowing across the square."

"What did they say?"

"I don't know, but when I showed her one of the pages—the one interviewing me—she turned pale and snatched it out of my hand, burying it in her bag, and looking around as if she was afraid someone might have seen me hand it to her."

"Did she say anything?"

"No, I asked her what was wrong, but she said 'nothing'. The rest of the questions were pretty routine. Repetitive, but routine."

"Yeah, me too." Acton flagged a taxi. "Let's get back to the hotel. We have an appointment we're almost late for."

FLAGS OF SIN

Shaoshan, Hunan Province, China
August 11, 1954

Li Mei heard voices in the shadows. *Who is it that disturbs me at a time such as this?* It took a moment to realize she had been dozing, and her eyes were closed. The voices continued, and she listened, rather than reveal she was awake.

It was Zedong. She suppressed a smile as her heart skipped a little faster in the knowledge he had made it. And Anhong, Zedong's child she had raised in secret now for almost twenty years. Zedong had only one son alive, at least publicly, and much to her dismay, Anqing was apparently starting to show signs of mental illness, most likely due to a severe beating he had received when only seven years old by a Shanghai policeman. The trauma over his other brothers dying seemed to have exacerbated the problem.

But she had her doubts.

The stories of his mental illness were just that—stories. She hadn't seen any evidence of it, other than the heartfelt sorrow over losing his siblings—but if that was evidence of mental illness, then in her opinion, they were all guilty of it.

He had visited her over the years, and seemed to be a fine young man. And he had been with the family, at her side, for the past three weeks, and they had spoken often, and long, and he seemed a perfectly sane, lucid individual.

And remarkably intelligent.

His time in Paris and Moscow had served him well, and he was now a linguist, translating scientific texts for the government from Russian into

Chinese. A valuable, honorable, contribution to the new empire, albeit not heroic in any sense. He shunned politics, and that may be why the rumors were being spread by Zedong's enemies, for he had them. Many. And if they had their way, they would remove him in a heartbeat. The power struggle within the country was constant, and Zedong had had to be ruthless to retain his power, but with each passing year, his grip tightened, his opponents were crushed, and he ensured the dynasty of his grandfather continued in secret.

And with that knowledge in her bosom, she was ready to pass. It had taken longer than she had expected. She had been ready when the little one had given his momentous speech, and cried in her arms, but it had finally come. She wasn't sure how old she was, she had long ago lost count, but according to some of her nieces and nephews who were more schooled than she was, she was almost ninety-five.

A good age to go.

She had led a full life, a happy life, one filled with love and adventure, more than any farm girl could have hoped for. She just wished that her beloved Jun could have lived longer to enjoy it with her.

Her chest heaved slightly at the thought of him, his dark, creased face, his eyes, so bright, his hair so soft to her touch. They had fallen in love on the road from Beijing, and in those desperate nights of trying to keep warm, the baby huddled between them, they had exchanged their first kiss.

She smiled as a warmth spread through her at the memory.

"I think she's awake."

It was Zedong.

She opened her eyes and smiled.

"Hello, little one, I'm so happy you are here."

Zedong sat on the edge of the bed, Anhong the other, and Anqing stood at the foot. She took Zedong's hand in hers, then looked at all three men.

"I have little time left, but before I go, I must be certain my task is complete, for I made a promise to my Emperor, and it must be kept if I am to be permitted eternal happiness in the afterlife."

"Great-Grandmother, please don't talk like that," said Anhong.

She patted Anhong, the boy she had raised since he was a toddler, hiding his true identity even from him. *Oh, the lies are what I most regret.* It had been a life of lies, a life of hidden truths, a life of deceiving both strangers and loved ones, and a life that was near a close.

It was time for all to be revealed.

She looked at Zedong.

"It is time to tell your son, Anqing, the truth about his family." She looked at Anhong. "And it is time to tell your *son*, Anhong, the truth as well."

Anhong's jaw dropped, and he looked first at her, then Zedong. Zedong smiled at him, nodding.

"Yes, it is true."

Anqing looked at her, his own jaw betraying his shock. "You mean we're brothers?"

She was delighted by the excitement in his voice, and when she nodded, he rushed around the bed and embraced Anhong as he stood, shaking him back and forth. Anqing stepped back, his hands still on his brother's shoulders, and smiled.

"I have a brother again," he whispered, his voice cracking.

Anhong appeared still to be in shock. He neither smiled, nor frowned. In fact, he displayed little emotion.

"Anhong, my dear, sit with this old lady one last time."

Anhong tore his eyes away from his newly discovered brother, and looked down at her. She beckoned him and he returned to his perch on her bedside.

"There is much more for you to learn, both of you, and I have little strength remaining. Should I not be able to finish, your father will reveal the rest. But know this before I begin. The restlessness you have always felt inside, the suspicions you have had of thinking you should be something more, something greater, are there for a reason. For you are of royal blood, and are destined to rule China."

Anhong's eyes were wide, and full of fear and doubt. He looked at Zedong, his father, who nodded.

"Yes, Anhong. I am the grandson of the Tongzhi Emperor, last legitimate emperor of the Qing Dynasty, and all I have done, has been to restore our family to the throne we rightfully deserve."

There was a thump as Anqing, still standing at the side of the bed, collapsed.

Anhong was too much in shock to even notice.

And Li Mei, with the secret out, the truth revealed to all those who needed to know, slipped away into darkness, as she heard the cries of Zedong in the distance, and the shudder of a stiff wind against the old farmhouse, as Heaven came to collect her soul.

Hilton Beijing Hotel, Beijing, China
Today

"Professor Acton?"

James Acton looked over at the front desk and saw one of the clerks waving at him. He didn't recognize him, and wondered how the man knew who he was. He fingered his room key in his pocket, and questioned if it had an RFID type chip in it that triggered something as they came through the doors.

Any other day he would have thought it cool, but after today's experience at the hands of the Chinese authorities, he found it rather chilling.

Acton walked over to the desk, and the man handed him an envelope.

"This arrived for you earlier."

Acton forced a smile, took the envelope, then headed toward the elevator with Laura in tow. They didn't say anything to each other, or even acknowledge the envelope, until they entered their room and had secured the door.

Laura looked at the drapes, and so did he. The windows were wide, the sun pouring in, and Acton knew what she was thinking.

How paranoid should we be?

Acton tossed the envelope on the bed and they both attacked the drapes, closing the room up tight from outside prying eyes, then turned on the television, radio, and ran the shower along with the sink taps.

As each precaution was taken, he found his heart beating faster, and by the time they were ready to open the envelope, though only a few minutes had passed, he found his hands shaking from the adrenaline.

He sucked in a deep, slow breath through his nose, filling his lungs and stomach, then slowly exhaled through his mouth, calming himself as he had been repeatedly trained.

Shaking hands can't shoot straight.

He tore open the envelope, and emptied its contents onto the bed.

And was disappointed.

It was a brochure, in English, for the Beijing National Stadium, or the Bird Cage as it had come to be known during the 2008 Olympics. Acton pulled it open.

"What's this?" asked Laura, as she leaned over on the bed, looking at the map inside.

"Not sure. There's nothing written on it that I can see." He flipped it over, then back again to be sure.

"Invisible ink?" she asked, her tone indicating she wasn't serious.

Acton chuckled. "He'd want us to be able to determine it was him."

Laura pointed at the front of the brochure. "Look at the 'B' in Beijing, and the 'D' in Stadium."

Acton smiled. They both had pen dots in them. In fact, there were pen dots and scratches all over the front that he hadn't noticed when he first looked at the brochure, his focus to open it and see the inside. But only those two letters of any words on the front had dots in them. And they could stand for only one person.

B.D.

Big Dog.

Burt Dawson.

Acton had known Burt Dawson for a couple of years, but only as a "good guy" the past year or so. His first encounter with him had been horrifying, and had resulted in a tremendous amount of heartache for him, and a terrifying rush for survival, that had eventually brought him to Laura for the first time. He had never forgiven Dawson completely for what happened, and every time he saw him he was haunted by the memories of his students, but he had eventually come to understand that Dawson and his team had been under orders, orders that had them believing he and his students were terrorists, and had even begun to question those orders at the risk of their own lives, and those of their loved ones.

It was something they didn't discuss, but both knew was there. They had since fought side by side, and had earned each other's respect, and trust, and Acton now considered Dawson a man he could rely on, and even call upon, in a time of need.

And now, for some reason, Dawson was reaching out.

"It has to be about what happened today," said Laura, almost reading his thoughts.

Acton frowned. "But how could he know what was going to happen?"

Laura's hand darted to her mouth. "You don't think he could be involved, do you?"

Acton's eyebrows shot up his forehead. "God, I hope not. I mean, this is China. You don't fuck around here. Saudi Arabia, Iran, Egypt? Sure. But here? You could start a war we'd actually care about."

"Okay, let's assume he didn't know about today. He's obviously trying to warn us about something. These pen dots might give us a clue." Laura opened the brochure again, and there was the odd dot on the page, the occasional scratch, but nothing obvious to him as to a message. "There." Laura pointed at the legend. There was a dot beside the number 6, the Metro station for the Olympic Sports Center.

"That has to be it," said Acton, finding the spot on the map. He glanced at his watch. "We have less than an hour to get there."

"Can we make it?"

"If we leave now, probably."

"We need to change first."

"No time," said Acton, getting up and folding the brochure so it would fit in his pocket.

"Have you seen yourself?"

"Huh?"

"Go look in the mirror, Darling."

He stepped in the bathroom and wiped the steam from the running shower off the glass. His eyes popped in surprise. Not only was he covered in dirt, he was covered in blood as well. The fact none of the hotel staff had said anything was a remarkable indication of their restraint and professionalism.

I can only imagine what the guests were thinking.

He immediately began stripping out of his clothes, and Laura did the same. Minutes later they were showered, dressed, and heading out the door with only half an hour to spare.

We're never going to make it.

FLAGS OF SIN

Building 202, Zhongnanhai Complex, Beijing, China
September 8, 1976

Li Anhong sat silently in his father's hospital room in Building 202 in the massive Zhongnanhai Complex in Beijing, where the People's Republic of China was actually governed. Mao Zedong had had a number of heart attacks, but his most recent, only days ago, was thought to be near fatal, and he might never recover.

Anhong had been working by his father's side since he had discovered the truth about him twenty years ago. But their relationship had been kept a secret, he still going by the family name Li. His father, the most powerful man in China, and in Anhong's mind, one of the most powerful men in the world, had enemies.

Not the least of whom was his wife.

Jiang Qing.

The *supreme bitch*, or so some of the staff called her behind her back if they dared.

Her and her Gang of Four had committed untold atrocities, resulting in the deaths of innumerable political enemies and rivals. Officially they were supposed to do his father's bidding, but with his weakening condition, and her lust for power, it was widely believed they often acted on their own.

And now with his father dying, he knew she would attempt to seize control.

Which was exactly what she appeared to be doing right now.

"Comrade, the doctor said the Chairman cannot breathe on his right side, he has a very bad lung infection."

"Mind your own business!" she screamed, as she rolled her husband onto the side Anhong knew was bad for him. Two nurses assisted her, and a doctor watched, frowning, having protested her orders. Yesterday she had sprinkled powder on him, despite the objections of the doctors, as it could worsen his lung condition.

But they were too afraid to push their objections.

Lest they find themselves dead like so many others.

But now, she had insisted he be rolled over onto his right side, and almost immediately, Anhong's father, and China's beloved leader, stopped breathing, and began to turn blue.

Anhong leapt to his feet.

"What have you done?" he screamed. She glared at him as the doctor rushed into the room, pushing her aside. They began CPR, and within minutes had him breathing again, but it was clear by the expressions on the staff's faces there was nothing more to be done.

The supreme bitch had succeeded.

She had effectively killed her husband, and was now free to make her grab for power. She stared at Anhong as tears streamed down his face.

"Why do *you* care so much if he dies?" she asked, the disdain for him and her husband clear in her voice.

"Because he is my father."

The room stopped, as if frozen in time, as everyone looked at him. It was well known that Chairman Mao had only one surviving son, and he was quite mad, in and out of mental institutions, and rarely spoken of.

"How dare you claim to be the relation of my husband!" she screamed, charging toward him. Anhong cowered into a corner, the doctor coming between the two of them before it came to blows.

"Leave us."

It was barely a whisper, but it silenced everyone. Anhong rushed to his father's side and took his hand.

"Everyone out except you and my wife, and Anqing if he is here."

The voice was weak, but clear, and the staff immediately obeyed, and Anhong looked up at the door as it closed behind them, then at Jiang Qing, still glaring at him, her eyes narrowed in hate.

He shivered.

She terrified him, and the thought of being alone in a room with her was almost more than he could bear. Before the door clicked shut however, it suddenly was pushed open again, and a smiling Anqing stepped inside the room, closing the door behind him.

He looked confident, strong. And completely sane.

Anhong sighed in relief at no longer being alone with that hateful bitch of a wife his father had had to tolerate for so many years. Why he had, was only known to his father, but the rumors of his sexual exploits outside of the sanctity of marriage seemed explained by the private relationship, or lack thereof, between him and his wife.

"Tell her the truth," whispered his father.

"The truth about what?" demanded Jiang, rounding the bed, her fists clenched. Anqing came up beside her, reassuring Anhong with a glance. He hadn't seen his brother in months, and it was a relief to see him well again. The years of cultivating the cover of him being mad had paid off, but also taken its toll, for he had to actually spend the time in the mental institutions for it to be truly believed.

He looks old.

"The truth about us. About our family. And about how you will never achieve what you have planned," said Anqing, his voice cold, even, menacing. A voice that sent shivers up Anhong's spine.

"What the hell do you mean?"

"*We* are direct descendants of the Tongzhi Emperor, last of the legitimate rulers of the Qing Dynasty, and it is *us* who will rule China after our father dies."

Jiang's jaw dropped, then she looked at her husband, as if looking for the truth.

He nodded as an alarm blared from one of the many machines monitoring his health. The door burst open, and the doctors and nurses rushed in, ending their conversation.

Jiang glared at both of them, then turned on her heel, storming from the room.

And Anhong knew they had made a mistake in telling her.

Metro Station, Olympic Sports Center, Beijing, China
Today

"You're late."

Acton nearly jumped out of his shoes at the voice. Laura's death grip on his hand indicated her own shock. He resisted the urge to spin around, instead freezing in position, while trying to look natural.

"Relax, Professors, otherwise you *will* draw attention to us."

Burt Dawson, leader of the Delta Force unit known as Bravo Team, rose from a park bench, and joined them. He was dressed in civilian clothes, much like the time they had seen him outside the Vatican. In fact, if Acton didn't know better, it might be the same disguise, save the camera he had been sporting back them.

"Sorry, ah, Mr. White. There was an incident today."

"At Tiananmen?"

"Yes."

"You were there?"

"Yes."

Dawson shook his head. "It's as if you two are cosmically drawn to trouble."

Acton had to admit it certainly seemed like it. In fact, he sometimes wondered if it would be safer for the world if he simply stayed home. He had done just that on December 21st, 2012, just in case the Mayan's had been right, and he was the catalyst. Since nothing had happened, *and* he had stayed home, he'd never know if he saved the world or not.

But judging from his history, being at home didn't seem to protect *him* regardless.

"I was going to warn you two that foreign tourists are being targeted by snipers. At least a dozen so far, if not more. We're still trying to put together the numbers, but they appear random to a point, in that we can't find a pattern beyond them being white, and being tourists. We're assuming it's politically motivated, but don't have any proof of that."

Laura reached into her pocket and unfolded the piece of paper she had picked up in Tiananmen.

"I found a couple of these floating around the square after the attack. The cop I gave a copy to seemed very nervous and grabbed it away from me."

"Do they know you have this?" asked Dawson as he took a photo with his phone.

"No, I don't think so."

Dawson pressed a few keys, then returned the phone to his pocket.

"Mind if I keep this?"

Laura shook her head.

"No, probably best I don't have it."

"Okay, I have to get back to the embassy. I suggest you two get your asses out of China tonight if possible, tomorrow at the latest. Charter a jet if you have to, but this is not the place you want to be right now. The Chinese are moving troops from outside the capital into staging areas. We suspect they're going to declare martial law and lock this place down tight until they can get a handle on what's going on."

"Sounds like Tiananmen all over."

"Exactly. And remember what they did then. They brought troops from outside the region. These are men with no ties to this area, or to the residents. They won't hesitate to kill if provoked. They will shoot first, and ask the proverbial questions later, if they even bother."

"When do you think the shit's going to hit the fan?" asked Acton.

"Could be any hour, any day, or never. It's hard to tell with the Chinese. But with the Ambassador now kidnapped, our government will be demanding action, and the Chinese version of action is different from ours. If it happened back home, we'd have every law enforcement branch looking into it. Here, they take a military approach. There is no Posse Comitatus Act here."

Acton's chest was tight, and Laura's grip hadn't loosened on his hand. His mind raced as he pictured scenario after scenario of all hell breaking loose like it so often did in his life, and how it always ended up with him and Laura in the thick of it.

"We'll go straight to the airport," he said, looking at Laura. "We'll send for our luggage, you call your agent and get us on the first flight out of the country. I don't care if it's North Korea. We need to get out of China."

Tires squealed behind him, causing them all to look. Several vehicles, lights flashing, raced down the road toward them. Acton gripped Laura's hand harder, and was about to run, when he felt a hand on his shoulder.

"Just stay calm, you haven't done anything wrong. Just remember, I'm Mr. White from the State Department. We met earlier this year arranging a dig permit for Egypt. You're tourists, and we arranged to meet here on the airplane."

"Unless they know that's all bullshit," hissed Acton as vehicles screeched to a halt from both directions.

He raised his hands, as did Laura.

But he never let go of her hand, as over a dozen police, or paramilitary, jumped from the vehicles and surrounded them, weapons drawn.

And out of the headlights partially blinding them in the dusk, strode the two investigators that had interrogated them earlier, and their apparent boss.

"It would seem we were never really let go," whispered Laura.

Acton's heart sank as the police advanced, cuffs in hand.

What do we do now?

FLAGS OF SIN

Chamber of the Spring Lotus, Zhongnanhai Complex, Beijing, China
October 6, 1976

"It must be stopped at all costs, and the only way to do it is to eliminate them all."

"But you are talking of his entire inner circle, his entire family. Your family! Think of the scandal! Your late husband will never rest in peace if you go through with this. His soul will haunt you until the end of your days, and into the afterlife." Wang Hongwen, terrified at her idea, shook his head. "I think this is wrong."

Jiang Qing frowned. *Pathetic. Weak. To think that I have included him in our meetings all these years, and now, when things are so close, nearly within our grasp, his resolve fails.* She made a mental note to add Wang to the list.

"I am the widow of our greatest leader, of our beloved leader. The people will follow me. The people will follow *us*. But we must act quickly. There are already those who plot against us, not the least of which are these fools who are working under the delusion they are descendants of the Tongzhi Emperor." She shook her head, her eyes closed. *How could my husband think such an insane thing?*

"I still can't believe it myself," said Zhang Chunqiao, a man she both trusted, and respected, his views on the bourgeoisie as legendary as his ruthlessness toward them. "But I will take your word for it that it is true. And since it is, I agree, they must be eliminated immediately. I will see to it today."

Jiang nodded. *I knew I could count on Zhang.* She looked at Wang, frowning. *If only you had Zhang's resolve, you would survive the night.*

"It is essential we act swiftly. We must be certain to have the support of the Generals before we move, and we must silence that cretin Deng Xiaoping. He is quickly gathering favor, and is popular with the people."

"It is unfortunate that *you* are not," observed Wang.

She glared at him.

"Because I did what was necessary, the people may not like me, but they respect me. And we do not need the support of the people now; we need the support of the military. The people will come later. For now—"

She stopped at the sound of shouting beyond the door, splintering wood, more shouting, and the crash of something as it broke on the floor. Then the doors of their meeting room, the doors of a room in her private residence, burst open, revealing a platoon of soldiers, and the man she least expected, striding through the doors.

"Anqing!" she cried as she jumped from her chair along with the others. "How dare you invade my private chambers!"

Mao Anqing, the crazed son of her late husband, smiled at her, then nodded at the others as more troops filled the room, weapons raised and pointed at the Gang of Four.

"Qing, it is good to see you on such a fine day."

Her heart pounded in her chest from the indignation of her privacy being violated, the hatred she felt for the man before her, a man she couldn't possibly take seriously or respect, and the fear. The fear of what was to come.

For she knew this was the end. There was nothing more she could do. Her husband had won. She knew she had lost his trust long before his death, and that even *he* had been plotting against her, but she would never have guessed that it would be the mentally ill brother who would be her undoing.

Li Anhong strode through the door, a smile on his face, his hands clasped behind his back. "Good day to you," he said, smiling at the four.

She spit on the ground, squaring herself defiantly against them, her bravado a false façade in the face of what was to come. She looked at the other three, all of whom had fear smeared across their faces. But not her. She wouldn't give these two vermin the satisfaction of seeing how she truly felt. One, a mental patient, the other, a pretender to the crown. Neither would know how she felt.

For she felt terrified.

She knew China. This was her China. She had helped build it. Shape it.

And it was ruthless.

And those who fell out of favor with the Party, could live to regret it.

She debated rushing the guards, perhaps earning a quick death, but she knew they would be too well trained to shoot her, their 8341 Special Regimental insignia revealing their skill level better than anything.

Her shoulders sagged and her head dropped.

"All I did, I did for China," she said.

Anqing whipped his hand toward her, signaling the formal arrest as two men stepped toward her, handcuffs at the ready. Within moments she was cuffed, and Anqing stood in front of her.

"And what *I* do today, I do for China."

Then he leaned in, and whispered in her ear.

"And I do it for my Emperor."

Leaving the Olympic Sports Center, Beijing, China
Today

James Acton sat with his hands bound by plastic ties in the back of a police van as it bounced along a road either in desperate need of repair, or with entirely too many speed bumps. He jostled Laura on one side, Dawson on the other, and wondered what the highly trained Special Forces operator was thinking right now. Could he escape the ties binding him? He had no doubt. He had been trained himself in how to defeat them easily.

But what would he do then?

He couldn't exactly kill the two police officers sitting across from them, nor the two investigators—or was it inspectors?—staring at them. They were innocent police, doing their job. The problem was the system they worked for wasn't.

And that terrified him.

He had visions of years if not decades languishing in a Chinese prison that would make a Soviet Gulag look civilized. And what of Laura? A woman? She would probably be raped repeatedly in a place like that.

His heart slammed in his chest at the thought.

We're getting out of here.

We have to.

"What's the charge, Inspector…Li, wasn't it?"

The man nodded.

"You will be informed when we reach the station. You have been arrested by order of our boss, Superintendent Hong."

"How long were we under surveillance?"

"No questions, please."

Suddenly the van jerked to a halt, and shouting could be heard from the front cabin. Several bursts of gunfire were accompanied by the van jerking several times, as if collapsing slightly, Acton guessing the tires were being shot out. The rear door was pulled open as the two armed guards in the back with them were still readying their weapons.

Both were shot in the head, instantly dead.

Three men climbed in, decked head to toe in black—gear he would associate with a special ops team—the first two holding handguns, the third holding a cellphone. At first Acton had the faint hope it was the Delta team coming to rescue them, but when Dawson didn't react, he realized this was something entirely different.

The man held the cellphone camera up to Dawson's face and pressed a button. A moment later it beeped, and he nodded. The first man grabbed Dawson and threw him out the back of the van and into the hands of another group that rushed him out of sight.

The man pointed the phone at Acton's face, then after a beep, shook his head, repeating the procedure with Laura. After the beep, he nodded, and the man closest to her grabbed her by the arm. Laura cried out, and yanked herself away from the man holding her, elbowing him in the head. He collapsed, and Acton shoved himself from his seat, launching his shoulder into the ribcage of the other armed man, who collapsed with a grunt, but without hands to steady himself properly, Acton fell into the laps of the two inspectors, who did nothing beyond shove him to his feet again.

He felt the barrel of a pistol press against the back of his neck.

"Professor Acton, be thankful we deem you to be of no value, otherwise you too would be coming with us." The sensation of the barrel disappeared for a moment, then he felt a jolt of pain as he was pistol whipped, the ensuing fog enveloping him as he slowly lost consciousness.

His last recollections were of Laura yelling for him, then Inspector Li shouting something in Chinese.

FLAGS OF SIN

Chongqing, China
November 14, 2011

Bo Yang sipped the 1963 Taylor Scion port, several bottles of which he had acquired in Europe, the rich liquid one of his few guilty pleasures. He kept himself clean—no drugs, no cigarettes, and minimal alcohol—and fit; a trim man by anyone's standards even at nearly sixty years of age.

For he had a purpose, a mission in life, that he had sworn to his father that he would fulfill. His father, Mao Anhong, who had died only four years ago, and had made him swear that he would fulfill the destiny laid out by his forefathers, not the least of which was his grandfather, Chairman Mao Zedong himself.

The two surviving children, his father, Anhong, and his uncle, Anqing, had failed. Deng Xiaoping had moved too swiftly after the death of his grandfather, Mao Zedong, and consolidated power before the brothers could act. But they had done nothing to draw attention to themselves, instead maintaining their covers, one the mentally ill brother with bouts of sanity, the other a former aide to the first Chairman of communist China, neither important enough to pay attention to, or eliminate. Instead, they receded into the background, and developed a plan for the next generation.

Him.

And he had done well. He had been groomed from an early age, and had risen to several positions of power, currently a member of the Central Politburo, and secretary of the Communist Party's Chongqing branch.

But how had he managed all of this with a father considered crazy, and a Communist party mostly hostile now to the policies of his grandfather? He had been raised as the son of one of the Eight Elders who had held sway over the Party, and the country, during the eighties and nineties, and had been groomed to be the future Paramount Leader. And if he played his cards right, and the markers he had been gathering were called appropriately, he would lead China soon.

Only his wife could screw it up now.

He loved her, which was the only reason he hadn't had her "disappeared" years ago. They had been married twenty-five years. She was a successful lawyer—*very* successful lawyer—and had founded a law firm that had gained national, and international, renown. But she had checked her ambitions once he had told her the truth, and instead gave up her career and worked silently in the background, cultivating the contacts, gathering the intelligence to be used against his enemies, and raising the funds to pay the necessary bribes, when the time was right.

She was instrumental in his success.

And now she was blowing it.

"Why did you do it?" he finally asked. She had come home almost an hour ago, had told him what had happened, and he had sat in stunned silence since, until getting himself the glass of port in an attempt to calm his nerves. "Please, explain to me how you thought this was the way out?"

"He threatened to tell the press our plans."

It was a matter of fact statement. Her voice was calm, as if she had done nothing wrong. As if what she had done was perfectly normal, a rational act that any sane person would have been expected to do.

"But you killed him."

She shrugged her shoulders, then rose, walking over to the liquor cabinet and pouring herself a vodka martini he had mixed her as she arrived—a pre-birthday treat for her, since in less than an hour, it would be the actual day celebrating her birth. Instead, it was the day preceding a death—by her hand.

"It was necessary. If we are to achieve our goals, we couldn't exactly have this man revealing our secrets, now could we?"

She was right. And that's what was infuriating about it. And he wasn't sure why the death of a businessman who had assisted them in several rather "delicate" transactions should bother him. After all, once he became Paramount Leader, he would probably order the death of thousands over his tenure.

He sighed.

"I'm more concerned with the fact that *you* did it. We have people for this sort of thing. If he has become a problem, we let them deal with it. That way our hands are clean. Now…" His voice drifted away as he tried to imagine what might now happen.

"He was going to phone a friend he had at the Times right then and there. I couldn't let him do that, and there was no time to call our people. So, I had to poison him. Don't worry, I made it look like he committed suicide."

"I doubt that will fool the authorities for long. It does worry me however that you had poison so readily available to you."

She smiled. "You know me, Darling, I'm always prepared."

He frowned. "Too prepared sometimes, it would appear. The correct course of action would have been to agree to his demands for more money, then have him killed."

She sat down beside him and sipped her martini. "You're right, of course, but what's done is done."

Bo Yang removed his cellphone and hit the speed dial for his fixer.

"This is Liang."

"We have a problem," he said to his trusted confidante. "A *big* problem."

7th District Police Station, Beijing, China
Today

James Acton was exhausted, sore, scared, and worried. Worried about Laura, and to a lesser extent Dawson. *He signed up for this shit. We didn't.* He frowned. *Yeah, if you had of run away from the shots like a sane person, Laura would be at the hotel, safe.* The thought triggered an epiphany. *What if we were arrested because we were with Dawson, and this has nothing to do with Tiananmen?*

The door clicked open and he looked up at the smiling face that entered the interrogation room he had been held in for hours. He had woken here, handcuffed to the table, his head pounding from where he had been hit, and nobody had yet had the courtesy to even let him know what was going on.

In fact, the man entering was the first person he had seen.

"Professor Acton, my name is Mr. Brown. I'm from the State Department, and am here as your representative with respect to this matter."

Acton frowned. "Mr. Brown," he nodded, as Brown took a seat across from him. "How did you find out I was here?"

A single eyebrow shot up Brown's forehead, and both eyebrows shot up Acton's as he suddenly recognized the man.

Spock!

He had no idea what the man's real name was, but he had met him several times, and knew he was part of Dawson's Bravo Team. He wanted to ask him what was happening, why he was there, why Dawson was in China, if he knew anything of Laura, and when the hell he was getting out of here—either through the front door as a free man, or rescued through the back door, as a fugitive.

But he knew he had to play along.

Spock seemed completely calm, as if this were a matter of fact situation he dealt with every day. He was every bit the professional operator Acton expected him to be.

"We received a call at the embassy about your arrest, and I was sent as soon as we located you."

Acton nodded. "I met a Mr. White on the plane. He invited me and my fiancée to meet him at the Olympic stadium. That's when we were all arrested."

"And where is Mr. White now?"

He doesn't know!

"The van was attacked and he was taken, along with Lau—"

The door was thrown open, the metal frame slamming against the concrete wall.

"Time's up!" yelled the man, apparently none too pleased at the information Acton had just revealed.

Acton stood, as did "Mr. Brown". Spock extended his hand.

"Professor, I hope to have you out of here as soon as we can clear up this misunderstanding."

Acton nodded, wondering how to fish something more definite out of him.

"Any idea how long I'll be here?"

Spock smiled as he released Acton's hand. He felt one of Spock's fingers press into his palm, and Acton closed his hand around the tiny object deposited there.

"I think you'll have to swallow your pride"—Spock seemed to incline his head slightly at this statement—"and wait probably four hours or so for further word."

Acton nodded as Spock was ushered from the room. The door slammed shut, and he sat back down, crossing his legs so he could open his hand slightly. In the palm, he saw a tiny metal ball. What it was, he had no clue, except that it must be some sort of tracking device, and Spock's none-too-subtle hint suggested he should swallow it.

Now.

He rolled it between his fingers, and faked a cough, covering his mouth and letting the device drop in.

He swallowed.

Then looked at the clock on the wall.

It was six p.m.

And he knew in four hours, something was going to happen.

Chongqing, China
Two months ago

Bo Yang sat quietly, sipping his port, waiting for the call. Everything was nearly lost. The secret had come out, it being too big to keep, and no matter how hard he had tried, he had been unable to protect his wife. She had been arrested, charged, and put on trial. The only question now was whether or not she would be put to death.

But it didn't matter.

She was no longer part of the plan, and no longer a hindrance due to her sometimes irrational acts.

And once you are in power, you can free her.

And it was power that he was about to achieve. The money had traded hands, the markers had been called, and the pieces were falling into place. They had tried to disgrace him, but the populace had spoken. No matter how they, the Party, had tried to discredit him, to stifle his support, it kept popping up on the blogosphere, the Internet, social media, and plain old print media. People had been arrested, people had disappeared, but the support continued, and the more it became a social phenomenon, and the more he injected his own disinformation surrounding his wife into the fray, the more the Party feared him.

For he was now an idol to the masses. Betrayed by the Party he had dedicated his life to, his wife framed for a murder she didn't commit, his career and life destroyed because he had chosen to stand by her side.

It was a PR campaign that would have made an American media mogul proud.

Because it had worked.

And now he awaited the final phone call, the call that would let him know he had the last piece of support he needed.

His phone vibrated on the table, and he placed his drink down. Taking a deep breath, he picked up the phone and flipped it open.

"Yes."

"We have their support."

"Very well."

He hung up and placed the phone back on the table, picking up his glass.

Then smiled as he looked across the room at the ancient flag, gold and blue, draped behind protective glass.

In two months, the Qing Dynasty will reign once again.

FLAGS OF SIN

Unknown Location
Today

Laura Palmer groaned, then righted herself. Opening her eyes, she blinked away the blur, and sucked in a quick breath as the memories of what had happened flooded back. *James!* She looked around but he wasn't there. She recognized the Delta Force commander, Burt Dawson, lying on a cot, apparently out cold, the female police officer, sitting with her legs tucked up under her chin, and an older man she didn't recognize. They appeared to be in a cramped room with no windows, several office-style halogen lights in the ceiling providing light, and four cots, one along each wall. Nothing else besides the locked door with a small grill blocking a Judas window.

"Good evening. At least I think it's evening."

It was the man sitting across from her. She looked at him and nodded. "Good evening."

"British?"

She nodded.

"How did you get mixed up in this?"

"My fiancée ran forward when he should have run back."

"Excuse me?"

Laura smiled.

"There was a shooting in Tiananmen Square. My fiancée tried to help. Then we were arrested later with our friend"—she nodded toward Dawson—"by her"—she tossed her chin at the female officer—"then were ambushed. They injected me with something—knocked me out." She looked at her watch. "I guess about three hours ago."

"I'm Ambassador Davidson," said the man, rising from his cot and extending his hand. "Call me Ian."

Laura rose as well and shook the man's hand. "Laura Palmer. I'm guessing it was you my fiancée was trying to save."

"What's his name?"

"Professor James Acton."

The man's eyebrows shot up. "Really! Heady company, your fiancée. I've read much about him. And you too, Professor."

Laura shrugged with a slight smile, then looked over at the cop.

"Are you okay?"

The woman nodded, but seemed to be nursing a head wound.

"Let me look at that," said Laura, stepping toward the woman.

The woman recoiled in fear, shoving herself against the wall.

"I won't hurt you. You know I'm not involved in this, otherwise I wouldn't be here with you."

The woman looked at her for a moment, then visibly relaxed, her shoulders slumping and the veins in her neck and forehead receding.

Laura sat down beside her and gently moved the woman's hair aside so she could see the small cut above the left eye.

"I'm Laura, Laura Palmer," she said as she examined the wound. "Forgive me, but I don't remember your name."

"Inspector Hu."

"Since we're all in this together, do you have a first name?"

The woman winced, jerking her head away.

"Sorry," said Laura, sitting back, her examination finished. "You'll be okay; it doesn't need stiches, but you should get it washed and put a plaster on it as soon as you get a chance."

The woman nodded, gingerly touching the wound then looking at her fingers. Apparently satisfied that there was no blood, she looked at Laura.

"Ping."

"Excuse me?"

"My name. Ping."

Laura smiled as broadly as she could, trying to reassure the woman she wasn't a threat. *We need everyone working together and trusting one another if we're going to get out of this.*

"Pleasure to meet you."

Laura pushed herself off the cot, and stepped over to Dawson's, looking him over. He didn't have any obvious wounds, and his breathing seemed steady and strong. She gently slapped his cheek, but there was no reaction.

"Out cold," she said to the others. "They must have really dosed him."

"Who is he?" asked Ping.

"Mr. White. He's State Department," said Ambassador Davidson. He looked at Laura. "You know him?"

She nodded, making direct eye contact with him for a moment, and he nodded, she hoped acknowledging that he realized exactly who and what Dawson was, and that it wasn't to be mentioned.

She turned to the Inspector.

"Ping, any idea where we are?"

The young woman shook her head.

"No, I woke up here only a few minutes before you did."

Laura sat back down on her cot, then quickly patted her pockets in the hopes they had missed her cellphone.

No such luck.

Ping smiled. "I checked as well. They took my phone too."

"I never carry one," said Ambassador Davidson. "Security reasons."

Laura nodded. Phones could be tapped and tracked. Not something you wanted happening to your ambassador.

A sound outside the door had them all start, their eyes fixing on the metal grate covering the Judas hole as it slid open. But any hopes at rescue were doused as the door opened, and two heavily armed men in body armor entered, followed by a third who carried a cardboard box that he tossed on the floor.

"Food. Water. Medical supplies," he said, pointing at the box.

Laura eyed the contents, and suddenly realized how thirsty she was. She reached forward for a bottle of water, when she saw a blur to her left.

FLAGS OF SIN

Chongqing, China
Two weeks ago

Bo Yang struck an imposing figure, his uniform freshly pressed, his rank and insignia, ceremonial and not yet official, classified him far higher than the top generals in the room. He sat at his desk flanked by two gold flags, their blue dragons boldly displayed, giving the impression they were clawing their way to the top of the poles that held them, locked in an ancient game of King of the Mountain.

And in Bo's mind, it was he who was that dragon, clawing his way back to the top of the mountain his family had been so unceremoniously kicked from. His grandfather, Mao Zedong, had ruled the country for decades, an emperor in everything but name only, but after his death, the family had been forced underground, but the reemergence was almost complete.

With billions of dollars, pounds and Euros, he had bought the loyalties of the men he needed, and most were in the room now, ready to follow his orders for a chance at ultimate glory and power, and if all else failed, escape from the country that would have them shot for even discussing what was about to happen.

"Everything is ready?" he asked.

His second-in-command, General Liang, nodded. "The killings will begin today across all major cities. We anticipate they will be covered up, but that is part of the plan. Leaflets designed to confuse the issue, will be scattered at the scenes, and the stories slowly leaked internationally. After one week, we will ramp up the killings, and the international community will demand a response. The Committee will meet to discuss this, and I will tell them I'm moving troops into position to restore order should it be necessary. This will satisfy them, and by the end of the second week, we will have armored and infantry divisions, along with air support, in place outside each of the target areas."

"How much air support?"

"Enough." General Liang leaned forward. "You must realize that we cannot hope to defeat the combined forces of the People's Liberation Army. We must defeat the forces in Beijing and the other target areas, replace the government, and then demand the loyalty of the unit commanders, eliminating those who refuse immediately, and replacing them with those loyal to us. It must be swift, decisive, and unwavering. And done within twenty-four hours of the start of our operation, or all will be lost."

Bo nodded, looking at the animated display of the planned Beijing assault on the large screen to his right. His heart slammed against his ribcage in anticipation.

It's so close.

"The essential piece is the kidnapping of the American Ambassador. We've analyzed his patterns, and found a weakness that should be easily exploited. Once we have him, the Americans will demand a response. This will allow me to move my troops in under the guise of providing that very response, which will allow us to take key positions within the city before they even know what's happening." The general leaned back in his chair, looking about the room. "If all goes well, the coup will be complete within hours, and you, sir, will be our supreme leader, and Emperor of a new China."

Bo sat back in his chair, having leaned forward during the description of the plan, it playing out in his mind like a Hollywood blockbuster.

Emperor Bo.

It wouldn't be his title at first, it would take time for the country to be prepped for such a change.

FLAGS OF SIN

But it was a change he was certain they would embrace.

If they knew what was good for them.

7*th* *District Police Station, Beijing, China*
Today

Inspector Li Meng stood dumbfounded in his boss' office. It had been everything he could do to prevent his jaw from dropping, and even now, it still begged to be open, if only slightly. He couldn't believe what he had just heard. It was incredible. It was insane.

It was so Chinese.

He stepped over to a chair and dropped in it as his boss, Superintendent Hong, stood up and closed the office door. Returning to his seat, he lowered his voice.

"I can't believe it myself."

Inspector Li, his head buried between his knees, looked up.

"Where did the order come from?"

Superintendent Hong waved his hands. "No no no no no!" he hissed. "Don't ask that. Not this time."

"But—"

Hong cut him off with a curt wave of his hand.

"You don't want to know. *I* don't want to know, but I do, and it terrifies me. Never before have I seen an order come from so high."

Li sucked in a deep breath, then sat up straight.

"When will the trials take place?"

Hong looked away.

"It's my understanding the trials have *already* taken place."

Li bolted from his seat.

"What! He hasn't even been in custody for more than a few hours!" Li paced the room, shaking his head. "And we don't even have the others *in* custody!"

"They were all tried in absentia. There was no defense. There will be no appeal. Justice will be swift and unwavering."

"But what were the charges?"

"Conspiring to overthrow the People's Government, and espionage."

Li's heart almost stopped. "Espionage?"

Hong nodded, staring out the window as if ashamed to make eye contact with Li.

"And you're certain about the sentence?"

Hong nodded.

"With espionage, there can be only one sentence."

Li knew he was right. And with the state apparently hell-bent on being seen as taking action on the shootings and now kidnapping of the American Ambassador, he knew the sentence would be carried out as equally swift as the trial.

"When?"

"Professor James Acton will be executed by firing squad tomorrow morning at six a.m."

Bo Yang's Mobile Headquarters, Beijing, China

"You were right to have us follow them, sir."

Bo Yang nodded as he reviewed the display in front of him. *Of course I was right. I am to be an emperor.* He looked up at the captain in front of him.

"They met with an American State Department official, most likely to give him information on what they had seen, but we ran his face." The man placed a file in front of Bo, opened to a summary page with a photo of the official. "He is *not* Mr. Virgil White. He's a special forces operative."

Bo's eyebrows went up slightly.

If things go wrong, someone to pin it on.

"I decided it was best to grab him, just in case. It was an easy takedown. The arrogance of the police knows no bounds—they had no escort vehicles so it was a low risk op. I figured foreign money, foreign operatives. We can leak photos and surveillance video of him, along with his true identity. Blame the Americans for what's going on. It could cause confusion while we consolidate power."

"Agreed," said Bo. "And the woman?"

"Facial recognition has her as Professor Laura Palmer, British subject," he said as he placed another folder on the desk.

"A professor? What the hell does that give us?"

"Nothing. But a *mega*-millionaire professor? That gives us a valuable hostage, just in case. She's worth over one hundred million Euros. *Well* over."

Bo pursed his lips. He didn't like to think of things going wrong, but it was best to plan for the worst. He pushed the file aside.

"I took the female cop as well. I figured it might be handy to have one of their own as a hostage. It might make them more reluctant to shoot."

"Or more eager to find us."

His subordinate frowned.

"Yes, perhaps taking her wasn't wise."

"It's too late now."

The man bowed in apology.

Bo nodded. "Where are they now?"

"I put them in the sleeping compartment with the Ambassador."

"Very well, you're dismissed."

"One other thing, sir."

Bo looked up, his attention already back on the monitors showing his forces' movements.

"Yes?"

"I took the liberty of having our contacts order the execution of the other passenger. He's the one who interfered with our operation earlier today."

"The would-be hero?"

"Yes. He'll be dead by dawn. Our people have already convicted him and the others of conspiracy and espionage."

Bo chuckled.

"Captain, you are thorough. I think you will go far in the new China."

The man bounced on his heels and thrust his shoulders back, chest out.

"Thank you, sir!"

Bo dismissed him with a wave of his hand. "Now go, I have work to do."

The captain bowed deeply, and began to back out of the room when Bo, constantly planning for every contingency, stopped him.

"On second thought, kill the American soldier. I don't want to risk having him getting loose in my headquarters."

The captain bowed even deeper.

"At once, sir. I'll do it myself."

The door closed and Bo leaned back in his chair, spinning it to face away from the desk. He stared at the gold silk that hung proudly on the wall, and debated if the flag should indeed stand side by side with the red Chinese flag when he made his announcement to the nation, and the world.

A shout from down the hall interrupted his reverie.

FLAGS OF SIN

7th District Police Station, Beijing, China

Inspector Li Meng sat at his desk, staring at the empty chair that should be occupied by his partner. *I hope you're okay, Ping.* He was at a loss as to what to do. Any time now they would be here to pick up his only witness for execution. He couldn't interfere with that without risking being accused of involvement and finding himself in front of the same firing squad. And of course nobody had seen anything. CCT footage was being reviewed, but not by him. That was another department. And would he be told if they actually found anything?

He doubted it.

He sighed and picked up the phone to call his wife. Punching the numbers from memory, he placed the phone to his ear and waited, but didn't hear anything. He hung up and waited a moment, then was about to pick up the phone to try again when he noticed that several others around him were looking at their phones, some yelling, "Hello, hello!"

Quickly picking up the phone, he held it to his ear.

No dial tone.

He stood up as the entire room went dark.

Shouts of confusion erupted from all around, and a moment later emergency lighting kicked in, lending a dull glow to the proceedings, long shadows cast from the glaring battery powered bulbs on the walls.

"Phones are down, power's out!" yelled someone as they rushed by him toward Superintendent Hong's office.

Li, still standing, looked through several sets of windows and saw three soldiers walking through security, unchallenged, the post seemingly abandoned in the chaos.

They must be here for the professor.

Li watched them calmly walk past police officers running in all directions, then proceed out of sight, toward the cellblock. Ignoring the confusion around him, Li strode from the squad room, something not seeming right about the soldiers.

Why aren't they wondering what's going on?

He hurried through the doors separating the squad room from the admin area, then through to the hallway that ran the length of the building on the outer wall. Turning left, he headed toward the cell block and saw the three soldiers at the end of the hall, one trying the door without success.

When the power goes out, the doors actually seal.

These couldn't be the soldiers here to pick up the prisoner. They would never head to the cellblock; they would merely wait at the front entrance for an officer to retrieve the prisoner.

There's definitely something wrong.

He started toward the end of the hall when he saw one of the men kneel down, then the three turn their heads. A popping sound and a flash of light from their position made him think of fireworks, but when the door to the cellblock opened, and the three men disappeared inside, he began to run toward the end of the hall.

Within moments he was at the door, weapon drawn, peering into the darkness. A lone emergency light over his head cast a beam down the corridor, and he could see the three men at the far end. There was a moan to his right, and he saw the officer on duty, who should have been behind a desk, actually lying in a heap on the floor.

He aimed his weapon down the hall.

"Identify yourselves!" he yelled as another small explosion flashed at the far end. Two of the men dropped to their knees, aiming weapons at him as the third disappeared into the cell.

Li continued to advance.

"I said, identify yourselves!"

The third man appeared, along with a fourth he immediately recognized as the professor.

Maybe they are here to pick him up?

He lowered his weapon slightly, then realized how ridiculous the thought was.

He raised his weapon again.

"Don't shoot!" yelled one of them, in English, the voice vaguely familiar.

It must be the professor.

"He's the cop who questioned me earlier. He was attacked in the van, just like I was."

The two men on their knees continued to aim their weapons at him, but Li continued to advance, realizing he was now committed, there was no escape to the sides as the cell doors were sealed, and there was no escape to the rear, it too far to go.

Adrenaline fueled his courage now.

And curiosity.

Who are they? And why is the American going with them willingly?

"I'll get you to stop where you are, Inspector."

This was a different man, one of the three soldiers, and the only one standing.

Li stopped.

"We're taking this man out of here. I suggest you turn around and forget what you saw."

Suddenly the lights flickered, then blazed above their heads. Li was momentarily blinded, and raised his hand to shield his eyes so they could adjust. In seconds he found himself in the grip of the two soldiers who had been aiming their weapons at him only moments before.

One removed Li's weapon, then covered him as the man's partner patted him down.

"You won't be getting out of here now," said Li when the man was finished. "This place will be swarming with my colleagues in seconds."

"Then help us," said the professor, stepping forward. "You know I'm innocent." He nodded toward the third soldier, who Li suddenly recognized as the man who had arrived earlier today from the embassy.

"Mr. Brown!"

The man nodded, an eyebrow climbing up his forehead.

"Inspector Li."

"What are you doing here?" asked Li, shocked at the realization that two of the soldiers were white, the third Asian, but not Chinese. *Korean?*

"You know very well that your government has given orders for Professor Acton to be executed tomorrow. We can't let that happen."

Li's jaw dropped.

"How could you know?"

Mr. Brown didn't answer.

"Inspector, you know I'm innocent. I don't deserve to die for trying to do the right thing."

Li looked at the professor, then slowly nodded.

He's right. He doesn't deserve to die. And I'm a coward if I let it happen without at least speaking up.

Li sucked in a breath and stood slightly taller, a decision made.

"I was serious when I said you won't get out of here. At least not that way," he said, jerking a thumb over his shoulder at the door they had all come through. "If you release me, I'll show you how to get out of here."

Mr. Brown waved off the other two men, dressed exactly like PLA soldiers, and he found himself once again a free man.

"Follow me," he said, stepping forward and past Mr. Brown and the professor. He broke out into a jog toward the end of the corridor, then turned right, continuing toward the far end. In less than a minute they were at an outer door, sealed, but unguarded.

"This is a special transfer area for dangerous or, shall we say, secret, offenders. It is never guarded as it is rarely used. Through here, you will be at the rear of the building. Fifty meters straight, and you are in the parking lot, where I'm sure you can find a vehicle. But you must hurry, the security computers will finish rebooting at any moment and the cameras will become active."

Li removed the pass that was clipped to his shirt, then slid it through the card reader. It beeped, displaying a green light, and the door lock clicked. He pulled the door open and urged them through. The two men who had guarded him went through first, then the professor extended his hand.

"Thank you, Inspector."

Li shook Acton's hand as Mr. Brown approached.

"Tell them you saw several suspicious looking people, came to investigate, we forced you at gunpoint here, stole your pass, and knocked you out. That way you should be okay."

"But—" started Li, about to ask about the knocking out part, when Mr. Brown's hand raised above his head, then came down hard, the pistol grip impacting his skull, immediately sending him to the ground in a rapidly darkening world.

Sleeping Quarters, Bo Yang's Mobile Headquarters, Beijing, China

Laura's head whipped to the left and it took a moment to comprehend what she was seeing. Dawson, thought to be out cold, was anything but. He was already on his feet, and had the closest guard in a choke hold with his left arm, his right hand reaching for the man's weapon.

And Laura reacted.

She pushed from her cot, sweeping her right leg along the floor, kicking out the legs from under the second guard. As he fell to the ground, she heard a shot ring out, and the third man jerked backward, toward the door as another shot rang out, her own man jerking from the impact. She looked up and saw the liberated handgun pressed against the only surviving guard's temple.

"How do we get out of here?" demanded Dawson.

The guard was terrified, and kept looking at his dead comrades. Laura meanwhile took the opportunity to strip the two dead men of their weapons, sticking a semi-automatic pistol in her belt, and slinging a Type 80 machine pistol over her shoulder, pocketing several clips. She tossed the other handgun to the cop, who still seemed in shock, then turned to the Ambassador, holding up the other Type 80.

"Do you know how to use this?"

"Three tours in 'Nam."

Laura smiled and tossed him the weapon and threw a few clips on the cot beside him. She grabbed the man who had brought the box of supplies and pulled his body inside, it blocking the door open. Taking up position at the door, she closed it over, leaving a slight gap she could look through.

"One target, twenty feet, coming this way, cautiously. He's got his weapon out."

"Ask him how we get out of here."

Laura glanced over her shoulder and saw Dawson push the prisoner toward Ping, the gun still pressed against the man's head, and the Ambassador going through the supplies that had just been delivered.

He looked up at her. "Don't mind me, Professor," he said as he filled his pockets with the military rations. "We don't know when we'll get a chance at supplies again."

"Good thinking," she said. She motioned with her chin at the cot. "Take a pillow cover, get some of the water and the med kit."

"Better thinking," said the Ambassador with a smile as he quickly complied.

"Five feet," she announced.

"Take him out," said Dawson.

"Taking him out," announced Laura, squeezing the trigger. There was a loud crack, and the man dropped. There was shouting, but not as much as she had expected.

It's as if there's hardly anybody here.

Ping asked something in Chinese, and the man quickly blurted out a reply.

"End of the hallway, there's a door, it leads outside," translated Ping.

"Where to then?" asked Dawson. Another exchange in Chinese.

"He doesn't know where we are, we're apparently in a mobile HQ."

Dawson coldcocked the man and he dropped in a heap. He stripped him of weapons as Laura threw the door open and exited, covering their escape. Dawson took point, the Ambassador and Ping following. Laura quickly backed her way toward the end of the hall as she heard several single shots ring out, each followed either by a cry or merely the thump of a body hitting the floor.

She walked by a room and felt her heart slam into her chest as the door suddenly jerked open. A man in his sixties, the uniform crisp, the insignia marking him as somebody high ranking, gaped at her, then jumped aside as she aimed at him and fired. She missed, his reaction time too quick, and the door was kicked closed from the inside, but not before she caught a glimpse of a Qing Dynasty flag mounted on the rear wall.

Odd.

She heard a door open behind her, and an engine roar to life. The entire building jerked, and it took a moment to connect what was happening with what had been said earlier.

Mobile HQ.

"We're in a truck!" she exclaimed.

"Let's go!" yelled Dawson. She glanced over her shoulder and saw him push Ping out the door, then the Ambassador, as the view from outside began to move. He grabbed her by the back of the shirt and she spun around, jumping out the back and rolling as she hit the ground, immediately regaining her balance and aiming her weapon directly in front of her as she surveyed their surroundings.

Ping spoke up.

"I recognize this area, follow me."

Shouts began to fill the alley they appeared to be in as they all followed Ping at a sprint. Gunfire erupted behind them, and the pounding of booted feet sent her pulse racing.

Somebody cried out in front of her, and she saw the Ambassador stumble. She rushed forward and ducked down, pulling his arm over her shoulder as she took some of the weight off of what was an apparently wounded leg.

"Let's keep moving, Ambassador," she said as she helped him around the corner and out of their pursuers' line of fire.

Ping was way out in front of them now, the Ambassador moving much slower.

"Ping!" called Laura. Ping looked back and stopped, then suddenly jumped out in front of a car as it turned the corner onto the small street they were on. She aimed her weapon at the windshield and the car skidded to a halt. Without hesitating, she opened the driver side door and yanked the terrified man out, tossing him on the ground as Dawson grabbed the Ambassador.

"Cover us," he ordered, as he hauled the ailing man toward their commandeered vehicle.

Laura spun around and backed toward the car, her machine pistol aimed at the opening of the alley they had just come from. The muffled boots continued to pound, and the shouts got louder, until they finally exploded into crystal clear clarity as several men erupted from the alleyway.

She squeezed the trigger, spraying the area with lead, two of the men falling prey to her well-aimed shots, the others scattering.

"Let's go!" she heard Dawson yell.

Tires squealed and she glanced over her shoulder as she fired several more rounds. The car was in the midst of a 180, repositioning itself for their escape.

The rear door was pushed open and she ran toward the car, emptying the last of her clip toward the alleyway blindly as she jumped into the back seat, and on top of a groaning ambassador.

The car jerked forward, sending her tumbling behind the seats. She heard several pistol rounds fire nearby, and saw through the confusion Dawson squeezing off rounds out the passenger side window to cover their escape. The rear window exploded as they were hit by return fire, and Dawson ducked back into the vehicle.

She forced herself to her knees and reloaded her Type 80 as the car suddenly jerked to the left, sending her hard against the door. It flew open and she found herself falling toward the pavement, both hands occupied by the task at hand.

An iron grip grabbed her by the shoulder, and pulled her back inside.

"We're clear!" yelled Ping.

As soon as the words were out of her mouth a car to their left exploded in a fireball that shot thirty feet into the air.

"Holy shit!" exclaimed Dawson as he reached over and jerked the wheel, sending them into another alleyway.

"What the hell was that?" asked Laura as she climbed into position to cover them through the now non-existent rear window.

But she didn't need to wait for the answer as she gasped at what came around the corner after them.

A diesel belching tank, its treads chewing up the pavement as it rapidly turned the corner, its turret swinging directly toward them as it lined up for a second shot.

"Get us out of here!" she screamed.

Sleeping Quarters, Bo Yang's Mobile Headquarters, Beijing, China

Bo Yang surveyed the carnage. His trusted Captain was dead, only moments after having spoken to him, and two of his guards were also killed. The HQ jerked to a halt and he reached for a wall to steady himself. The rear door burst opened and he glanced down the hall to see several of his staff jump aboard, led by guards from one of several support vehicles.

He took one final look at the bodies, then strode quickly to his office as the officers followed him inside.

"Status!" he yelled.

"We've relocated here," said General Liang, pointing at a map on the wall. "One of our staging areas. Our men are in pursuit of the escaped prisoners."

A thunderous sound was heard that caused the entire room to shake.

"What the hell was that?"

But he knew what it was. It was a tank firing; he recognized the sound from his visits to various military installations over the decades, fostering goodwill for this very day.

"Who the hell ordered a tank to open fire?" he demanded.

No one in the room dared answer, so he fixed his glare on his armored commander, whose eyes darted to the floor. "I will look into it at once, sir!" he said, jumping up on the balls of his feet then running out the door.

An orderly rushed into the room, handing General Liang a dispatch. Liang smiled as he read it.

"Sir, martial law has been declared until the perpetrators of the sniper attacks, and the kidnapping of the American Ambassador, are in custody. Apparently somebody just effected the escape of Professor James Acton and they're in a panic!" Liang smiled, waving the page. "This is what we've been waiting for! We've been given orders to send our troops into the city to restore order."

Bo dropped into his chair, leaning an arm behind him and absentmindedly running his fingers along the silk of the flag he honored.

And smiled.

He looked from man to man in the room, realizing the order he was about to give would change China forever. Leaning forward, elbows on the arms of his chair, hands clasped firmly in front of him, he took in a deep, slow breath, the rehearsed speech he had planned for this moment gone in the excitement.

"It's time to take China into the future, gentlemen. Commence the operation."

They all snapped to attention, saluting, then rushed from his office. The door closed, he spun around and stared at the dragon, its seemingly futile attempt to climb the pole about to succeed.

The coup d'état had begun.

FLAGS OF SIN

Approaching Tiananmen Square, Beijing, China

Laura Palmer gripped the back of the seat, trying to keep her balance as Ping maneuvered the car in a zigzag pattern up and down alleyways and side streets, trying to keep ahead of the tank by at least one corner, but several dead ends and alleyways blocked with delivery vehicles had caused them to double-back several times, leaving the tank always just out of sight.

"Stop!" yelled Dawson. "Reverse!"

Ping complied, slamming the car in reverse and driving like a maniac in the direction they had just come, but not nearly as straight. Several garbage cans fell prey to her swerves, and Laura desperately wished she were behind the wheel, her driving skills apparently far superior to the young police officer's.

Laura ducked as the contents of a bin flew up and over the car, some of it pelting her through the rear window. She looked down the alley where they had been heading, and saw the tank roll up, its turret rotating into position.

"We've got about five seconds!" she yelled when she felt the car screech to a halt.

"Forward!" yelled Dawson.

Ping complied, but followed it with an "are you crazy?" look as the car surged toward the tank. Laura glanced through the rear window and saw a delivery truck had just cut them off, blocking the alleyway. Looking forward, her heart hammered faster with each meter they closed between them and the metal beast hell-bent on destroying them.

"Get ready to bail!" yelled Dawson, one hand already on the door handle. Laura slid over to his side, and opened the door slightly. "Brake when I tell you, then get out and start running away from the tank."

Ping nodded, saying nothing.

"Brake!" yelled Dawson. The car jerked to a halt, sending Laura against the back of the passenger seat. For a moment she was disoriented, but felt her door jerk open, and a hand grab her. She stumbled from the car, then was pushed forward by Dawson. "Keep running, don't look back!"

But she had to.

She glanced over her shoulder and saw Ping at least a dozen paces behind her, terror etched on her face, her eyes bulged with fear, and Dawson pulling the Ambassador from the backseat and heaving him onto his shoulder in a fireman's carry. The alleyway compressed the sound, and the round belching from the turret sent a shockwave toward them. She couldn't tell if it hit them first, or if the car they had just been in erupted into a fireball first, either way, they were all thrown to the ground.

Dawson was up first, pulling Laura to her feet. "Keep going!" he yelled as he picked up the Ambassador. Laura grabbed Ping and ran toward the delivery truck, its driver and the lumper standing, mouths agape, staring at what had just happened.

"Get out of here!" yelled Laura, waving her hands to the sides, hoping they'd understand to get out of the alley.

But they just stood, frozen.

She reached the driver first, and saw an open door to the left.

"Over here!" she yelled, shoving the driver through the doorway, and diving inside after him. Another round erupted from the tank, slamming into the delivery truck, shoving it farther down the alleyway before it exploded.

FLAGS OF SIN

A body flew through the door, landing on the driver as Laura jumped to her feet. Another followed, and just as the fireball roared toward them, she saw Dawson pushing toward the door, obviously having taken time to save the innocent bystander. She reached out and grabbed his outstretched hand, yanking him inside, providing that little bit of extra momentum that allowed him to clear the threshold just as the fireball exploded through the open doorway. She slammed the steel door shut, and the roar instantly dulled as they all tried to catch their breath.

Dawson let go of her hand and jumped to his feet, pulling everyone else to theirs and collecting the Ambassador. "Let's get out of here."

Ping asked something in Chinese, and the men pointed deeper into the building. She replied with her hands, urging them forward.

She didn't have to urge hard.

They ran fast, dodging between boxes stacked to the ceiling, and through a dizzying number of doors and small rooms, but with each step they were farther from the tank, and Laura began to relax. A little.

And suddenly they were outside, the fresh cool nighttime air a relief compared to the claustrophobic thickness inside.

"We need to get somewhere public, and get the Ambassador to a hospital," said Dawson.

Ping pointed to their right. "One block, Tiananmen Square," she said. Dawson nodded. "Let's go!"

They broke into a sprint, and the two men ran with them, probably not entirely certain as to why. One of them pulled out a cellphone, which Ping immediately grabbed. They ran past an alley and Laura caught a glimpse of the tank pursuing them, already rushing toward the street they were now on.

"We're gonna have company!" she yelled as they suddenly burst onto a large boulevard filled with a steady stream of nighttime traffic, but to Laura's dismay, there was almost no pedestrian traffic to mingle with.

The screeching of treads behind them added a new sense of urgency to their situation as they looked about for somewhere to hide.

Oh James, I wish you were here!

FLAGS OF SIN

En Route to US Embassy, Beijing, China

Nothing much had been said since the breakout. Acton was still in shock from the knowledge he was about to be executed, and with the further knowledge that he was now an escaped fugitive.

In China.

They had to make it to the embassy so that at least he would be protected, and then negotiations could begin for the charges to be dropped. Clearly something was going on that none of them knew anything about. The death penalty for trying to help? He could understand being arrested and questioned, then released. He could even understand deportation. But sentenced to death, with the execution to be carried out within twelve hours of the arrest?

To him it sounded Iranian, not Chinese.

If he weren't paranoid—which after everything that had happened to him over the past couple of years it was a miracle he wasn't—he'd think he was being targeted for some reason. But no one could have known he would be where he was, so that couldn't be it.

But if he had injected himself into the middle of something he wasn't supposed to, perhaps that's why he was being targeted. But then why did they take Laura?

And who were *they*?

They couldn't be the authorities. The authorities already had him. *They* had to be the people at Tiananmen. And those people were well equipped. He recognized the sound of a sniper rifle, and those weren't easy to come by. It was as if they were being targeted by—

"Holy shit!" he exclaimed.

"What?" asked Spock, looking in the rearview mirror.

"Do you guys have any intel on what's going on?"

Spock said nothing. Neither did Jimmy or Niner.

"Come on, I'm in the loop now."

Spock looked at Niner who sat in the passenger seat and nodded. Niner turned back.

"Okay, here's the dealio. Over the past two weeks foreign tourists have been murdered, most by sniper rounds, with anti-foreigner propaganda leaflets thrown about. Today they targeted our ambassador, and that's what you stumbled upon. We were called in to do a security assessment, and had warned against taking the exact route he took, because he takes the same goddamned route every effin' day."

"Take a breath, dude!" urged Jimmy.

"Sorry, Doc, but it just pisses me off when politicians ignore perfectly sound advice, then get themselves up shit's creek. Then it's guys like us that have to go and rescue their asses, or die trying."

A phone rang and Spock fished it from his pocket, handing it to Niner. Niner flipped it open.

"Green here."

His eyebrows shot up and his eyes widened as a smile spread across his face.

"BD! Where the hell are you?" he asked as he put the phone on speaker.

"We're pinned down near Tiananmen."

Spock jerked the wheel to the left, pulling a one-eighty with no warning.

"Pinned down?"

"Yeah, by a tank."

"Are you fuckin' with me?"

"I wish I were. I've got Professor Palmer with me, a local cop who was kidnapped with us, along with our ambassador and two innocent bystanders. The Ambassador's badly wounded. Won't make it if we don't get some real cover and a chance to dress his wound."

"We're on our way, ETA…"

"Ten minutes!" yelled Spock.

"You get that?"

"Yup. Listen, they arrested me with both professors. I don't know where Professor Acton is—"

"I'm right here, Sergeant. Tell Laura I'm okay."

"Good to hear your voice, Professor. Spock, get your asses over here but be careful. Something big is going on and I'm not sure what. There's a lot of heavy equipment involved. If I didn't know better, I'd say we're in the middle of a coup d'état."

There was silence in the car at these words and they all exchanged glances, and the concern in the eyes of these men made Acton all the more scared.

"Understood, Bravo One. We'll be there ASAP. I assume you can be reached at this call display number?"

"Confirmed. Contact us when you arrive."

Niner flipped the phone closed and looked at Spock.

"Should we notify the embassy?"

Spock nodded. "Give them a sit rep, and tell them to expect a contingent of US citizens coming in hot."

Niner nodded and began to dial the phone.

Acton leaned back in his seat and looked out the window and gasped.

"What the hell is that?" he asked as they rounded a corner.

On the opposite side of the road was a column of tanks, armored personnel carriers and troop transports, racing in the opposite direction.

"What are those markings?" asked Jimmy, leaning over Acton's lap.

Acton looked, but they appeared to merely be a solid gold, oddly reminiscent of the background of the Qing Dynasty flag, but without the blue dragon emblazoned across it so boldly.

"Regimental colors?"

"Doubt it," replied Niner. "Those usually have symbols of some type. That's a solid color. I'd guess it's meant to distinguish them from other units."

Acton frowned, looking at the armor as it roared by.

"I have a feeling your sergeant's hunch is right. We're in the middle of a coup."

FLAGS OF SIN

North-East Corner, Tiananmen Square, Beijing, China

The sense of déjà vu was almost eerie. With the exception of there being no natural light, she was in nearly the exact same spot as earlier today, only the characters had changed. She, Dawson, Ping, the Ambassador and the two Chinese delivery men were huddled behind a large planter. Across the square, instead of a white van, was a tank. But for some reason it hadn't fired; it was merely holding its position.

Ping was furiously texting, and had been since Dawson had relinquished the commandeered phone. Dawson was now lying flat on the ground, peering around the side of the planter at the tank across the square.

"If he decides to fire, we're dead," he said matter-of-factly.

Laura thought of James, and how he had rushed off to try and save the Ambassador earlier, and how he was now rushing to try and save her this very minute. Her heart was tight in her chest as she realized what Dawson said was so true. Just one shot from that tank and they would be finished. It wasn't like the horror she had gone through earlier when she watched the snipers try to chip away at the planter her beloved had hid behind, the only thing saving him the large amount of soil it contained. If it had merely been concrete, it would have split in two with the first shot, and James would have been exposed.

But tonight, soil or no soil, that tank's round would slice through the planter like brie. And right now she could think of nothing to do about it.

She tied off the tourniquet she had made from the Ambassador's tie, having cleaned the wound as best she could with the water Ping had managed to keep carrying, and wrapped it with a bandage from the med kit contained in the pillow case, but the wound was deep, and still seeping blood. The Ambassador was weak, and could barely speak.

He won't make it if we can't get him to a hospital soon.

"Okay, here's the plan," said Dawson, shuffling over to them. "Right now that turret is pointing down the street, perpendicular to us. The tank's at zero degrees from us, like a compass. We're at one-eighty, the turret's pointed at ninety. The moment he starts to aim at us, you two"—he pointed at the delivery men—"go that way"—he pointed to their left—"since that will give you the best chance at surviving. Just keep running until you're out of sight, and lay low. They don't know who you are and aren't looking for you."

Laura had to smile to herself that his thoughts were to protect the innocent bystanders first. He looked at her after Ping had finished translating.

"Professor, you and the Inspector head this way"—he pointed at a forty-five degree offset from the deliverymen's escape route. "Get behind those cars, then keep moving down the street as best you can. Watch for the tank in case he repositions. If he does, switch to the other side of the cars. Keep retreating until you can get out of sight, then try to make your way to the US Embassy. Hail a cab or something. Just get the hell out of here."

"What about you?"

"I'll follow you with the Ambassador, but we'll be slower. I don't want us holding you up."

"That's bollocks, Sergeant. I'm not leaving you behind."

Dawson gave her half a smile. "You and Professor Acton were made for each other," he said, shaking his head. "Listen, there's nothing you can do. I have to carry him alone, and you can't provide cover fire, since it's a tank we're dealing with. My duty is to you and the Ambassador. He's an

American citizen, and you're the citizen of an ally. This is my job, let me do it."

She realized he was right. There *was* nothing she'd be able to do. The best thing she could do would be to take care of herself so he wouldn't have to worry about her.

"You're right, of course, Sergeant."

He seemed relieved to hear her say that, and he shuffled to get a look.

"Something's happening."

Laura looked up and her heart sank. Two columns of tanks were roaring toward them on either side of the boulevard they had just crossed. Cars were slamming their brakes on, swerving to avoid the armor that advanced like a juggernaut, what they hit and who were in their way of no concern. Several vehicles tried to reverse out of their path, and she winced as one car, a Jaguar convertible, its top down so its occupants could enjoy the evening air, stalled out as its driver panicked. She sighed as they managed to jump clear of the vehicle moments before the column of tanks rolled over it as if it were nothing more than a tin can.

Other more reliable vehicles were able to mostly scramble out of the way either by heading headlong into the sidewalks, or by reversing direction and jumping the boulevard to the other side. Some even tried to bail into the square itself.

Her eyes were focused on the civilian chaos, but when she noticed the closest column turning to flank the square, alongside where their pursuit tank had already taken up position, she caught a glimpse of something that made no sense.

"Those tanks!" she began, but stopped. At first she could have sworn she saw the blue of the Qing dragon on the bright gold flags flying proudly from the rear of the tanks, but she couldn't spot it again. *Your mind is playing tricks on you.* She flashed back to the Qing flag she saw in the room of the mobile HQ, and it was clear to her what these flags represented.

Dawson looked at her. "What?"

"That gold flag they're flying. It's exactly like the flag I saw at the headquarters when we were escaping, except for the blue dragon."

"What are you talking about, Professor?"

"Sergeant, they're essentially flying the flag of the Qing Dynasty," she said as she looked back at the column, the flag fluttering on the back of each of the tanks as they approached. "I think you're right, Sergeant. We're in the middle of a coup!"

FLAGS OF SIN

Bo Yang's Mobile Headquarters, Beijing, China

"Everything is going according to plan, sir."

Bo looked up from the screens displaying active updates of his troop placements in over a dozen cities across China. His heart hammered in anticipation of the upcoming days as he consolidated power, and returned his family to its rightful place on the throne of China. Chairman Bo. Emperor Bo. It mattered not. What flag flew behind him, mattered not. All that mattered was China.

And China would embrace his leadership, he was certain of it. He intended to be a firm but caring leader, to let the private sector he had embraced himself, thrive under his watchful eye, and to become the cult of personality so necessary in today's modern world. He would embrace the young through Twitter and Facebook, or at least their Chinese equivalents. One day he hoped that he wouldn't have to continue the policy of a filtered Google, or IP addresses blocked due to hosting information critical of the regime.

Because he knew, in time, there would be nothing to be critical of.

After consolidating power, he planned to bring an end to the killings, the imprisonments, the disappearances. Chinese emperors were once loved by their subjects, and he intended it to happen again. Not a love through fear, but a love like that in the United Kingdom, where the populace adored their Royals. His own son, currently being educated in the United States, would return home and marry a commoner, China's very own Will and Kate.

But unlike England, China's new monarch would remain in control.

He let out a slow breath through his nose, his focus returning to the General.

"And our escapees?"

"We believe they are pinned down in Tiananmen Square. Our ground forces are moving in now, and we should have them in custody shortly."

"Very well. Once you have them, bring them back here and execute them all immediately."

General Liang's eyes opened slightly wider.

"Even the Ambassador?"

"Yes. We'll blame it on the *former* regime if need be."

"Very well, sir."

General Liang snapped to attention, then left the room, leaving Bo alone with his thoughts.

We will have complete control in less than an hour.

FLAGS OF SIN

7th District Police Station, Beijing, China

Inspector Li winced as the medic treating him dabbed the gash on the back of his head with what was probably iodine or some equivalent. What it was, he didn't care, all he cared was that it stung.

And his head throbbed.

He waved his hand at his coworkers, urging them away. It was becoming claustrophobic. He realized they were all concerned, all furious, all wanting revenge on whoever had done this, but he also knew that he had pretty much 'literally' asked to be hit.

He had helped the proverbial enemy.

And he'd do it again.

There was no way that American professor should have been sentenced to death for what had happened. As the medic announced he would live, but should go to the hospital just in case, he waved him off.

"I'll be fine."

"Back up! Back up! Back up!" rapid fired Superintendent Hong, flicking his wrists to make a path. "Give the man some air, he needs to breathe!"

The crowd obeyed their superior's orders, and finally gave Li the space he so desperately wanted. Hong stopped in front of him and Li raised his head, wincing at the pounding that seemed to increase four fold.

Hong wagged a finger at him.

"You go to the hospital. I don't want you dropping dead tonight when you get home to that beautiful wife of yours. Go to the hospital, get checked out, and take two days off. More if the doctor orders it!"

Hong's shouting didn't make things any better, and he was probably right. The medics helped him to his feet and he scratched his last thought.

He's definitely right. His head pounded, and he felt slightly light headed as they helped him toward the door, the shouts of encouragement from his fellow officers, torture.

As they reached the parking lot, one medic let go of Li's arm to open the door of the ambulance as his phone vibrated in his pocket. Fishing it out, he read the text message and froze. He reread it, then yanked his arm free of the other medic, and marched toward an idling squad car, the medics shouting after him.

But he didn't hear them above the pounding in his head, and the concern that gripped his chest. He looked at the message again.

Its ping. Trapped at tiananmen square ne corner. Help!

FLAGS OF SIN

North-East Corner, Tiananmen Square, Beijing, China

"What the hell is that?" asked Dawson, pointing behind them.

Laura rolled on her back and looked where he was pointing. There were dozens of people—scratch that—hundreds, running up the boulevard toward the square, waving what appeared to be phones over their heads, all sporting the loudest of outfits imaginable.

"I have no idea," she murmured.

"It's a flash mob," said Ping with a smile. "That's who I was texting. They are very popular in China, hundreds occur every day. I tapped into several networks we monitor and organized a bunch of them to happen right here, starting about now. They'll keep happening over the next half hour, probably growing with each one as the word spreads. They only last five minutes."

"What's with the clothing?" asked Dawson as Laura admired Ping's thinking. It was genius. Create a flash mob that would fill Tiananmen with young people, blend in, then disappear with the crowd.

"Usually you have a theme. This one is 'wildest outfit'."

As the crowd approached, policemen who had been distracted by the arrival of the tanks just moments ago started swarming from the square, whistles blowing, waving their arms.

"Uh oh," muttered Laura. "This might not work after all."

She watched in dismay as several dozen formed a line, halting the advancing partiers, who merely continued to hold up their phones, recording the proceedings, their laughing and dancing not interrupted in the least. This was the new China, and these were the new Chinese. A generation for whom Tiananmen Square was a public park, not a shrine to the victims of a massacre.

Suddenly the idea didn't seem such a good one. She looked at Dawson, and the concern in his eyes suggested he was having the same thoughts. In fact, if she didn't know better, she'd say he *never* thought it was a good idea.

Never bring civilians into a military situation.

Watching or reading the news, she was the first to criticize when civilians were used as cover, or "meat shields" as James liked to call them, and now, here they were, hoping to do the same thing. Slip away amongst a crowd of kids, counting on the tanks lining the other side of the square to not open fire.

But this wasn't back home, or the United States. This was China.

Those who cannot remember the past are doomed to repeat it.

The often misquoted statement from George Santayana echoed through her mind, memories of watching the Tiananmen massacre when she was the same age as some of these kids flashing by like an old movie reel.

She turned to Ping. "Can you cancel the flash mobs?"

"Why would you want to do that?" she asked, her eyes revealing how idiotic she thought the request was.

It was Dawson who replied.

"These are civilians, we can't risk their lives to save ours."

Horror spread across Ping's face as the realization of what she had done sank in.

"Oh no! Oh no! Oh no!" she cried as her thumbs flew over the keyboard, but they were interrupted by a cheer from the crowd. They all looked to see the crowd pointing to the south end of the square. Laura spun around and saw hundreds if not thousands of people rushing into the now unguarded square, the majority of the police meant to prevent just such a thing crowded in the north-east corner where the initial crowd had arrived.

"What are they doing?" asked Laura as she saw the square get swarmed with more and more kids, who appeared to sit down and do something with their arms.

"Pretending to have a picnic," said Ping, her shoulders slumped.

Immediately police began to redeploy, running toward the new crowd, which freed up the original crowd to rush around the officers that remained, their numbers having swelled while they were blocked.

"How many of these did you organize?" asked Dawson.

"Five."

"Here comes another crowd," said Laura, pointing toward the tomb of Mao Zedong to the south.

"Hats," muttered Ping. She dropped the phone in her lap. "It's too late. There's no way I can stop it."

"Then we might as well take advantage of it," said Dawson. He pointed at the deliverymen. "Next group that walks by, you two join it," he said. Ping translated, and the men rose to their knees. A group of youth rushed by, their colorful outfits an unfortunate contrast to the drab outfits the men wore, but in seconds they were lost in the crowd.

Laura peeked over their hiding place and could see no reaction from the tanks, but noticed something else that sent her pulse racing.

"Something's going on."

Dawson looked then rolled over, grabbing the phone from Ping's lap. He quickly dialed.

"ETA?"

He frowned.

"We've got infantry starting to deploy here, plus thousands of civilians filling the square."

He listened for a moment, his frown getting deeper.

"Understood."

He flipped the phone closed and looked at Laura.

"Things are about to get a lot worse."

FLAGS OF SIN

Approaching Tiananmen Square, Beijing, China

Acton looked out the window, his frustration growing. *We need to get there, now!* Something was definitely happening, and it wasn't good. Traffic was getting heavier, most of the cars flowing in the same direction they were, causing a slowdown, exacerbated by dozens of cars just stopping randomly, letting out their passengers, mostly young people, who then began rushing down the sidewalks toward Tiananmen.

Sirens wailing from behind caused them all to look.

Lights flashed in the distance, approaching far too quickly to be in the same traffic they were in.

"They're serious," said Niner. "Looks like they're coming up the sidewalks."

"Shit!" exclaimed Spock. "Look."

Acton spun around and saw a sea of red brake lights as the entire side of the boulevard they were on came to a screeching halt. Spock, apparently already anticipating this, cut across several lanes and jumped the curb, pulling a one-eighty and roaring away in the opposite direction, the traffic fairly light on this side.

"We're going the wrong way!" protested Acton. His visions were of Laura trapped in the square, the tanks and soldiers apparently already there, opening fire.

Tiananmen all over again.

"That's a police blockade they just put up. Last thing we need is to get questioned with an escaped fugitive in the car," replied Spock, who cranked the wheel sending them into a side street. Another turn and they were heading back toward the square, but on a smaller street that appeared to not yet have attracted the attention of the authorities.

"Call BD. Give him a sit rep. I think Tiananmen is going into lockdown."

Niner nodded and began dialing when Acton's heart slammed against his chest. In a nearby parking lot were a mass of soldiers, tanks, and a large semi-truck, bristling with antennae.

This is a staging area.

But for what, he feared to ask.

FLAGS OF SIN

North-East Checkpoint, Approaching Tiananmen Square, Beijing, China

Inspector Li showed his ID to one of the officers manning the blockade and the man nodded, waving for the gate to be raised. Li had intended to take his own car, but the idling squad car had been too good an opportunity to pass up. He'd probably be reprimanded tomorrow, but he'd just blame his head wound if need be. The squad car's lights and sirens had allowed him to push through the traffic, and eventually take the sidewalk up to the blockade.

And now he was through.

A staging area was to his right, and he could see hundreds of People's Armed Police assembling in riot gear. Whatever was going on at Tiananmen had been deemed unacceptable, and the rapid response team set up after the 1989 incident was moving in.

But what could she mean? Trapped?

Trapped by who? By what?

As he sped toward the square, he could see thousands jumping around and dancing, others sitting, and more arriving, the security cordon obviously not completely in place.

Please don't let my daughter be here!

He couldn't believe the idiocy of these kids. Didn't they know what happened the last time something like this occurred?

But they didn't.

It was a stain on the regime's history that had been washed away with the fire hose of censorship, like the hoses used to clear away the blood of those crushed under the treads of the tanks as they roared toward the square. These kids weren't alive when it happened, or if they were, they were still in diapers. They would never hear about it at school, never hear about it on the censored Internet, and their parents would never tell them about it, for fear they might repeat it to their friends, and it would get back to the authorities.

If you can't learn your history, then whose fault is it when you repeat it?

He pulled his phone from his pocket and dialed home. He sighed when his wife answered quickly.

"Where are you?" she asked groggily. "I fell asleep waiting for you."

"There's a problem. Is Juan there?"

"No. She went to some party with her friends, said she'd be back a little after midnight."

Li sighed. A party was fine. A party meant someone's apartment most likely, with he hoped adult supervision. But at this point he didn't care. As long as she wasn't anywhere near here. But midnight?

We need to set an earlier curfew.

He pulled to a stop on the boulevard north of the square, the crowd less than a hundred meters away.

"Where's the party?"

"Tiananmen. Some dance was being organized or something."

Li's heart froze as his world closed in around him.

Juan!

FLAGS OF SIN

North-East Corner, Tiananmen Square, Beijing, China

"Now what?"

Dawson looked across the square, filled with revelers, their five minute flash mobs having converged, the time limit now ignored. It was turning into an impromptu gathering in defiance of the authorities, everyone naively in such a good mood, they must have figured themselves invulnerable.

Kids always think they're immortal.

"That's not one of mine," said Ping as she peered over the planter. Hundreds more were arriving from Mao's tomb, but this group carried gold flags, some on poles, some held over their heads, others wrapped over their shoulders.

But they all had them.

"That's the same flag as on the tanks," observed Laura.

"What did you say it represented?"

"I'm assuming the Qing Dynasty. They were the last of the emperors. I saw the full flag, with the blue dragon, hanging on the wall in an office as we were escaping their HQ."

"So, what? Somebody's trying to reestablish the dynasty?"

Laura shrugged.

"It's been almost a hundred years since they were in power. It doesn't make any sense. More likely someone is using it as a cover. It's been almost romanticized today in Chinese popular culture, with many of their traditions still carried on. It's plausible that someone thinks a coup staged with the Qing symbolism might succeed where yet another communist regime, under a different dictator, might not."

Dawson looked back at the new arrivals who swarmed into the midst of the already massive crowd, their flags fluttering above the throngs. Whatever was going on, he knew it didn't concern them. He had to get the Ambassador to safety.

"Okay, let's get out of here. Our friends' departure doesn't seem to have triggered any reaction, so chances are they've given up on us." He pointed at Laura then Ping. "Next group, you two mix in, then get out as quickly as you can."

"What about you?" asked Laura.

"I'll take the Ambassador as originally planned. Hopefully the crowds will keep us out of view."

Laura frowned. "I think you have a better chance if you and I carry him out, as if he's drunk or something, rather than a fireman's carry."

Dawson shook his head. *She's determined to get herself killed.*

"Absolutely not." He pointed at a group passing nearby. "Now go!"

Ping jumped up, far too quickly for his liking, and rushed toward the group.

A snapping sound rung out, followed by several screams. Dawson popped his head up as another clap rang across the square, and more screams were heard.

And to his horror, he saw bodies being thrown toward their position as snipers opened fire across the square, trying to take out the police officer. He turned toward her as she stood frozen in horror.

"Get down!" he yelled, but it was too late. Her body jerked and was blasted backward, her arms and legs dangling in the air as if she were a ragdoll, finally coming to rest near the road they so desperately needed to get to.

They know exactly where we are. But why aren't they moving in to get us?

FLAGS OF SIN

East Chang'an Street, North-East of Tiananmen Square, Beijing, China

"Start calling her and texting her now. Don't stop until you hear from her. Tell her she has to get out of Tiananmen Square immediately, the police are moving in. Tell her anything you need to tell her, just get her out of there!"

"You're scaring me, Dear, what's happening?"

"There's no time to explain," said Li as he climbed out of his car, his eyes now peering into the crowd, desperately trying to find not only his partner, but his daughter. "Just do it, and call me when it's done." Suddenly something occurred to him. "Wait!"

"What?"

"Don't mention the square or police or anything. They might look at the messages later and we don't want them knowing she took part."

"Took part in what? You're *really* scaring me!"

"I'm scared too, Dear. Just get our baby home!"

He hung up then quickly typed a text to his daughter.

This is daddy. Go home now. You are in danger!

A cracking sound followed by screams ripped across the square, followed by several more. He peered into the throng and was almost sick as he saw the crowds scattering, large pools of emptiness created as whatever they were running from was abandoned.

And each space contained several bodies, and even from his vantage point, he recognized the damage from his previous crime scenes. Another shot slammed into the crowd, and another area opened, and he immediately noticed the line formed across the square. He followed it to its source, and gaped in horror at the line of tanks and infantry on the other side.

What is the PLA doing here? This is a police matter, not army!

The sniper was obviously amongst the group of soldiers, but why was only one gunman firing? He followed the widening gap through the square to see what the target might be, and he gasped when he immediately recognized Ping, frozen in place.

"Get down!" somebody yelled in English, and his eyes darted to the source to see the American man and British woman that had been kidnapped earlier, then his eyes snapped back to Ping as her body was tossed toward him like a doll on a string.

"No!" he cried out, but he knew it was fruitless. She was dead. There was no way she could survive that hit, not with the type of damage he had seen earlier.

Willing his own frozen legs forward, he rushed across the street toward the square, and dropped beside her body, momentarily forgetting the danger that lay on the other side. He cradled her head in his hands and wiped the hair from her face. Her eyes, the life draining out of them, stared back at him and a slight smile emerged from the corners of her mouth, then nothing.

"Get down!" yelled the voice again, and Li suddenly snapped back to reality, looking across the square realizing there was now a clear line of sight between him and the sniper on the other side. He placed Ping's head back on the concrete and jumped up, racing toward the concrete planter the foreigners were hiding behind just as a shot echoed.

A sharp pain in his side and he gasped, tumbling forward as he lost his balance. He hit the ground hard and felt strong hands grab him by the shirt, yanking him across the ground, but he knew it was too late.

He was hit, and was dying.

Please God let Juan get out of this!

FLAGS OF SIN

Bo Yang's Mobile Headquarters, Beijing, China

"Flash mob is in place, sir, but there's something else going on."

Bo Yang didn't like surprises. Not on this of all nights. He looked up at General Liang.

"What?"

The General shifted his feet.

"It appears that several other flash mobs have convened in the square. Before us."

Bo sat back in his chair. He didn't believe in coincidences. This had to be related somehow to the events he currently orchestrated. Flash mobs never convened in Tiananmen. The armed response would be swift and ruthless.

Which was exactly what he was counting on.

But with this added wrinkle, he had to think.

Does it affect the plan?

"Any intel?"

General Liang seemed to ease slightly as he flipped open a file.

"Yes, sir. It appears five flash mobs were called for, all around the same time, all from the same mobile number."

"Whose phone?"

"We're tracing it now, should know shortly. They seem innocent enough. Crazy clothes, crazy hats, pretend to be on a picnic. Seems like kids being kids."

Bo shook his head and jammed his finger onto the surface of his desk.

"Not on this night, of all nights." His mind raced. He knew the plan. Would it matter if there were more in the square when it was executed? He looked at Liang, decision made.

"Proceed as planned."

General Liang snapped to attention, then hurried from the room.

If there are thousands more, then so be it. More martyrs for the cause.

FLAGS OF SIN

North-East Corner, Tiananmen Square, Beijing, China

"Is he okay?" asked Laura as Dawson, lying on his side, quickly assessed their new arrival. She recognized him as one of the police officers that had interviewed them, and arrested them, earlier. *Ping must have been his partner!* She felt her chest tighten at the pain he must be going through, losing his partner like that. She glanced over at the body, so close yet so far, the widening pool of blood evidence if any were ever needed that she was most certainly dead.

Why is this happening?

A nice vacation. That's all she had wanted. To get away from it all. To get away from the Triarii, the Vatican, the Pope, the Priests, the Imams, the Jihadists, the ancient cults and the millennia old vendettas. She had thought long and hard of where to go, and China had finally been chosen for the very control people criticized. What had been happening to them just didn't happen in China.

Or so she thought.

Now here they were in the middle of a coup d'état, people dying all around them, and James only God knows where.

"He'll live," pronounced Dawson. "He just got a sliver of concrete in his side from when that shot hit the ground behind him."

"Can you take it out?" she asked, her journey of self-pity interrupted.

"Already did and there's hardly any bleeding, but he's in shock. Keeps muttering something."

Laura helped Dawson roll the officer onto his back, then fished some water from the pillow case and held it to the man's lips. The water dribbled down the sides of his mouth at first, but then he began to come around and was quickly drinking the water thirstily. His eyes fluttered then focused on Laura.

"Juan!"

Laura smiled at him reassuringly, she hoped. "I'm sorry, I don't speak Chinese. You're going to be okay. You were just hit by a piece of concrete. You're going to be fine."

"Juan," he whispered, then suddenly shoved himself up on his elbows. "My daughter, Juan, she's in that crowd."

Laura's hand darted to her mouth as her eyes filled with tears, and her head with a prayer for the safety of a girl she knew nothing about.

FLAGS OF SIN

Approaching Tiananmen Square, Beijing, China

The sound sent waves of fear tingling up and down Acton's spine. The whoosh of helicopter blades as they sliced through the air was unmistakable, and never seemed to bring good news. Spock brought the car to a halt and they all looked up.

"Jesus Christ!" exclaimed Niner. "Somebody's going to war!"

Acton watched as at least a dozen heavily armed attack helicopters passed overhead.

"Where are they going?" he asked, but he already knew the answer.

"They're heading straight for Tiananmen," replied Niner as he dialed the phone. A moment later he was giving a rapid update to Dawson. "Helicopters approaching your position. You should see them any second. BD, you gotta get out of there, now!"

There was a pause as Spock put the car in motion again, racing down the side street, slowing at each intersection to peer up the road, but each time they found the same thing.

A blockade.

It was clear the authorities were blocking any and all access to Tiananmen, but the question was why? Why were they blocking off access and sending columns of tanks and squadrons of helicopters because of a bunch of kids? He knew the Chinese didn't tolerate dissent, and would rapidly remove anybody who looked suspicious from the square, but this seemed an overreaction, even for them.

And if there was a coup, why would they converge on Tiananmen? It wasn't a military target, it was purely civilian. A coup should be taking control of the key government and military installations, not public squares.

He could understand setting up road blocks, spreading your presence throughout the capital, but to concentrate forces on Tiananmen made no sense.

Then suddenly it did make sense, and his heart slammed against his ribcage as blood rushed through his ears.

"Tell them they have to get out of there, now!"

FLAGS OF SIN

North-East Corner, Tiananmen Square, Beijing, China

"We've got incoming," announced Dawson as he spotted the lead chopper clearing the roofs of the Forbidden City to the north. Inspector Li rolled over, climbing to his knees and looked as Laura twisted her head. They both gasped.

"We have to get out of here!" cried Laura, looking about desperately for a route, but they all knew there was none.

Another sound distracted Dawson, and he looked behind them to see a column of vehicles, mostly troop carriers, moving toward them from the south-east side of the square. They appeared to be People's Armed Police as opposed to military, most likely the standard riot squad response that would be deployed in the event of a flash mob.

Dawson pointed.

"Police are arriving."

"Thank God!" exclaimed Laura, but he didn't share her sentiment. These were lightly armed police, who were riding into something far bigger than they had planned for.

"They're going to be slaughtered." He looked at their new arrival. "Inspector, you have to warn them off!"

Inspector Li looked at the arriving column and shook his head. "There's no time!"

Dawson looked at him, then over his shoulder at the flash mob that continued to party, their numbers in the thousands, if not tens of thousands.

This is going to make 1989 look like a random shooting.

Tiananmen Square, Beijing, China

Somebody had a boombox blaring the latest Gaga, and Li Juan belted out the words along with all her friends. She couldn't remember the last time she had had this much fun. Whoever's idea this had been was clearly a *partaay* genius, and should be getting full social cred tomorrow for their accomplishment.

She was so happy when her mother had let her go. She knew getting home so late would be a little unusual, and if her dad, the disciplinarian of the household, had been home on time, she had no doubt he would have refused her pleas.

But he hadn't shown up for dinner, and for that she was eternally grateful.

She exchanged hugs with her friend Ching. They both tilted their heads back and screamed at the night until they were out of breath, then broke down into a fit of laughter as a tune from the Biebs roared at them, and as much as she hated to admit it, she secretly loved Justin and looked about to make sure others were singing before breaking out into full voice.

She began rhythmically jumping in the air with the rest of the crowd, when she felt her phone vibrate on her hip.

It was her mother.

Aww, Mom!

She answered but couldn't hear a thing, for which she thanked God.

"I can't hear you, Mom! I'm okay! We'll be leaving soon and I'll call you when it's quieter!"

She tried to listen for a reply but there was nothing she could make out, so she hung up and was about to shove the phone in her pocket and return to her dancing and singing, when she noticed a message indicator. She hit the button.

12 missed calls

7 unread messages

She hit ignore, and slipped the phone back in her pocket, determined not to let her overprotective parents ruin what was turning out to be the best night in her sixteen years of existence.

They worry way too much. It's just a party. And in a public square. What could possibly go wrong?

The song ended and she stood with her feet on the ground, rather than splitting the time between the concrete and the air just above it, and before the next song could kick in, she heard the roar of an engine to her left. In fact, several more large engines, like trucks, seemed to start, but were soon drowned out by the next tune from a local band.

She shouted in delight and grabbed her friend by the hands as they spun around in a circle, her friend soon losing her grip and careening into the crowd. Fortunately it was so thick with people, she didn't actually fall, and was helped upright by the others, as Juan grabbed her knees, laughing so hard she thought she might puke.

And that's when she noticed her feet and legs, in fact her entire body, was vibrating.

It wasn't in time with the music, it was something else.

And it was ominous.

She slowly reached into her pocket, and retrieved her phone. She opened the list of text messages, and saw half a dozen from her mother, and one from her dad. She selected it.

This is daddy. Go home now. You are in danger!

Her chest became tight and she stopped even the slightest movement that she may have been involuntarily performing in synch with the beat. She pushed herself up on her tiptoes to try and see where the sound she had heard earlier had come from, but could see nothing but the crowd. *Why do I have to be so short?* She continued to peer through the throng, and for one fortuitous split second, everyone dipped as they imitated the music video they all knew by heart, and she alone stood erect.

And cried out.

A row of tanks lined the square, and their turrets were turning toward the crowd. She spun around and saw the other side of the square lined with trucks, police pouring out of them and spreading to the north and south sides of the square, cutting off any escape.

But she knew what she had to do. She grabbed her friend by the hand, and began to run through the crowd.

Away from the army, and toward the police. For the police were her daddy's friends, and if she could reach them, they might stand a chance.

Oh Daddy, I wish you were here!

FLAGS OF SIN

North-East Corner, Tiananmen Square, Beijing, China

Laura watched the trucks jerk to a halt and the police begin to pour from the rear of the carriers, their crowd control gear at the ready, and their weaponry apparently at a minimum. They were here to break up a party, not a riot. She had no doubt they knew about the flash mobs, and the fact it was thousands of children they were dealing with.

And she had no doubt they had no idea what faced them on the other side of the square.

As the police fanned out to their left and right, creating a cordon along the entire eastern side of the square, she heard an ungodly boom, and she spun toward the crowd to see a burst of dust and concrete, and something else, flying through the air near the center of the square.

"What was that?" she asked.

"A tank just fired on the crowd," replied Dawson. He dialed the phone and it was soon answered.

"They're opening fire on the crowd. Do *not* approach the square. What's your location?"—he nodded—"Got it." He flipped the phone closed.

"Where are they?"

Dawson pointed north. "Side street east of the Forbidden City." Another boom, and this time she was watching as the shell hit and bodies were blown to pieces, limbs and other unrecognizable body parts, mixed with shattered concrete, tossed into the air. Bile began to fill her mouth.

"We need to stop this!" she cried, knowing how ridiculous it sounded. She turned to the policeman. "You need to warn your people what is going on, what they're getting themselves into!"

But he was already on the phone, shouting in Chinese, then furiously typing out a series of text messages.

Automatic weapons fire rattled across the square and the crowd finally began to realize what was happening. Screams of terror pierced the night, and the crowd began to surge, but in every direction. Those nearest the police ran away from them, those nearest the army ran away in turn. Laura watched in horror as a young girl was knocked down, then repeatedly trampled by the panicked crowd.

She wanted to look away, to drag her eyes from the carnage in front of her, but she couldn't. It was a horror that demanded to be remembered, demanded to be witnessed, and she, a historian, an archaeologist, was now witness to history, a history so horrible, she wasn't certain she wanted to survive, lest she should have to remember the events of this night.

Dawson slapped her on the arm.

"We're getting out of here, now."

He heaved the Ambassador over his shoulder, then rushed to the next planter, dropping to the ground. He motioned with his head for her to follow, and she grabbed the cop by the shoulder.

"Come on, let's get out of here!"

But he shook his head.

"I have to save my daughter!"

He jumped to his feet, and rushed headlong into the panicking crowd.

7th District Police Station, Beijing, China

"Why aren't you at the hospital?"

Superintendent Hong Zhi-kai stood behind his desk, having leapt to his feet the moment he recognized Li's voice. The paramedics who were supposed to have taken him to the hospital had just left empty handed, and the officer whose car had been "borrowed" stood in Hong's office this very moment, his head bowed in shame at having just been reprimanded for leaving the keys in the ignition and losing a valuable piece of state property.

"There's no time for that!" yelled Li above a raucous noise Hong couldn't make out. In fact, he could barely make out Li's voice.

"What's going on? What's that noise?"

"Would you shut up and listen, sir!"

Hong's eyes shot wide open, and he dropped in his chair. He couldn't remember the last time anybody had spoken to him like that, and was quite certain he had never been spoken to like that by a subordinate.

"I'm standing in the middle of a coup!"

Hong, still stinging from the shock of the rebuke, took a moment to process what was just said.

"Can you hear me?" yelled Li.

"Yes, yes I can," muttered Hong as what Li had said sunk in. *But that's impossible.* "Please repeat what you said."

"We're in the middle of a coup. Somebody is trying to take over the government. Our men at Tiananmen Square are going to be slaughtered, tens of thousands of kids *are* being slaughtered! My daughter—"

Li's voice cracked, and Hong couldn't be sure if it was the choppy reception, or Li himself who stopped talking.

"Repeat that last part!"

"My daughter is among those being slaughtered. You need to notify the government and have them send in the army. Our rapid response squad is trying to fight tanks with rifles. They don't stand a—oh my God!"

"What?"

"Helicopters! Helicopters are opening fire on our men. You need to send help now! Tell them the hostiles are flying gold flags on their equipment. Did you hear me? Gold flags!"

"Gold fl-flags, I g-got it," stuttered Hong, still trying to process what was happening. A pounding on the glass of his office caused him to jump in his chair.

"Sir, you have to see this!" said one of his men, pointing at the television screen.

Li's voice demanded attention. "Sir, I have to go, call in reinforcements, you're our only hope."

"Okay, Li, okay," he murmured as he walked around his desk and into the outer office. It was a YouTube video streaming on their smart TV. If he hadn't just heard what Li had said, he'd have no clue what he was looking at, but with a context to put the confused imagery to, he dropped into the nearest chair, everyone else in the room standing, mouths agape as they watched tanks firing upon a group of teenage children, dancing only moments before.

Hong closed his eyes, and imagined his own son, only thirteen, and prayed he was at home, safe with his mother and mother-in-law. He reached for his phone when he realized it was in his hand.

"Hello?" he said, but there was no one there.

What should I do?

He heard his mother-in-law's voice scream in his head. *Make a decision for once in your life!*

He sucked in a deep breath then stood.

"Listen up!"

The room turned toward him. He pointed at his secretary. "Get me the Commissioner, tell him it's urgent."

"But it's after midnight, sir."

"Do it!" he yelled. She jumped and grabbed her phone. Hong turned to the rest of the room. "We are in the middle of a coup. Elements of our own armed forces are attempting to take over the city, and are slaughtering our own men, and our own children, as we just sit here. Li is on site, and just phoned in a situation report. His own daughter is caught up in this mess, our own men are dying. This affects us! This affects our families! This affects our country!" He strode toward the TV, another YouTube clip playing showing a different vantage point of the slaughter. "Call in everyone, I don't care where they are, get them in here, then notify the hospitals, the other stations, every government office you can think of, and let them know what's going on. The hostile forces are flying gold flags on their equipment. That's verified by Li on site."

Nobody moved, nobody said anything, everyone stunned.

Hong slapped his hands together.

"Move!"

The entire room bounced, then rushed into action, phone calls being made, text messages sent, emails typed, as Hong watched with satisfaction, and a pride in his men, and in himself.

Mother-in-law, if you could see me now.

"Sir! I have the Commissioner."

Hong nodded and strode into his office, closing the door behind him, as he picked up his phone.

I just hope he's on the right side of this.

North of the Forbidden City, North of Tiananmen Square, Beijing, China

The thunder of the gunfire was unmistakable. Acton had heard enough of it in the Gulf War to know what an exploding round from a tank sounded like. It was terrifying. The screams that erupted along with the automatic gunfire left little doubt that whoever was firing, was firing on the crowd.

Acton jumped from the car, Spock shouting after him to no avail, and sprinted toward the gunfire. Bursting from the alleyway they were stopped in, he turned and rushed up a more significant road, the square becoming visible and the horror it contained causing him to slowly come to a halt, his hands flying up to his head as he pulled at his hair, unable to comprehend the carnage in front of him.

Footfalls came to a stop beside him as the rest of the Delta team caught up, nobody saying anything. To the left were what appeared to be a riot squad of nearly a thousand men, to the right a row of tanks and infantry, and in the middle a mass of living and dead flesh, an undulating sea of panic that ebbed and flowed in all directions, those to the left seeing the police, thinking they were the ones firing, and those to the right, seeing the army, and knowing they were firing.

Acton looked up and saw a squadron of helicopters hovering overhead, and his heart stopped as they tilted forward slightly, streams of rockets erupting from their weapons pods. He followed them as they streaked through the air, then dropped to a knee as the police vehicles erupted into flames, scattering shrapnel in all directions, police and kids alike blown apart, impaled, or tossed like kindling onto an open fire.

Laura!

He had no clue where she was, where to even begin looking. He pushed himself to his feet as Niner sucked in a quick breath.

"Oh my God!" he gasped.

Acton followed his gaze, and they all watched in horror as the tanks spun their treads in opposing directions, and took up new positions facing the crowds, rather than perpendicular as they were a moment before.

Please, God, no!

The first tank jerked forward, followed by the rest, as they roared into the square, those closest to Acton's position rushing forward along the boulevard to the north of the square to cut off any escape.

"They're killing them all!" he cried, his mind an explosion of sensations, it being exposed to too much at once. He turned away, unable to look any more, but the roar of the tanks continued, the shells firing indiscriminately into the crowds continued, the small arms fire, continued.

And the screams.

The screams continued.

Bo Yang's Mobile Headquarters, Beijing, China

"It's working, sir, exactly as you predicted."

General Liang gushed with praise, Bo ignoring it. *Of course it worked.* It only worked better than he could have ever imagined. The other flash mobs added to what he had intended a hundred fold. The original plan called for the death of perhaps several hundred. It was intended to shock the world, and would be used the next day to justify his takeover, as it would be blamed on the government.

The previous government.

He would claim his troops moved in to try and protect the protesters from the police and army forces attacking them, and with his helicopters having taken out the People's Armed Police rapid response team, the proof of his intended target was clear. Were innocents killed by his men? Yes, but only by accident, in their zeal to protect the many.

That would be the story.

"Sir, look at CNN International!"

Bo looked at one of the screens, a red Breaking News banner emblazoned across the monitor with YouTube video playing, showing the massacre, and a talking head commenting as if he were an expert on everything.

Bo smiled to himself. He knew it would take at least half an hour for any PLA units to respond. *His* units were supposed to be the very PLA forces used in a situation like this, and they were already rolling into position for *his* purposes. If everything went according to plan, if he could just get that thirty minutes, he would have the city bottled up, with complete control by the morning.

General Liang scanned a report handed to him by an underling, then turned to Bo.

"Sir, every major news network in the world is carrying the story. And they are all reporting it as PLA firing on its own citizens!"

Half a smile climbed Bo's cheek.

"Any response from our *leadership?*" The last word dripped with sarcasm.

General Liang shook his head. "There's been no response."

Of course not. In their arrogance, they sleep through their downfall.

North-East Corner, Tiananmen Square, Beijing, China

Laura cried, her chest heaving, her shoulders sagging as she sat on her knees, watching the carnage unfold. She was helpless, she didn't know what to do. The horror of it all was just too much. She felt someone shove her shoulder and push her back to the ground.

"Keep down!" yelled Dawson.

She felt like asking, "What's the point?" but thought better of it. She could honestly say she had never seen anything like this before, but she had been in situations that had seemed hopeless at the time, and survived. But as the tanks rushed into the crowd, Dawson had pointed out that their escape route to the north was being blocked off by armor, and when the helicopters had opened fire, a wall of flame and burning flesh blocked their escape to the east.

She could see no way out.

Dawson looked at her. They had cleared two of the concrete planters without being shot. There was one more, the very one her beloved James had been pinned down behind earlier, yellow maintenance tape surrounding it, the mess and blood all washed away as if the events had never happened.

Dawson pushed himself to his feet, the Ambassador still over his shoulder, and rushed to the final bit of cover between them and the tanks surging to close the gap. She looked across the square, then ran. Another volley erupted from the helicopters overhead, and she dove for the ground, rolling in behind the planter, and beside Dawson.

The tanks were tearing forward, the lead one hung up on a car it had decided to crush rather than go around, but they would have the road, their escape route, blocked in moments.

"We have to go, now!" yelled Dawson, who stood and rushed toward the street, exposed. She jumped up and chased after him, her mind no longer controlling her actions with reason, instead going on instinct in an effort to just survive the next few minutes. She focused on Dawson's back, her arms pumping at her sides, her legs pushing hard against the concrete as she quickly caught up to him, the warrior slowed by the burden he carried.

An explosion erupted from her right, a round from a tank landing not thirty feet away. Dawson was blown off his feet first, he and the Ambassador tossed half a dozen yards to the left as she felt herself lifted in the air and thrown like a marionette, its owner tired of pulling the strings.

Instinctively she rolled, and was in a crouching position within seconds, the training she and James had been receiving paying off. She rushed toward Dawson, noticing he was holding his leg, and gasped as she saw a large piece of shrapnel protruding from his calf.

The screech of metal and the roar of a diesel engine caused her to spin around as the lead tank barreled down on their position.

And she did the only thing she could do.

She stood up and turned to face the oncoming metal beast, her stance wide, her shoulders squared, her arms held high in the air, not in surrender, but outward in defiance, as if she could physically stop the tank herself through sheer willpower. She knew if it didn't stop, there was no way she could move Dawson and the Ambassador herself, and had already decided her life was forfeit, there being no way she would be able to escape the carnage unfolding around her.

She was already dead.

And she wasn't going to spend her last few moments cowering in fear. She was going to face them as she had faced life. In control, and in defiance of the odds.

She only wished she had a chance to say goodbye to the man she loved.

And the fact he wasn't here with her, by her side, facing his death with her, was the only thing she was grateful for this night.

For the tank didn't stop, it didn't slow down. It continued to surge toward her, and her visions of stopping a column of tanks like the brave soul dubbed 'Tank Man' in 1989, were about to be crushed under the treads of a juggernaut with no scruples, no compassion, no concern.

An automaton obeying its orders to the letter.

Crush all those who oppose you.

FLAGS OF SIN

Tiananmen Square, Beijing, China

Li pushed through the crowd, his phone in hand, desperately trying to locate his daughter through the thousands of panicking youth. He had long since abandoned ducking with each volley of gunfire, or each clap of thunder from a tank. He knew he'd be dead regardless.

The phone vibrated in his hand and he immediately hit the button to read the message.

Daddy, help me!

His heart slammed against his ribcage, his chest tight as he typed a reply.

Where are you?

It only took a few seconds.

In the square. I don't know where.

His thumbs flew as fast as they could, which was far slower than his younger partner might have accomplished.

Are you closer to the tanks, or the police?

Police.

He sighed.

Keep moving toward police and toward the forbidden city road. Meet me at corner.

He pushed through the crowds, racing toward a rendezvous he prayed he could keep, as another shell exploded amongst the crowd. Reaching the corner, he took cover near a tourist kiosk, his own comrades, cowering behind the burnt out hulks of their troop transports, or worse, dead, their bodies or body parts strewn across the concrete, those that could were beginning to retreat.

And leaving a crowd, in hysterics, not sure where to go. Glancing at the street, where he hoped to cross in the next few minutes, he saw a column of tanks race from their positions, pushing their way down the boulevard, and any escape to the north.

"Daddy!"

He spun as he heard the cry of his daughter slice through the crowd. He couldn't see her, but definitely had heard her, a father always knowing the sound of his baby's cry even if amongst a thousand others.

"Over here!" he yelled, hoping his voice might guide her.

He heard her call again, then two forms burst through the confusion, rushing directly toward him. He jumped up and waved at them. His daughter rushed into his arms, her tear streaked face flushed, her friend equally terrified. He took them each by the hand and turned toward the boulevard.

He gasped as he recognized the British professor standing in front of a tank that barreled down on her, her companions lying on the ground behind her. But there was nothing he could do for her, and for now, his priority was his child and her friend.

He ran toward the street, knowing full well he had to cross it and get to his car before the tanks arrived, otherwise all hope was lost. His eyes fixated on the squad car across the road, then his jaw dropped as all hope drained from him, the car erupting in a ball of flame as it was taken out by one of the choppers overhead.

He came to a halt, wondering what to do, his eyes returning to the professor as she stood defiantly, his mind drifting back to his own actions over twenty years ago, when he had stood down a column of tanks exactly as she was doing.

But he feared today's outcome would be different than it had been for him.

FLAGS OF SIN

Forbidden City, South-East Bridge, North-East of Tiananmen Square, Beijing, China

"Laura, no!" screamed Acton, breaking from the grip Spock and Niner had him in. When he saw Laura, his immediate instinct was to run to her, but they had held him back as she had stood to face down the tank, to sacrifice herself in one final, insane act, hoping those operating the tank would have heart enough to not run over a woman standing in front of them.

But these men had no morals, not if they could participate in something like this. This slaughter, senseless in its intensity, could only be ordered by an insane man, and could only be followed by those either too scared of the insanity, or those devoid of emotion or caring, those who thought in 'us and them' terms, where only 'us' were humans deserving of compassion, and 'they' were mere animals meant to be slaughtered.

All he knew as he raced across the footbridge toward the boulevard was he wanted to kill them all, to see the horror in their eyes as he tore their throats out. Anger and hate filled his heart as the tank continued roaring toward his beloved, promising her last moments in life to be ones of fear and terror, but even from here he could see her eyes were wide, defiant. She was going to reach those inside with her bravery and self-sacrifice, or die with dignity, displaying the ideals he had learned were dear to her heart.

Protect the innocent.

And teach by example.

She had taken him in, a desperate man, on the run from the most powerful and determined authorities in the world, when she could have called the police. Because she had recognized he was innocent. Then she had helped him, nearly at the expense of her own life, and they had fallen in love.

And that love was still as intense now as it was then. More so. As his legs pumped, pushing him closer to her, the several dozen lanes seeming endless, their relationship flashed before his eyes as his heart cried out to God to save the one he loved, and to take him instead.

A thunderclap from behind him barely registered, but the tank, almost on top of Laura, suddenly jerked to the side, away from him, away from her, the turret erupting in flames, the shockwave from the blast sending Laura flying backward. As he rushed forward the wave hit him, causing him to lose balance slightly, then the turret erupted with a massive explosion that finally sent him tumbling to the ground, rolling several times before coming to a stop.

Pushing to his hands and knees, he looked across the street to where Laura had been, but saw only smoke and flame as a column of tanks advanced from behind the Forbidden City, and engaged the hostiles.

FLAGS OF SIN

West Chang'an Street, North Edge of Tiananmen Square

Laura's head throbbed, her ears pulsed with white noise, her eyes, shut, burned orange through the eyelids, her nose, filled with an acrid smell, the air so hot it threatened to singe her lungs with each breath. But all this went almost unnoticed as her entire body seemed to be getting cooked from an intense heat. Her mind tried to cut through the fog, to try and remember what had happened, then was suddenly snapped back to reality as she felt hands grabbing her, pulling her upper body off of whatever surface she had been on, then arms enveloping her and hugging her tight. She still couldn't hear beyond the roar in her ears, but she recognized the feeling of his arms, his chest, his lips on hers.

James!

She opened her eyes and saw his tear streaked face looking down at her. His lips were moving, saying something to her, but it was a dull murmur on the other side of a wall of noise that was only now beginning to ebb. She looked around and saw several members of Delta Team Bravo grabbing Dawson and the Ambassador, then motioning for James to get moving.

As she pushed herself to her feet, she saw the inspector race past them, two young girls in his grip, and she felt her chest tighten with relief as she assumed one of the girls was his daughter. James pulled her up and she began to walk, then jog, across the street as her senses slowly came back.

Her hearing came back with a pop, and she looked up to see the choppers overhead banking and raining fire down on a column of newly arriving tanks.

Will this ever end?

Bo Yang's Mobile Headquarters, Beijing, China

"We've taken the television station!" yelled one of Bo's underlings, pointing at one of the screens as it flashed to a standby message.

"Excellent," said General Liang, smiling at Bo. "When we're ready, we'll broadcast your message, and the people will be on our side."

Bo nodded, watching the carnage unfold on CNN and the BBC, almost all television stations across the world running live broadcasts showing cellphone footage being posted by those inside the massacre. How these teenagers managed to not only record, but post video, while running for their lives, was beyond him.

Today's children are too obsessed with gaining Facebook friends and Twitter followers.

Even in China, where everything was strictly controlled, children were posting video while running for their lives, more concerned with making it known they were in the thick of it, so they'd be the center of attention at school tomorrow, all the while forgetting the most important thing.

You need to be alive to enjoy your new found fame.

Suddenly several of the monitors went blank, and several showing streaming YouTube feeds flashed to a standard firewall message.

"What's going on?" he asked as he stood.

"They've shutdown the Internet!" answered one of his men, furiously typing on his keyboard. "Cellular network is down as well!"

Bo slammed his fist on the desk, causing its contents to rattle.

General Liang approached, his voice low. "That's almost thirty minutes ahead of schedule."

FLAGS OF SIN

Bo frowned, dropping back into his seat, as his plan played out in his head with this new wrinkle. They needed the Internet and the cellular network for the message to be spread, but as he looked at the monitors still showing the international stations, it was clear the message was already out.

China was in chaos, and the international community was already demanding somebody take control.

"Broadcast our message."

East of the Forbidden City, Beijing, China

Missiles erupted from weapons pods overhead as Acton, still holding Laura by the hand, raced after Niner, who had Dawson over his shoulder, and Spock, who had the Ambassador. Both were making good time with Jimmy out front, taking point, one of the commandeered weapons held surreptitiously at his side so as to not attract attention. Inspector Li and the children were behind him, and all had eyes on the tanks to their right, and the helicopters overhead, engaging the armored column.

He quietly cheered on the army units responding to the chaos, but it quickly became evident they were losing. With no air support, they didn't stand a chance against the attack helicopters hovering overhead. He glanced over his shoulder and saw one good thing that had come of their arrival—the tanks in the square had stopped their advance on the crowd, and had turned their attention to the bigger threat.

Which meant their fire was now concentrated in the direction Acton and his companions were fleeing.

A tank erupted into a fireball to their right, the screams of the crew inside heart wrenching. Machine guns mounted on the turrets were turning their attention to the helicopters overhead, but if things didn't change quickly, the column sent to engage the hostiles would be eliminated.

Screeching of metal from behind caused Acton to look back and see the only functional tank in the front of the column pushing the two lead tanks out of the way, trying to end the bottleneck they were caught up in. He breathed a sigh of relief as he saw a hole punched through allowing the tank to break from the road they were trapped on and out onto the large boulevard they had just run across. The entire column surged forward, pushing the burning hulks of their companions along with them if necessary, and as the breakout continued, a new sound filled the air causing them all to look up.

Fighter jets streaked overhead, their contrails reflected against the night sky by the lights of the city. This battle was about to be ratcheted up a notch, and if they were hostiles, they'd be firing missiles right where Acton and the others were running.

He tightened his grip on Laura's hand as he exchanged a glance with her. The fear in her eyes matched his own, but there was nowhere else to go but forward. They were hemmed in by the moat surrounding the Forbidden City on their left, and the column of tanks to their right. They had to reach the end of the ancient fortification before they stood any chance of surviving what Acton feared would be an aerial bombardment of the armor only feet away.

Bo Yang's Mobile Headquarters, Beijing, China

"—many of you are aware, a massacre of unprecedented proportions is being undertaken by your government in Tiananmen Square at this very moment. These actions are unacceptable, an overreaction of unheard magnitude to a gathering of young people participating in an impromptu party, a 'flash mob' as they call it.

"Early reports are that hundreds, if not thousands, are dead. This cannot continue, and as such, I have ordered the troops under my command to take any and all action necessary to stop this atrocity. This includes directly engaging these renegade forces, and seizing the command and control infrastructure that has permitted this outrage to take place.

"Your leadership has failed you. Your country is at risk. I am Bo Yang. You know me. You know what I stand for. It is time to fight back. It is time to take China back. It is time once again for the Chinese people to stand up, and demand what is right. So I call on all those who love their country, who love the progress we have made, and who want it to continue, to unite under my banner, and to fight back against those who would oppress us, and slaughter our children. Rise up, and take back your country, resist those who would threaten our future and our prosperity. Rise up and protect your children. Take to the streets and support those troops under the gold flags. Take—"

The screen they were all watching went dead, then a test signal appeared.

"What the hell happened?" screamed Bo, his glare moving from station to station in the cramped control room, but no one dared look.

General Liang had his head buried in a phone, then hung up, turning to Bo. "Sir, an airstrike has just taken out the broadcast towers. There's no way for our message to get out!"

Bo slammed his fist on the table, then stood up, sucking in a deep breath.

"Where's the goddamned air support you promised me?"

"It's on its way, sir! ETA two minutes. We weren't expecting them to react so quickly, somehow they knew what was happening sooner than they should have."

Bo clenched his fists, tight, the fingernails biting into his palms. *Somehow they knew.* Either they had a traitor in their midst, or word had leaked. And he had a pretty good idea how.

Those fucking escaped prisoners.

North of the Forbidden City, Beijing, China

"There it is!" shouted Spock as he pointed at a car parked on the street they had just come out on. They rushed toward the vehicle and it was quickly apparent to Acton and everyone else it was far too small for their current numbers. "Get the wounded inside first," said Spock, using the fob to unlock the doors.

"There's not enough room," said Laura as she helped get Dawson into the passenger seat, Jimmy and Niner loading the Ambassador into the back. "We need another car!"

"Please, take the children!" begged Inspector Li. "Please, take my daughter and her friend!"

Dawson jerked a thumb at the backseat. "Get the kids in the back, behind the seats if you have to."

"Thank you!" cried Li as he hugged his daughter and gave her a kiss. "You two get out of here now, get home, okay?"

Li's daughter Juan cried, holding onto her father. "No, I don't want to leave you, I want to stay with you!"

"No, you have to go with them, you'll be safe!"

Two helicopters raced down the street, between the buildings, banking up the road the motley crew had just fled, their cannons opening fire on the column of tanks, momentarily distracting them all from the drama unfolding between father and daughter.

Niner grabbed Juan's friend, pushing her into the back seat, then picked Juan up, placing her behind Dawson's. Li slammed the door shut before she could try to get out.

"Spock, you're in charge. Commandeer a vehicle, get to the embassy." Dawson tossed Spock his weapons. "We don't want to be caught with these on us."

"Yes, Sergeant," replied Spock. Pointing at Jimmy, he said, "You drive." He tossed him the keys which Jimmy caught easily as he ran toward the driver side of the vehicle. Jimmy slid his weapon over the roof of the car then jumped inside. Spock pulled a phone out of his pocket and handed it to Dawson. "Satellite phone. We've got another." Two more choppers raced toward them as the car gunned to life. Jimmy immediately executed a three point turn and roared away. They all stood for a moment as they watched the car make a quick right turn, and disappear.

"Let's get the hell out of here!" yelled Spock. He pointed at Li. "Name!"

"Inspector Li."

"Li, you lead the way."

Li nodded and they began to run in the same direction the car had left, when two more choppers appeared, nearly at ground level, their noses pointed steeply forward as they rushed toward the action. The first chopper's cannons flashed as it belched lead at them, tearing up the road in front of them.

Acton shoved Laura aside, landing on top of her as he shielded her with his body. The heat from the engines, forced down by the chopper blades, washed over them, and within seconds they had passed. Before he had a chance to pick himself up a missile streaked after the choppers, eliminating the one bringing up the rear, the fireball knocking them flat. Acton rolled again, covering Laura as shrapnel and flaming fuel sprayed across the street.

"Everybody up!" yelled Spock, and Acton leapt to his feet, grabbing Laura's hand and hauling her up. He quickly looked for his companions and saw they all appeared uninjured, Li already running away from the burning hulk of the attack helicopter, and toward the same street Jimmy had turned down.

We need a vehicle!

Approaching East Tiananmen Blockade, Beijing, China

Dawson had rescued enough civilians in his time to know there was no point asking the girls huddled behind the front seats to be quiet. The explosions in the distance each signaled the possible death of Li Juan's father. He wasn't about to tell her to keep quiet so he could think. Besides, it wasn't necessary. His training had taught him how to think under circumstances louder than the wailing of two teenage girls.

But not much louder.

He winced at one particularly shrill wail.

"Shit, BD! Look!"

Dawson saw Jimmy eying the rearview mirror. He leaned down and looked out the side mirror.

Shit, indeed!

Two choppers were roaring up the road behind them. Dawson knew they weren't the intended target, but these guys seemed to be engaging targets of opportunity whenever it suited them, and they could definitely be classified as one based upon the indiscriminate killing he had seen take place.

"Evasive maneuvers, Sergeant."

"You got it!"

Jimmy cranked the wheel to the left, pulling on the emergency brake, sending the car into a rapid ninety degree turn while killing its speed, the car bouncing sideway on its tires before he disengaged the handbrake and floored the accelerator, sending them leaping into an alleyway there was no way a chopper could follow them into.

He raced toward the street lights at the end, the choppers roaring past them, then spilled out onto what looked like the massive boulevard north of Tiananmen where they had been earlier. Dawson looked over his shoulder and saw the square, enveloped in smoke and flame, about a mile back.

"Problem!"

Dawson's head spun forward, and he cursed as he looked for a way around the blockade half a mile ahead. The blockade they were on the wrong side of. Traffic was backed up on the other side, being turned around, but their side was devoid of almost anything beyond police and army vehicles. He looked for gold flags but didn't see any.

He was about to tell Jimmy to just pull up to the blockade when four Z10 attack helicopters roared over their heads, rockets rapidly erupting from their weapons pods, 30mm cannons blazing, the barricade and several police cars exploding into fireballs that flashed against the cloud cover overhead.

"Gun it!" yelled Dawson.

"Gunning it!"

Jimmy floored it and the car leapt toward the remains of the barricade as the helicopters turned for another pass. The lightly armed police were firing on the choppers, to no avail, their armor too thick for the small caliber bullets to make any difference. Jimmy angled the car toward a section of the barricade that had been torn apart, and gripped the steering wheel hard as he braced his arms.

"Hold on!" he yelled as Dawson turned around to shove the girls' heads down. A jolt, slicing half the speed off the car, sent him flying forward, his side slamming painfully into the dash, the girls in the back screaming as the Ambassador rolled onto them. Dawson shoved with his foot, pushing himself back toward the rear seat as Jimmy barreled through the debris.

Dawson, with the help of the two girls, lifted the Ambassador back into the rear seat, then turned around just as another volley of rockets streaked over their heads. He instinctively ducked, picturing one of the rockets streaming through the front window and out the rear, but thankfully the imagined moment never occurred, the rockets instead passing overhead, slamming into the vehicles and barricade behind them.

Dawson looked forward and saw something glint off a glass and steel tower. He stuck his head out the window and looked up as an entire squadron of fighters banked toward their position. He looked down the road, realizing this was the ideal route for a strafing run.

"Get off this road, now!"

North of the Forbidden City, Beijing, China

"Keys!" exclaimed Niner, climbing in the abandoned car. It turned over, then roared to life, a triumphant Niner gunning it several times. "Get in!" he yelled. Laura, Acton and Li scrambled in the back, Spock in the front, and Niner peeled away from the curb, their commandeered vehicle fortunately bigger than the cramped car their companions had been forced to take.

"Weapons check!" ordered Spock, removing the clip from the Type 80 machine pistol, inspecting it, then slapping it back in. "Ammo?"

"I've got two clips," said Acton, handing them to Spock.

Spock took one. "I've seen you shoot, Professor. You keep that."

Laura offered up her two clips.

"You definitely keep one," said Spock with a grin, stuffing the clips in his pockets, and a handgun in the back of Niner's belt.

"Oooh, Sergeant," cooed Niner. "Dinner first!"

Acton chuckled, then looked at Spock as an eyebrow shot up his forehead. Then he outright laughed. Laura began to giggle, and soon the entire car was laughing. Acton wasn't even certain Li had caught the joke, but whether he was laughing at the joke or just at them, he had tears coming from his eyes. The tension of the past hour let up a little as they laughed at what might have been the corniest, oldest joke in the book, but it didn't matter. Their minds demanded relief from the horrors they had witnessed, and Niner's typical inappropriate humor was just the ticket. Acton wrapped his arm around Laura's shoulders and planted a kiss on top of her head, his nerves calming for the first time since the opening shot had been fired in Tiananmen earlier that afternoon.

Suddenly Niner hammered on the brakes and they all tumbled forward. He slammed the car in reverse and floored it, retracing their path using only the mirrors, Acton assumed so he could continue to see what was in front of them that had him so worried. As Acton righted himself, he looked down the street and saw nothing, but in the distance an office tower reflected the sky above, and a fireball lit up the glass, followed by another explosion. But it was so distant Acton couldn't believe that was what had Niner reacting like he was.

"Hang on!" yelled Spock, who had apparently seen what had Niner so concerned. Acton noticed Spock was leaning forward and looking up. Acton did the same, leaning between the seats.

"Holy shit!" he exclaimed as what appeared to be the fuselage of a fighter, with only one wing attached, plunged from the sky. He pushed himself back, throwing his body over Laura as Inspector Li did the same, he having spotted the excitement through his open side window.

The car shook as the plane impacted the ground. Acton dared a glance over his shoulder and saw the wreckage sliding across the pavement, disintegrating into thousands of deadly pieces, secondary explosions bursting forth as the ordnance detonated along with the remaining jet fuel. Niner continued to reverse as the jet gained on them, it seeming to follow them as it slid across the road, toward them, and into their lane.

"It's fucking following us!" exclaimed Niner as he swerved into the other lane. Acton watched as the plane continued to drift across the road, then sighed as it slammed into the curb, bouncing up and burying itself into the façade of a commercial building he hoped was deserted at this hour.

Niner hit the brakes and they all exchanged glances, checking each other to see if everyone was alright.

Spock turned to face the back seat.

"Inspector, is there an underground parking lot around here?"

Li nodded. "Just down this street—"

"Wait! What's that?" interrupted Laura, pointing at an electronics store across the street, several televisions playing in the windows. Inside and out, people from the neighborhood seemed to have gathered, watching the screens, a CNN International logo in the corner of one of them, the carnage from Beijing prominently displayed.

"I didn't know you got CNN here," said Acton.

"We don't," said Li. "That's an unauthorized signal. They probably have a satellite dish." Li looked at his phone. "No signal. The cellular network must be down."

"Taken out?" asked Niner.

"More likely shut down by the authorities. Which means the Internet is probably down."

"I know that man," said Laura, pointing at the screen as a recording played on the background. "Who is that?"

"It's Bo Yang. Very prominent businessman or at least he used to be. His wife was accused of murdering a British subject. That's probably where you recognize him from."

Laura shook her head then gasped.

"The flag!"

"What?" Acton leaned closer to try and make out the image.

"He's got a gold flag behind him."

"Just like on the tanks," said Spock. "He must be the guy behind this little operation."

Laura jabbed her finger at the screen.

"But he's the guy I nearly shot when we were escaping that mobile headquarters!"

Bo Yang's Mobile Headquarters, Beijing, China

"Our aerial units are being engaged, sir!"

Bo Yang's head spun at the junior officer shouting the report from his console. General Liang looked panicked, and his General who had guaranteed him air superiority was nowhere to be seen.

"By who? I thought we had the airfields surrounding Beijing secure?" His voice was almost a growl, the fury he felt barely contained. Things were starting to go wrong. The armored response had been swifter than expected, the Internet and cellular shutdowns far ahead of schedule, and the destruction of the television broadcast tower was executed so swiftly, it was as if they had been prepositioned to do it. And now their air superiority was threatened.

"Elements of the 32nd from Qionglai Air Base, several squadrons of J-10 fighters, sir!"

"Qionglai! That's nowhere near here!"

"We've been betrayed!" hissed General Liang. He looked about. "Where is that coward?" He stormed from the room, Bo barely noticing as this new piece of intel percolated. If fighters had already arrived from Qionglai, they were either betrayed, or someone had tipped off the Politburo at least fifteen minutes ahead of schedule.

Again his mind came back to the escaped prisoners.

It's always the unanticipated eventualities that scuttle a well-laid plan.

"Send everything we have at Tiananmen to the Zhongnanhai Complex. We need to take down the bureaucracy now, before it's too late. Our message has been sent, our job there is done."

En Route to Hospital, Beijing, China

"Fuck me!" exclaimed Jimmy. Dawson looked forward as the car slowed, his attention having been momentarily on the Ambassador. Two tanks were positioned across the road they were on, dozens of PLA regulars surrounding it, rushing toward the lone vehicle stupid enough to still be out during a coup.

Jimmy came to a stop as a platoon's worth of soldiers rushed their position.

"Gold flags, Sergeant, gold flags," muttered Jimmy.

Dawson grunted, having already seen them. He turned back to the girls, who he had learned spoke nearly perfect English.

"Stay calm, tell them the truth. Your dad is a police officer, and he begged us to take you. You don't know who we are, and neither does he. Understand?"

Both girls, still crying, thankfully quietly now, nodded, the terror in their eyes, the trembling of their entire bodies, indication enough to Dawson that they understood the gravity of the situation.

Somebody yelled something in Chinese, a lieutenant, judging from Dawson's understanding of Chinese insignia. Both Jimmy and Dawson raised their hands slowly.

"What do you think, BD? Make a break for it?" Jimmy's voice was low, his lips barely moving.

"Too risky. We've got civilians here. They could have shot us already. Let's hope this unit has different orders than those at Tiananmen."

"And that they aren't looking for you and the Ambassador."

Jimmy rolled down his window and leaned out, his hands held up and out the window.

"I'm sorry, I don't understand. I'm American, from the Embassy." He patted his shirt pocket. "Identification, okay?" He slowly reached into his shirt pocket, the weapons seeming to take a bead on his chest as he did so. Dawson controlled his breathing, pretending to be intent on the exchange about to take place, but in reality assessing the troops that surrounded them. There were twelve, all armed with standard issue weapons, nothing heavy.

Except the two tanks.

But tanks reacted slowly. They weren't designed to take out small cars, swerving on civilian streets. They were meant to take out prepared defenses, roadblocks, other large military vehicles.

And to roll over infantry positions, or based upon tonight's performance, civilian.

He glanced down at the gearshift and observed Jimmy had the vehicle in reverse, ready to go at a moment's notice. The passport was out of Jimmy's pocket now, and being handed out the window. A glance in the side view mirror showed two of the troops were directly behind the car, facing away from the bumper as they covered the approach. Hitting reverse should take them out of the picture.

That left ten.

All with automatic weapons, who would pour down a rain of lead on them so thick they'd be lucky to find enough pieces of them to ship back in a FedEx envelope.

It was best to play along.

At least for now.

The lieutenant took the passport, examined it, then handed it back to Jimmy, but as he approached, his eyes opened wide and he pulled his handgun from its holster, shouting in Chinese, pointing at the back seat.

Jimmy shook his hands gently, still gripping the passport as he put on a smile that would have won him Miss Fort Bragg.

"It's okay, we're taking him to the hospital. Can you help us get there quicker? Perhaps an escort?"

The lieutenant, his weapon drifting between the rear seat, Jimmy, and back, suddenly focused on Jimmy, his eyes narrowing as he appeared to make a decision.

Oh shit!

Dawson wished they had kept some of those guns, but even then, the situation would have been hopeless.

But at least you'd have gone down fighting.

Endless years, countless missions, and he'd always made it out alive. Sometimes it was by the skin of his teeth, sometimes it was with a sucking chest wound, but he always made it out. To die in China, as a bystander in a fucking coup?

That just wasn't acceptable.

"Now."

Jimmy dropped his right foot hard on the accelerator, lifting the left foot from the brake, his two foot driver technique saving him a precious half-second. The car surged backward, shocking the lieutenant, who fired. Dawson ducked as the bullet slammed into the windshield. There was a thud then the car bounced several times and Dawson saw the two soldiers who had been behind them roll out from the front of the car as if deposited by the tiny vehicle.

Gunfire erupted and they all ducked when Jimmy cursed.

"What?"

"Look!" he said, pointing behind them.

Dawson looked forward first and saw the soldiers were all shooting at the sky as opposed to at them. He spun around and saw two fighters racing down the road directly toward them.

"Hope that's not for us!"

"Can't be, BD, why waste ordnance like those things are carrying on a civilian vehicle?"

A missile dropped from the lead fighter's wing, followed by a second, both streaking toward them.

"I hope you're right!" yelled Dawson, his voice getting louder with each word as the missiles neared.

"You and me both, boss!"

The missiles roared past, the jets not far behind, their cannons opening up, Dawson and Jimmy both ducking, realizing the pilot would have no worries about wasting bullets on them. Dawson spun around and felt a surge of hope as the two tanks blocking their way took direct hits, blasting their hulls open, tossing them back a dozen feet.

"Do you see what I see?" he asked as Jimmy raised his head.

Jimmy nodded and slammed the brakes on, then put the car in drive, hammering on the gas. They surged forward, Jimmy jerking the car to the side, the street torn to shreds by the cannons, their would be killers lying either dead, wounded, or scattered. The car raced past the carnage, directly toward the flaming tanks.

"We're not going to fit!" yelled Dawson as one of the tanks spasmed forward, closing the gap by several feet.

"We'll fit!" yelled Jimmy, still accelerating. The rattle of automatic weapons erupted from behind them, and the rear window took several hits causing the girls to scream and the Ambassador to moan. Dawson reached back with a hand and put it reassuringly on Juan's shoulder as the car raced toward the two flaming hulks, one of them still partially operational, its engine engaged, jerking forward inches at a time, sometimes feet.

"Hang on!" yelled Jimmy as he aimed the car at the tank that was slightly farther back, its partner slowly shuddering toward it. They blasted past the spasming tank then Jimmy slammed on the brakes, spinning the wheel with one hand, hauling on the emergency brake with the other. The car skidded sideways, slamming into the rear tank, then Jimmy floored it again, releasing the hand brake, and darted forward, the hull of the other tank mere inches from Dawson's door as they pulled clear.

"And the letter of the day is fuckin' A!" yelled Jimmy with a smile as the car turned a corner, out of the line of fire.

Dawson simply sat back in his seat, performing some tactical breathing to bring his heart rate down. His eyes darted to a group of signs and he pointed.

"Hospital."

Jimmy nodded, cranking the wheel down the street indicated.

As they did they both sucked in a breath as two choppers made a low pass overhead, apparently not interested in them.

We've gotta get off the streets.

FLAGS OF SIN

North of the Forbidden City, Beijing, China

"You're certain that's the man you saw?"

It was Inspector Li that asked the question, and Laura furiously nodded. "Absolutely. And there was a Qing Dynasty flag on the wall behind him."

"Qing?" asked Niner.

"They were the last of the emperors to rule China. Gold flag with a blue dragon," explained Acton. He turned to Laura. "You're sure you saw *that* flag?"

"Absolutely."

Niner made an expression suggesting he found the thought 'cool', and put the car back in gear with a motion from Spock.

"Where are you going?" demanded Laura.

Spock turned around to face them. "Away from here, Professor. We're in the middle of a war zone."

"But we need to stop this."

"I'd love to, and I'm open to suggestions how."

Acton frowned at the tone, but realized the pressure and frustration Spock must be operating under, especially considering Laura's demand. *How do we, five people in a car, stop an army hell-bent on taking over?* And that wasn't the only thing that came to mind. He also wondered if they should. Should they interfere in the natural course of a country's development?

He thought of the Arab Spring, and how the West was so eager to get involved, especially in Egypt and Libya. Now what was the result? Most of the countries that had successfully overthrown their secular dictators had fallen under Islamist control, with Egypt even bringing in a new constitution so heavily laden with Islamic philosophies, they risked becoming the next Iran.

I'd hate to be a Christian in Egypt now.

And here they were in China. A country slowly progressing politically, rapidly progressing economically. Would this coup bring in greater freedoms for their people? It might, but he doubted it. If someone was using the Qing Dynasty as their reasoning, then most likely a megalomaniac was at the helm, with visions of a throne and worshippers dancing through his head. And if his method of takeover was to massacre thousands of innocent children, then one thing that could be said with all honesty, was that the new regime was certainly no *better* than the old.

But Inspector Li had apparently already made up his mind.

"The professor is correct. We must stop this if we can."

"And again I ask how?"

"We need to find the headquarters we escaped from. If we can find that, then we can stop them," said Laura.

Spock nodded, and Acton could see the wheels turning through the thoughtful eyes.

"Where is it?" he asked.

"It moved." Laura sighed. "I don't know where to. When we escaped, we had to jump out of the back because they were repositioning."

Something flashed in Acton's mind, a memory of something he had noticed on their rush here.

"What's it look like?" he asked.

"Like a huge semi-trailer, armored, camouflaged, with a bunch of antennae and satellite dishes on the roof," replied Laura.

Acton's heart pounded a little faster as the description matched up with what he was remembering.

"I've seen that!" he exclaimed. "On our way here, we drove right past it!"

This had Spock turning in his seat to face him.

"Where?"

"I don't know Beijing, I just know we passed a parking lot, and the vehicle Laura described was there, with a bunch of other military vehicles. I thought it was some sort of staging area."

"Was it before or after the road block we avoided?"

Acton had to think about that for a moment.

"After, *just* after as a matter of fact. You had pulled the u-ey, and we had just turned onto a side street, parallel to the main road that was blocked. Niner called in a sit rep."

"I know exactly where that is," said Niner, pressing down on the accelerator a little harder. "We'll be there in less than five minutes."

Li leaned forward. "How do you know Beijing so well?"

Spock and Niner exchanged glances.

"As part of our embassy training, we're required to familiarize ourselves with each city we visit."

"Uh huh." Li leaned back in his seat, apparently unconvinced.

They drove in silence for several minutes, everyone just catching their breath for the action yet to come. Spock pointed ahead.

"Slow down, I think we're coming up on it. We'll cover the last bit on foot."

Niner nodded, easing off the gas then pulling into an empty parking spot. They all climbed out, probably making a none too innocent looking group, all of them disheveled in some way. As they quickly walked down the street, toward the presumed location of the headquarters coordinating this insanity, Acton tried to straighten his hair with his fingers.

Laura took him by the arm and shook her head.

"Don't bother, Dear, it's hopeless."

He smiled as he brushed the matted hair from her face, then looked ahead at a gap between two tall apartment buildings, realizing they must be almost there.

I hope it didn't move again.

Bo Yang's Mobile Headquarters, Beijing, China

The crack of gunshots brought the room to a halt. Bo didn't react, he already expecting what had just happened. And the fact there was no additional shouting or shots, pretty much confirmed it. The door to the control room opened, and General Liang entered, holstering his weapon.

"The traitor is dead," he said matter-of-factly. "But we have a problem."

"What?"

"He hedged his bets."

"Meaning?"

"He played us and them. He had his air units from Qionglai dispatched on a training exercise, flying Combat Air Patrols near the city, fully armed, as soon as our operation started."

Bo could feel himself turning red with anger. He let go the breath he was holding with a burst, trying to ease the death grip he had on his palms.

"What do you mean?" he asked through gritted teeth.

"Before I shot him he said he wanted them in place in case things went wrong, then they could be ordered in by the regime, and if they prevailed, he would look like the hero. If we prevailed, he would claim it wasn't him who gave the order. Either way he'd come out a winner."

"And you showed him otherwise."

Liang shrugged.

"He got what he deserved as a traitor."

"Some would call us traitors," muttered Bo.

Liang shook his head and strode to the head of the room.

"No, we are patriots. We are doing this not for ourselves, but for our country, to make it strong again, under one man. *You.* And with one man in power, unanswerable to those who have only their own interests at heart, China will be even greater than it is now. The world will tremble at the roar of the dragon once more!" He stretched out his arms, encompassing all that were sitting at their terminals, monitoring the situation. "Who do we serve?" he yelled.

"Bo! Bo! Bo!" they all responded in rapid unison.

Liang smiled as he walked back to Bo's desk.

"We serve *you*. *You* who would make us strong again." He sighed. "But, our traitor's actions have caused a problem. We *will* lose air superiority very shortly."

Bo nodded.

What else can go wrong?

"Sir!"

"What is it?" demanded Liang.

But the subordinate didn't reply, his expression suggesting he was too terrified to speak the words. Instead, he handed a report to his General.

"What? That's impossible!"

"What?" asked Bo, preparing himself for more bad news.

"Our units at the Zhongnanhai Complex are reporting that they are already being engaged by the 32nd!"

"What?" exploded Bo, smashing his fist into the keyboard in front of him, snapping it in half. "Send in everything we have! We *must* have control of that complex or all is lost!"

FLAGS OF SIN

Outside Bo Yang's Mobile Headquarters, Beijing, China

"Something's happening."

It was Inspector Li who broke the silence with his whispered observation. Engines were firing up, and the several hundred troops who were idle a moment before, were rushing toward their vehicles. Tanks, troop carriers and what Acton would describe as jeep-type vehicles began to roll from the large parking lot that had indeed been a staging area as Acton had originally thought.

A staging area that protected the mobile headquarters containing Bo Yang with so many troops, any type of attack by a five person squad would be useless. Li had already phoned his boss on Niner's satellite phone, a Superintendent Hong, giving him the location, but they had no idea when help might arrive, if ever.

And the sounds of the battle in and around Tiananmen were mere blocks away, the viciousness of it evident by the flashes on the clouds covering the night sky, and from the plumes of smoke rising around the city, the violence by no means appeared contained.

As they watched the parking lot empty of men and vehicles, Acton began to worry the mobile HQ may move again, and expressed his concern.

Spock agreed. "Niner, better go get the car, bring it a little closer. We'll tail them if we have to."

Niner nodded and sprinted back from where they had come. By the time he returned, the parking lot was nearly empty, with only two jeeps and four men outside.

"Ballsy leaving your HQ undefended," observed Niner.

"Or desperate. Those guys left here in a hurry. I don't think that was planned," replied Spock.

"Either way, it's an opportunity," said Niner. "We could take out these guys no problem, clear the HQ, and Bob's your uncle, coup over."

Spock shook his head. "We've interfered enough by reporting the position. It's up to the Chinese to sort this out. If *we* get caught involved in this, it would cause an international incident that could ultimately lead to war."

Li looked at them both, then chambered a round in his weapon.

"I *am* Chinese, and I'm going."

And with that he strode across the road, walking directly toward the parking lot, his white dress shirt untucked and covered in the blood from his dead partner, and the dirt and soot from hitting the deck countless times.

"We can't let him go alone!" cried Laura.

Spock frowned, all eyes on him, as he weighed his options. Finally sighing, he nodded. "But I want you two to stay here," he said, pointing at Acton and Laura.

Laura shook her head.

"Your chances at success are better with us. We're trained, you know that."

Spock sighed again, apparently not liking the fact he was dealing with civilians who were right, but still a liability, his training going against everything that was about to take place.

"Fine. Six of them, four of us here, Li's not in on the plan so we'll count him out. Professor Acton, you take the target on the left, Palmer the second from the left. Niner the next two, I'll take the two on the right. We're drunken tourists, people, so let's put on a show."

Acton threw his arm around Laura, Niner around Spock, and they strode around the corner they had been hiding.

"I shware, if she spoke Engrish, Ida married her," yelled Niner, stumbling over the curb. "But she di'nt undershtand a word I was shaying. But she was sooooooo bewteeful!"

"That she was," agreed Spock as he half carried Niner across the street.

"Yer so lucky, Jim. You gotta girl who loves you, and is hot to boot!"

"You got that right," laughed Acton, grinning at Laura who was shaking her head at Niner.

"You'll find someone," she said. "But even if she speaks English, I don't think she'll take too kindly to you throwing up on her like you did that poor girl."

They all laughed as they climbed the curb beside the parking lot, Inspector Li having heard them and had stopped to wait, apparently figuring out what was going on.

"We're drunken tourists, you're leading us back to where we can get a cab," whispered Spock.

Li nodded and pointed through the parking lot.

"Right through here, then one block, we'll be on the main road. You can get a cab to your hotel there," he said, a little too loudly, his days of roleplaying apparently long behind him.

They left the sidewalk and entered the parking lot, the six guards having taken notice of them, all now standing, weapons at the ready, but aimed at the ground for now.

"Oh, Laura, if you weren't engaged, I'd be all over you right now," slurred Niner who then stumbled to his knees and pretended to dry heave.

"Ready," whispered Spock without moving his lips.

Acton reached behind his back, scratching it, as one of the soldiers approached, yelling something in Chinese and waving with his hands, apparently suggesting, or more likely insisting, they go around.

Spock's voice was a whisper. "On three, two, one, now."

Acton gripped the handgun tucked in his belt, pulled it out and took aim at the target on the left as he stepped away from Laura to give her room. Before he could squeeze the trigger Niner and Spock had taken out their four targets. He quickly fired two rounds, and his target went down, just as Laura did the same.

Niner and Spock rushed forward, confirming the kills and began dragging the bodies out of sight. Acton grabbed his kill, pulling him toward the rapidly building pile near the side of the mobile HQ. He felt kind of queasy looking down at the man whose life he had just snuffed out, this, if memory served, being the first time he had killed someone then dragged their body somewhere. He had killed before, even with his bare hands, but after the kill, he had quickly disassociated himself with the body, but now here he was struggling to pull the dead weight of a human being out of sight so he could kill more of his comrades.

Acton looked back and saw Inspector Li still standing on the sidewalk, his mouth agape, apparently stunned at the efficiency in which the six men had been dispatched. Acton was still shocked at how slow he was on the draw, the two Delta Force operatives having eliminated two targets before he had even the chance of eliminating one. And if he knew them, they probably could have eliminated the other two, and were probably prepared to do so, if he or Laura had missed.

But they hadn't. Double tap to the chest, just as they had been trained. Don't try to go for the headshot, that was the movies. Two in the chest, he'd be down, and most likely dead, the heart considered by some to be an important, if not vital, organ. Headshots would kill, but the target was much smaller and much more likely to move when you least expected it.

With the bodies cleared, Spock began handing out flashlights that had been on the soldiers' belts, then pointed at the generator rumbling between the truck and the trailer. "Cut the power on my mark," he said to Niner, then motioned for the rest to follow him to the door at the end of the HQ. Li had now joined them, the shock at the speed of what had just unfolded seeming to have worn off.

Niner grabbed the handle and turned to Laura.

"Layout?"

"A long hall down the left side to the end. Rooms are all on the right, five of them I believe, but I can't be certain. The last one is the sleeping quarters we were held in."

Spock nodded.

"I go first. It may be dark, so use the flashlights. People could come out the doors in a hurry, trying to figure out what's wrong. Don't think, just shoot. We're not concerned with friendlies here. We clear the hallway first. If that's empty, we'll each cover a door, Professor Palmer, you cover our sixes. When Niner joins me, he and I will begin clearing the rooms, the rest of you provide cover."

They nodded, and Acton flicked on his flashlight, readying his weapon.

"Give him the signal," said Spock.

Acton leaned around the side of the truck and gave Niner a thumbs up.

Dongzhimen Hospital, Beijing, China

Jimmy swung the car into the hospital complex, gunning it toward the ramp at the front entrance. As they turned Jimmy cursed, immediately cutting their speed as they rapidly approached over a dozen heavily armed PLA regulars. They rolled to a stop in front of the entrance and were immediately surrounded.

"Everybody stay calm," said Dawson, his hands raised and a smile on his face. "Girls, remember, you just tell them the truth, you've done nothing wrong, your Dad asked us to take you to safety, you don't know us, he doesn't know us. You just want to go home."

The doors were hauled open, the startled girls screaming, which actually seemed to calm the troops a bit, their weapons turning their focus to the two white men in the front seats.

Dawson slowly climbed out, his hands raised. He was shoved to the ground by one of the troops, and two Type 80s danced in his face. Shouting on the other side of the vehicle, and Jimmy's calm, reassuring voice, told him the same was happening to his fellow soldier.

A blur to his side and an excited shout had the weapons pointed at his head suddenly swing to the back of the car, and at the terrified Chinese girl who burst from the backseat. She was babbling in Chinese, a language Dawson had not even a basic understanding of, pointing at the backseat then at Dawson. The weapons re-aimed at Dawson's head, and he wondered what the hell she was saying to them, when she jumped in front of him, hugging him, shielding him from their weapons.

Dawson wasn't sure what was going on, but when several white coats came running out the front entrance, then congregated at the backseat, he breathed a sigh of relief that the Ambassador might finally get the medical attention he so desperately needed. He wasn't concerned about his wound, he already having pulled the piece of shrapnel out and treating it with the med kit Professor Palmer had handed over. He'd be out of commission for a few weeks, but would live.

Juan was pulled away by one of the soldiers, the weapons now regaining their clear shots at Dawson, as she was carried inside the building, kicking and screaming, shouting in Chinese, her friend, carried between two soldiers, her feet stumbling, merely whimpered, the shock of the entire night apparently too much, what little control she had had now gone, her young mind having decided this was the end of her ordeal, and it was time to shutdown to protect itself.

A gurney was rushed up and the Ambassador loaded onto it, then pushed inside. Dawson heard Jimmy offer up his identification, identification that Dawson no longer had, his having been confiscated by the police when he was arrested. Which probably meant the moment he gave them his Virgil White, State Department cover, he'd be tossed in a cold dark cell somewhere.

It's time to let Jimmy do the talking, and get us a phone call.

The clapping of helicopter rotors triggered a bout of shouting, the soldiers rushing away from the car and toward the edge of the elevated ramp. Dawson ventured a glance and saw four attack helicopters hovering a few hundred yards away, their cannons and weapons pods highlighted by the street lamps below. He looked back at the hospital entrance and saw the two girls were nowhere to be seen, and neither was the Ambassador, his charges now inside and hopefully safe from whatever was about to happen.

He glanced to his right, and down the ramp they had just come, then to his left. The exit was blocked by a jeep, which would provide cover, but might also be a primary target. Forward toward the hospital entrance would simply mean he'd be running with the bullets, and they were a hell of a lot faster than his legs.

He turned slightly toward the ramp they had just driven up and exchanged a glance with Jimmy who had repositioned himself with apparently the same conclusion. They traded barely perceptible nods, and Dawson's eyes refocused on the choppers, still hovering nearby. He tried to see into the cockpits, to sense what they were thinking, to anticipate when they might open fire, but it was no use. The chopper to the right dipped, and Dawson's legs began to push him to his feet, then he froze.

The chopper banked away, followed by the other three, revealing their gold flags emblazoned on their tail section, and leaving him and the soldiers sighing in relief, firing on a hospital apparently not on the agenda of those attempting a takeover of the most populous country in the world.

Which meant the weapons once again returned their attention to him and Jimmy.

Out of the frying pan and back into the fire.

FLAGS OF SIN

Inside Bo Yang's Mobile Headquarters, Beijing, China

A burst of weapons fire, muffled by the insulated walls of the trailer they were in, had the room at a standstill. Bo Yang, standing in the corner while his keyboard was replaced, looked at General Liang. Liang pointed at one of the guards.

"Go find out what that was!"

The soldier left the room on the bounce and Bo returned his attention to the screens occupying almost every square inch of wall space.

"Status?" asked Liang, his voice almost hysterical, the usually in control soldier apparently beginning to lose that veneer of the calm, professional that had attracted Bo to him. Liang had been groomed for over a decade for this very night, and Bo knew the man had invested his life in their cause, and, like Bo, stood to be executed, after lengthy torture sessions, should they not succeed.

"We have lost air superiority, sir," replied a young officer manning one of the tactical stations. "Our squadrons have either been eliminated or have bugged out."

"Cowards!" screamed Liang. "Miserable inept cowards!"

"And the assault on Zhongnanhai?" asked Bo, returning to his seat as the technician indicated his computer was working again.

"Our Tiananmen units have encountered heavy resistance, and have not yet arrived. Our units from here are on their way, but have not yet arrived. The 32nd is just too large a force, sir."

Liang looked ready to tear the head off the poor bastard who had just delivered the bleak assessment. Bo's shoulders slumped as the lights flickered, then went out.

What now?

FLAGS OF SIN

Outside Bo Yang's Mobile Headquarters, Beijing, China

The door burst open before Spock had a chance to pull on the handle, a soldier apparently sent to investigate the earlier gunfire, poking his head out. Spock reached up and grabbed him by the jacket, yanking him from his elevated position and into a controlled slam onto the ground. Two quick punches to the face, the man's head smacking on the pavement each time, had him out cold.

Acton and Laura took up positions on either side of the still swinging rear door of the headquarters, Acton peering down the hallway and seeing it was deserted. The lights flickered and went out, and he heard Niner's shoes pounding on the pavement. Spock and Niner charged up the few steps and into the hallway, their weapons at the ready, flashlights illuminating swaths of the darkened interior.

A lone emergency light flickered on at the end of the hall, casting long shadows of every nook and cranny along the walls and floor, as Acton and Inspector Li climbed inside, rushing to cover their respective doors, Laura remaining outside to watch their backs. Confused shouts could be heard, most from the far end of the hall, most in fact coming from the other side of the door Acton found himself covering.

He dropped to one knee and focused his weapon on the door, chest height, ready to eliminate anything that may come through. He glanced down the hall as Niner threw open the first door, apparently unlocked, and Spock entered. A single gunshot echoed down the hall, and the confusion on the other side of his door seemed to suddenly find order with silence.

The next door down the hall was kicked open by Niner, with Spock stepping inside, the flashlight flickering on the walls, but no shots fired, the room empty.

A single voice snapped an order on the other side of his door and he tensed up, regaining his attention as the final door between him and the Delta duo was kicked open. A burst of gunfire erupted from the room, causing Spock and Niner to both twist away from the door. They stepped back, then emptied their clips into the walls, waist height, leaving a row of holes torn through what, based upon the dust, Acton judged to be gyprock. There was no return fire, and Spock stepped inside for only a moment.

Shots blasted from the other side of the door Acton stood on, and he found himself falling backward in shock, then rolling to the side on instinct. He looked back at the door, it now shredded at chest level, the wall behind where he had stood moments before pockmarked with bullet holes, the only thing having saved him was the fact he had been on his knee.

Spock and Niner rushed past him, motioning for Li to leave his door and cover Acton's, they apparently having decided the final door was the sleeping quarters Laura had been held in, and most likely to be empty. They cleared the room with no shots fired as another burst of gunfire sliced through the door of the final room, sending Li diving to the floor. The shots stopped, and a lone voice yelled something.

"He's out of ammo!" yelled Li as he jumped to his feet and kicked the door down, screaming something in Chinese.

"Shit!" muttered Spock as he and Niner rushed in after the Inspector, Acton following. Gunfire erupted, and before Acton could get inside he found Li with a weapon pointed at the man Laura had recognized on the television, Spock with a gun on an elderly man in full military regalia, and Niner covering a room of corpses.

FLAGS OF SIN

And at the back of the room, the proud flag of the Qing Dynasty hung on the wall, stained with the blood splatter of one of its adherents who had died for the cause.

Bo Yang's Mobile Headquarters, Beijing, China

Could it be over? If it was, this was never how he would have expected it. Bo looked at the people in the room. A police officer if he ever saw one, two Caucasians, probably American, another Asian man, possibly Korean in origin, but based upon his companions, probably an American as well. Three people who shouldn't even be in the country, let alone interfering in its politics, and one lone cop.

How could his plans, laid out in intricate detail, over decades, be unraveled by these people? He, an emperor, superior in intellect, title and station, halted by a group of Americans and a police officer. His mind reeled from the shock of what his eyes were taking in.

He looked at Liang, his comrade, his friend, his partner in all of this, and could tell that he too was just as shocked. They had expected to succeed, but if they hadn't, they had at least expected to have died fighting troops loyal to the regime, dying in a blaze of glorious gunfire, martyrs of the empire, their deaths eulogized in story and song for centuries to follow, hopefully inspiring the next generation to victory.

But instead, here they stood, hands in the air, prisoners. Prisoners of three Americans and a cop. He couldn't accept this. It was intolerable. It was unbelievable. It was an eventuality that had never occurred to him.

It was an eventuality that couldn't stand.

The American covering Liang spoke in English.

"Tell him to give the stand-down order."

The impudent man who dared to point a weapon at his emperor, spoke.

"I am Inspector Li of the Public Security Bureau. You are under arrest for crimes against the State. I am ordering you to notify your troops that this coup is over, and to stand down so that no further lives are lost."

Bo evaluated the man delivering the ultimatum. This man, this Inspector Li, impressed him. Li was clearly out of his league, probably from some lower caste family considering his age and limited title, but here he stood, daring to try and put an end to the most important event in Chinese history since his grandfather had taken control of China. A simple policeman, doing his duty, serving his country faithfully, yet ignorantly, but with the courage to hold a weapon to the head of a man he knew far greater than him, and far more powerful.

Bo smiled.

"Do you have any idea who I am?" he said in English for the benefit of the room filled with foreigners.

"I know exactly who you are. You are Bo Yang, criminal and traitor."

Bo shook his head, lowering his hands. Inspector Li jerked his weapon up several times, implying Bo should put his hands back up, but he chose to ignore the order, instead placing them defiantly on his hips.

"Do you not recognize the flag that stands behind me?"

Li nodded. "Everyone would."

"For those of you who don't know," he said, looking at the Americans, "that is the flag of the Qing Dynasty."

One of the men, the last to have come through the door, stepped forward.

"I recognize it. But it hasn't been an official flag for almost a century. What does it have to do with you?"

Bo smiled at the man.

"To whom do I have the honor of addressing?"

"Professor James Acton."

The name rang a bell with Bo, his mind flashing back to the report he read on one of their former prisoners.

"I trust your fiancée is safe?"

This appeared to catch the man off guard, something Bo always enjoyed seeing. Information was power, and possessing it when no one else thought you had it, was even more powerful. To catch your enemy in a lie was one thing, to reveal to your enemy you knew their secrets, was something entirely different, for it left them wondering what else you knew. Reveal one tiny tidbit, even if it were the only item you knew, and it left their minds reeling with the possibility you knew far more.

Which could lead to further revelations, revelations of things you may never have discovered.

Play along, and let them hang themselves.

For he knew something none of the new arrivals knew. He knew if he drew this out long enough, the defense force that should have been here guarding them, that had been dispatched to the Zhongnanhai Complex assault, would return at any minute, Liang having ordered their recall as soon as the power went out, with an old style walkie-talkie that never left his hip. The SOS had been received, and it was only a matter of time.

Professor Acton recovered from the shock of his question.

"Yes, she's fine. No thanks to you."

Bo shrugged.

"This is war. She interfered."

Acton took a step forward.

"Actually, *I'm* the one who interfered." He raised his weapon, pointing it at Bo. "And I believe our friend here"—he motioned at Inspector Li— "gave you an order."

"You expect me to order my troops to stand-down?" Bo laughed. "Never."

"It's over, and you know it," said Li.

Bo looked at Li. "I find it highly doubtful that a mere inspector in the Public Security Bureau would know the status of the armed conflict now unfolding."

Li smiled from half his mouth, his eyes narrowing.

"Even I, a mere inspector, knows that if a battle is going well, you do not dispatch the very troops guarding your headquarters."

Bo covered the surprise he felt with a smile and a nod.

"Very good, Inspector, very good. You are more astute than I gave you credit for." Bo leaned forward, his fists in balls, pressing against his desk. "But what are you going to do about it? You have no way to communicate with the outside world, and you have shut off the power, so I have no way to give the order you demand of me."

One of the men nodded to the Asian American, who immediately left the room, Bo assumed to turn the power back on. It didn't matter. Every moment of delay meant his forces were closer, and this interruption would be over.

"Professor Acton," he said, returning his attention to the American professor, and pointing at the flag of his ancestors. "You asked what this had to do with me."

The man nodded, saying nothing.

"My great-great-grandfather was the Tongzhi Emperor."

Professor Acton smiled.

"Nice try, but he had no children."

"That is where your history fails you, Professor. He did indeed have a son, born only days before he was murdered by the Empress Dowager's forces, his memory sullied by rumors of his death from smallpox and later syphilis, when his name continued to carry more honor than his mother could stand."

"Okay, I'll bite. If he had a son, how come no one knows about it?"

"He was hidden away, raised by my adopted great-great-grandmother Li Mei, the governess of the baby emperor." Bo raised a hand to cut off the professor. "Let me finish. That baby was named Shun-sheng by her and one of the imperial guards, Mao Jun, who married and raised him as their own, in Shaoshan, Hunan Province."

"Shaoshan?" muttered Acton, his eyes narrowing. "Hunan?"

Bo smiled.

"What are you a professor of?"

"Archaeology."

"So you know your history."

Acton nodded.

"Then why don't you answer the question that is burning in your mind?"

Acton frowned. "Are you suggesting that your grandfather is, or rather was, Chairman Mao Zedong, the founder of Communist China?"

"Fuck me," muttered the other American under his breath.

Bo clapped his hands, startling Li who for a second Bo thought was about to shoot him. He held his hands out, open, to calm the excited police officer.

"Very good, Professor. Yes, indeed, my grandfather was Mao Zedong, who led China for decades, inspired by the knowledge his grandmother Li Mei imparted."

"You're suggesting Mao Zedong was inspired to rule China because he believed he was the legitimate emperor?"

Bo nodded. "You sound doubtful."

Acton shrugged. "We're here, aren't we?"

Bo chuckled, his head bobbing. "Yes, indeed. We *are* here."

"There's just one problem," said Acton as the power kicked back on, the computers beginning to reboot around them. "You're not one of Mao's grandchildren."

"Ah, but I am. My grandfather had a son, Anhong."

"Who disappeared when he was three, and was presumed dead at the hands of the Kuomintang."

"That was *presumed* dead, but was actually delivered to my great-great-grandmother Li Mei, to be raised in secret. He had a son, me. I was raised under a false identity, so I could one day reclaim the throne, and lead China into its ordained future, as the most powerful and ancient country under the Heavens."

The Asian American returned, his mission accomplished, and whispered something in the other man's ear. The man nodded, and the Asian American disappeared again.

"Is any of this possible," asked the man.

Professor Acton nodded. "It's all circumstantial, but yes. The Tongzhi Emperor died when he was eighteen. If he had had a son, it would have threatened the Empress Dowager's control over him, as he would have an heir, and it might have emboldened him. At the time he was already challenging her control over him, and she was known to be ruthless. If he had a son, and he had been secreted away, they never would have admitted it, since that child would be the rightful heir to the throne. Instead the Empress Dowager installed someone she could control, and ruled in the background until her death. Shortly after that, the empire fell."

"But Mao?"

Acton shrugged his shoulders. "The names fit, the timeframes fit, but without DNA tests, there's no way to know for sure. However, it might explain why Mao was initially a proponent of democracy and Western ideals, then suddenly turned to Communism and its inevitable dictatorship."

The professor shrugged his shoulders, again looking at the other man. "I just don't know. He"—he nodded at Bo—"certainly seems to believe it, though."

"Because it's true, Professor."

The wall panels snapped to life, and radio communications could be heard faintly over the headsets still either on the heads of the fallen, or dangling beside their terminals.

"I'll get you to send that stand-down order now," said the man covering General Liang.

Bo looked at the panel showing troop placements, and saw the column rushing to their rescue only minutes away. He shrugged his shoulders, and nodded to Liang. Liang looked at the same display, then back at him, his eyes conveying that he too knew the column was mere minutes from rescuing them. He stepped over to one of the consoles, pulled the headset off the dead lieutenant that had been manning it, and placed it on his head. Tapping a few keys, he was about to speak when the American stepped toward him.

"And if you think that column on Dawang Road is going to save you, you probably didn't notice they haven't moved in the past two minutes. I'm guessing they've been engaged."

Bo's eyes darted to the display, and his heart sank as he realized what the American said was true. He hadn't noticed it before, the scale of the displayed map too small, but the blinking dot had indeed not moved any closer. Liang looked at him, his eyes resigned to their fate, and snapped to attention, saluting. Bo returned the honor, and Liang spoke into the microphone.

His words sent a surge of pride through Bo's heart, his chest swelling with the implications, the bravado, the ballsy audacity just displayed by his second-in-command, and the complete and utter cluelessness of their captors as to what had just been said.

Except one.

Inspector Li's eyes shot wide open and he began to spin toward Liang as he shouted the translation.

"He said to fight to the death!"

Bo reached forward, grabbing the pistol from the distracted Li's hand. Liang, seeing this, surged forward and grabbed the American's gun, trying to twist it out of his hand. A shot rang out and Liang dropped, the weapon he had been struggling for, his downfall.

All weapons turned toward Bo as he raised the Inspector's gun to his own head.

"For my family, for my Emperor, for my China."

He squeezed the trigger, his last images that of blood splattering on his beloved flag, then the sensation of his body collapsing backward against the wall, his hand reaching up, grabbing the gold and blue silk, pulling it from the wall. He collapsed to the ground, and with his life moments from ending, he watched as it rippled down, covering him as he would want to be buried, draped in the flag of his ancestors.

Dongzhimen Hospital, Beijing, China

The helicopters had left, and the attention had returned to the two Americans that had arrived in a screech of tires and brakes, their car shot up, the occupants covered in blood and dirt.

Dawson didn't blame them for not trusting them.

The question was how far did that lack of trust go? How much did these men know of what was happening in their city? In their country? The highest rank he had seen was a lieutenant, and he seemed just as young and green as the men he led, a group of men who appeared terrified, and if he didn't know any better, a group of men who had no standing orders beyond protecting the hospital.

And that could be dangerous. With no rules of engagement, two suspicious Americans could easily be construed as the enemy, and prime sources of intel. Intel that would not be forthcoming.

Dawson was grabbed by two men and forced toward the hospital entrance. He spoke reassuringly, his hands up, his body language that of someone cooperating. A glance over his shoulder, which was rewarded with the butt of a rifle between his shoulder blades, showed Jimmy between two guards, trying to reassure them he was no threat.

The doors opened automatically and they were shoved through, the entire lobby stopping and staring at the two disheveled foreigners. The lieutenant led the way deeper inside. Dawson's trained eye took in everything. The route they were taking, the location of elevators, stairwells, emergency exits, cameras. He knew this could get ugly, and though he didn't want to kill any innocent Chinese soldiers, he wasn't about to sacrifice himself or Jimmy due to their ignorance.

If he had to, he would kill to free themselves.

But for now, he had to assume they were going to be interrogated, and hopefully that meant time. Time for things to settle down. Time for a message to hopefully get through to the embassy. Time for the chaos outside to end.

The lieutenant opened a door and Dawson was shoved through, followed by Jimmy. The door was slammed shut, and two guards posted on either side, the lieutenant shouting orders in Chinese.

"You okay?" he asked Jimmy.

Jimmy nodded. "You?"

"I'll live. We're dealing with amateur hour here."

"Which is never good."

"Agreed. Speaking of amateurs, I still have Spock's satellite phone," said Dawson, reaching into his pocket and pulling it out. "Watch the door." He placed his back facing the door, and rapidly dialed the embassy number. He put the phone to his ear and leaned on a cabinet, pretending to relax as the phone rang.

"United States Embassy, Beijing. How may I direct your call?"

"I don't have time, I need you to take a message," whispered Dawson.

"You'll have to speak up, sir, I can barely hear you."

Dawson felt his chest tighten. He raised his voice a few decibels. "I need you to take a message."

"I'm sorry, sir, I'm just the switchboard operator. Let me know how I can direct your call and you can leave—"

"Listen lady, you tell your Marine Detachment Commander that Ambassador Davidson, Mr. White, and Mr. Black, are being held by Chinese troops at Dongzhimen Hospital. We need embassy assistance immediately or we may be executed. Do you understand me?"

There was a pause.

"Yes, sir. Dongzhimen Hospital."

"Yes, now get that message to your Marines right a—"

The door burst open and Dawson spun around to see the lieutenant storm toward him, rifle raised in the air. The butt came down on his nose as he made the split second decision not to react, and the world went black.

FLAGS OF SIN

Bo Yang's Mobile Headquarters, Beijing, China

"What did he say?" asked Acton, standing over the body, the flag of the Qing Dynasty covering the upper half of Bo Yang's body like a cloak, shielding him from any further indignities.

Inspector Li stood up, having checked the man's pulse to confirm he was dead.

"For my family, for my Emperor, for my China."

"Important words," said Acton. "This is history we're living right here, right now, and those words deserve to be remembered, to be written down. I'll bet what happened tonight will be erased from official history by the authorities, but someday, people will want to know what happened, and historians will want to investigate whether or not his claims were true. Was he indeed Mao's grandson? Was Mao the grandson of the last true Qing Emperor?" Acton shook his head at the wonder of it all, vowing himself to attempt the undertaking. "Fascinating," he muttered as he stepped toward the flag, removing a handkerchief from his pocket. He wiped it across the flag, then carefully folded the bloodstained cotton, placing it in his pocket, preserving the DNA.

"Fascinating indeed, Professor," said Spock pointing at the screen. "But we need to get the hell out of here now!"

On the screen the column that had been stationary was moving again, as was a rapidly approaching series of triangles that appeared to Acton to ignore all roads.

Incoming aircraft!

Spock grabbed Li and shoved him out the door, Acton following right behind him. They sprinted down the short hallway and burst out the rear entrance, jumping to the ground. Laura and Niner, covering their sixes, both spun around.

"What's going on?" asked Niner.

"Incoming!" yelled Spock, pointing up. Acton looked and gasped as four fighter jets streaked toward them. He grabbed Laura by the arm and they sprinted from the parking lot, back toward where they had left the car, Li, Spock and Niner close on their heels.

The roar of the engines began to echo between the buildings, and was joined by several higher pitched whines. Acton glanced over his shoulder and saw missiles streaking toward the mobile HQ, their contrails like the lines painted on the road to Hell, the source moving too fast for his eyes to pick out, but their effect when they slammed into the large, armored trailer spectacular. The massive machine jerked sideways, toward them, as if bent in half at the middle, then a ripping sound was followed by a giant fireball that erupted from the holes punched in the far side by the missiles. The entire structure at first bulged as if preparing to release something held tightly inside, when finally, the pressure proving too much for the armored lining, it tore open like a tin can, flame pouring out, a shockwave rolling toward them as the unleashed fury tried to consume all who had been involved.

Acton was knocked to the ground, as were the rest of them. He hit hard, his chin smacking the pavement. Instinctively he scrambled toward Laura, throwing his body over hers, and looked back at the flames rolling toward them. Spock and Niner were shielding Inspector Li, and were wisely not looking in the direction of the oncoming flames.

"Hold your breath!" yelled Spock.

Acton turned away, burying his head under his arms, sucking in a lungful of air. A wave of heat rushed over them, chewing through the oxygen, then just as quickly rushed back, retreating toward the source of all the night's chaos.

"Everyone okay?"

It was Spock. Acton rolled over, letting go his breath with a burst, and sucking in several fresh ones as he looked at Laura who was thankfully doing the same.

"I'm good," he said, Laura echoing him. He jumped to his feet and pulled Laura to hers. Li was limping, trying to avoid putting any weight on his right foot.

"Sprained ankle," he said as tires squealed behind them. They turned as one and saw a jeep, gold flag flying from the back, bounce over the curb and enter the parking lot, three of its four occupants standing, weapons ready, staring at the burning hulk that had been their headquarters. One of new arrivals pointed at them, shouting, and the driver gunned it toward the armed group. The one in the passenger seat lowered his weapon, taking aim.

Niner took him out, and Spock emptied a clip into the engine block, bringing the jeep to a halt. Acton grabbed Li, throwing the man's arm over his shoulder. Laura got on the other side and they began to move the injured man as quickly as they could toward the vehicle parked around the corner. More gunfire erupted from behind them but Acton didn't look, instead focusing on reaching the corner and safety, however fleeting it might be.

"Doc!"

Acton spun to see Niner throw the keys for the car, he watched them arc through the air as he continued to move forward with Li. He jumped and grabbed them, Niner already having returned his attention to the gun battle.

They rounded the corner and Acton pressed the fob twice, unlocking all the doors. They loaded a groaning Li into the back seat, and Laura climbed in with him as Acton started the car. He put it in gear and hammered on the gas, sending it hurtling toward the corner. Rounding it, he turned to the right then cranked it to the left, the car skidding to a halt, its passenger side facing the two Delta Force Bravo Team members.

"Get in!" he yelled, reaching over and pushing open the passenger door as Laura did the same with the rear. Niner and Spock backed toward the car, then climbed inside. As soon as Acton saw their feet clear the pavement he hammered on the gas, just as a tank rolled over the jeep they had destroyed.

"Where to?" he asked as he whipped back around the corner they had just come.

"Embassy!" yelled Spock.

"Turn left here!" yelled Li, pointing. Acton spun the wheel, skidding around the turn, and floored it, hoping to put as much distance as he could between them and the tank he had just seen. "Keep going straight, I'll tell you when to turn. The embassy is only ten minutes from here."

Unless we run into more roadblocks.

FLAGS OF SIN

Dongzhimen Hospital, Beijing, China

When Dawson came to, it was to the sound of thuds followed by grunts. He had the impression of Rocky Balboa pounding flesh in the meat locker, but as the fog cleared and his eyes opened, he found himself looking up to see Jimmy tied to a chair, a Chinese soldier punching him in the face and the stomach, each punch carefully lined up, intended to inflict maximum pain, the black gloves the soldier wore, protecting the bastard's knuckles from any damage, or evidence he had inflicted the beating.

Another soldier, apparently meant to cover Dawson, wasn't doing his duty, instead watching the show and assuming Dawson was still out cold. The lieutenant screamed questions at Jimmy in Chinese, the apparent purpose of this entire exercise not interrogation at all, but punishment under the guise of questioning.

They were mad, they were scared, and they were dangerous.

Terrified men without orders.

Dawson checked his wrists, and they were still unbound. So were his ankles.

Sloppy.

A quick survey of the room showed the door was closed, no evidence of anyone outside, and only the three soldiers.

Dawson kicked his leg out, sweeping the soldier supposedly guarding him off his feet. Rolling over, he planted an elbow directly on the man's windpipe, crushing it and snapping his neck. Still rolling from planting the elbow, he reached up and grabbed the soldier assaulting Jimmy by the belt, positioning his other leg behind the man's feet, and yanked. The man fell backward, toward the floor, his arms flailing for something to hold onto.

He hit the floor, his head smacking hard on the tile, and Dawson slammed the side of his open hand into the man's throat, leaving him gasping for air that could no longer reach his lungs.

Dawson rolled to a knee, punching forward hard, nailing the stunned lieutenant in the groin. He doubled over in agony, a high-pitched wail erupting from his mouth as Dawson stood, shoving his palm upward into the man's chin. The lieutenant flipped over, landing on his back, dazed and grabbing his boys.

Dawson fished a gun then a knife off the man's belt, quickly cutting Jimmy loose.

"Can you stand?"

Jimmy made a valiant effort, then shook his head.

"Sorry, BD, I can't move."

Jimmy's voice was weak, barely audible. Dawson looked around and saw a gurney on its end in the corner. He unhooked it from the wall and it slammed on the floor with a crash. Pulling it beside Jimmy he was about to load him on it when the door clicked open behind him. He shoved the gurney hard, slamming it into the door, the surprised guard who had come to investigate staring through the window.

Dawson looked at the handle and frowned, pressing the little button on the door knob to lock it, knowing it wouldn't hold a good stiff shoulder. Reaching up, he grabbed hold of a large cabinet on the side of the door and pulled. It tipped then finally fell with a thunderous rattle, blocking the door. He shoved it tight against the frame, then hauled the lieutenant, still groaning, to his feet, pressing the man's weapon against his temple.

"If I don't hear from the United States Embassy, he dies."

Now he just hoped somebody spoke English out there to understand him.

FLAGS OF SIN

Tanze Road, Beijing, China

"Left at the next big intersection, just ahead, then the gate is on the right!" yelled Li.

Acton nodded. It had felt like the longest ten minutes of his life. They had been lucky for the most part, their speed and the openness of the side streets Li had led them on limiting their pursuers to three jeeps, the tanks unable to keep pace. But the small arms fire from the lead jeep managed to occasionally hit them, leaving their rear window shattered, to which Niner had replied, "Finally!", repositioning himself so he could return fire out the rear window as opposed to the side window that had a built in child safety feature, limiting it to lowering halfway. A limitation that had only lasted a few minutes before Niner got frustrated and smashed it out with the butt of his weapon.

"We've got company!" yelled Spock.

Acton glanced in his rearview mirror but saw nothing other than the jeeps several hundred feet back. He adjusted his side mirror up with a push and nearly shit his pants. Two attack helicopters were barreling down on them, and flashbacks of London filled his mind as he debated whether or not he should slam on his brakes to let them pass overhead.

But this wasn't London, this was Beijing. And this time they were being pursued on the road too, not just in the air.

He pressed harder on the accelerator, the intersection he knew led to the embassy within sight. Spock fished the satellite phone from his pocket, taking the call he had placed earlier off hold.

"ETA sixty seconds, we're coming in red hot!"

The cannons opened fire, tearing up the pavement, steadily approaching their rear bumper. Acton swerved to the left, but the guns tracked him, either automatically or manually, how he didn't care. All that mattered is there appeared to be no way to outrun or outmaneuver them. He cranked the wheel to the right, again to no avail.

Something flashed in front of him and he gasped as his eyes focused on the new threat.

"Look out!" he yelled, everyone turning to see what he was shouting about. Two missiles were screaming down the road toward them, the plane that had fired them burning up the pavement with its afterburners, as if chasing the instruments of destruction it had just unleashed.

Acton slammed the brakes on, his thinking that if they were the target, perhaps a hotter heat source, like helicopter engines, might attract the missiles. The helicopters overshot him, both splitting off in opposite directions, the missiles splitting as well, chasing the choppers down their respective side streets, their heat signatures their doom.

Acton hammered on the gas, the car leaping forward as the jet passed overhead, the three jeeps now upon them. Bullets tore into the driver side. Acton swung the car to the left, slamming it into the jeep that had overtaken them. The driver lost control, crashing into the rear of a parked car, flipping it spectacularly end over end, the occupants spilling out onto the roadway, or atop the line of stationary vehicles.

They were at the intersection. Acton cranked the wheel to the left, skidding around the turn, the embassy, well lit, now on their right, the gate, normally closed, opening as soon as he had made the turn. Behind them in his rearview mirror were the two remaining jeeps, not fifty yards behind them, guns blazing, the muzzle flashes unceasing, the rattle as rounds impacted the light skin of their car, threatening at any moment to take out a tire or rupture the fuel tank, or worse, penetrate the compartment and kill one of its occupants.

"Hang on!" yelled Acton, spinning the wheel to the right as he slammed on the brakes, then lifting his foot and shoving the accelerator to the floor, sending the car surging through the gates, two dozen Marines, their M27 Infantry Automatic Rifles at the ready, letting them pass, then rushing the gate as it began to inch closed.

Acton hit the brakes, bringing the car to a stop, as they all turned to watch. Their pursuers made the same turn he just did, but unlike with their arrival, the uninvited guests were met with a wall of lead, two dozen weapons opening fire, shredding the first vehicle to pieces the moment it passed the gate and entered US soil. The engine exploded, and the vehicle careened to the side, slamming into a concrete fortification, the driver and passengers full of far more holes than God had intended.

The second vehicle slammed its brakes on, the front tires crossing the gate, but the men immediately threw their hands up, and when the Marines didn't fire, bailed from their vehicle, running down the street and out of sight.

Several Marines pushed the jeep straddling the gate out of the way, then the iron bars rumbled shut as Acton closed his eyes, resting his head on the steering wheel, the shouts from outside the vehicle, all in precious English with the occasional twang he loved so much, counteracting the adrenaline that had fueled him for hours.

He felt a hand on his shoulder, a hand he immediately recognized, and gripped it, tight. His precious Laura, safe, their friends, safe, and one Chinese Public Security Bureau Inspector, safe.

Dongzhimen Hospital, Beijing, China

A face appeared at the window, shouting, and Dawson pressed the barrel harder against the lieutenant's head. This face was older, probably fifties or sixties, and judging by the artwork on his shoulders, a full-bird Colonel.

Finally, someone who can make a decision.

There was shouting, orders being given, yelps from soldiers obeying those orders, and the confusion on the other side of the door seemed to settle down.

There was a knock, and the man's face peered through the glass.

"Mr. White? I am Colonel Peng. I am here with a Mr. Redford from your embassy."

"Let me see him!"

Dawson wasn't going to fall for any tricks. His guard would remain up until he was back at the embassy.

Colonel Peng's face disappeared, replaced a moment later by Redford, a face he instantly recognized from the security briefings, briefings Dawson remembered the Ambassador not taking seriously, but which Redford did. Dawson relaxed. Slightly.

"Can I come in?" he asked, giving a small wave.

"Just a second."

Dawson looked at Jimmy, still sitting in his chair. "Can you hold a weapon?"

"'Til they pry it from my cold dead hands."

Dawson gave him half a grin, pressing the gun into Jimmy's outstretched palm. He pushed the lieutenant against the wall, then with hand gestures that would make it clear to the young man, said, "If he moves, shoot him."

Jimmy nodded, taking aim, as Dawson grabbed another weapon from the body of his first kill, then unlocked the door, pulling the cabinet out about a foot.

Redford poked his head inside, frowning at the storage unit still blocking him from entering.

"Can I come in?" he repeated.

"What's the situation?"

He waved two passports. "I have two temporary diplomatic passports here, that entitle you to unfettered transport to the embassy, then out of the country. All you need to do is drop your weapons, and we can leave. I have an armored vehicle outside, with two of your friends providing security."

Dawson exchanged glances with Jimmy, breathing a sigh of relief that their comrades were safe.

"And the professors?"

"Safe, along with a Chinese police inspector."

"And his kids, the ones we came here with?"

"They've been released."

"And the Ambassador?"

"Under Chinese care here, but with our embassy physician observing until he can be transported back home."

"I want the hallways cleared," said Dawson. "All the way to the vehicle, no soldiers."

Redford looked back and Dawson heard orders being snapped in Chinese from the other side of the door. A few moments later Redford's head poked back in.

"Done."

Dawson pulled the cabinet out of the way, then lifted Jimmy to his feet. They stepped out of the room, Jimmy covering the lieutenant until they were through the door. Dawson looked up and down the hall, and the only green uniform he saw was the Colonel's. Dawson flipped his weapon around, and handed it to the man butt first. The Colonel took the weapon, snapping out a respectful nod, acknowledging it not as a surrender, but as a negotiated peace.

Jimmy handed his over to Redford, then collapsed in Dawson's arms. Dawson scooped him up, then carried him down the hall, through the lobby, and out the automatic doors. Their car was still parked where they had left it, but a black SUV, American flags proudly flying from the front corners of the hood, was parked behind it.

The doors opened and out stepped two of the filthiest bastards he had never been more happy to see.

Spock and Niner.

They helped their comrade into the back seat, then Dawson climbed in beside him, along with Redford. Spock took the passenger seat, while Niner drove.

Nothing was said as they returned to the embassy, but when they passed through the gates, Dawson couldn't help but notice the jeep lying off to the side as they entered, and another one torn to shreds, bodies covered in sheets lined up beside the vehicle.

"What the hell happened here?"

Niner brought the SUV to a stop beside a civilian vehicle that had more bullet holes than body work left.

"Apparently we got Actoned," said Niner.

"What the fuck does that mean?" gasped Jimmy.

But Dawson had a pretty good idea as a smile spread across his face.

Li Residence, Beijing, China

Li skipped the elevator, it too slow for his purposes, and instead rushed up the four flights of stairs to his humble apartment. The moment his key hit the door it was pulled open from the inside, and a pair or arms wrapped themselves around him. He buried his head in his wife's shoulder, inhaling her scent, hugging her hard.

"Daddy!"

The cry from deeper in the apartment filled his heart with relief and joy. He let go his wife and rushed toward his daughter as she ran around the corner, arms outstretched, tears already flowing freely down her face. He dropped to his knees and she threw her arms around his neck, her chest heaving as she clung to him.

"I'm sorry, Daddy, I'm so sorry!" she cried. He held her tight, so tight he was afraid he'd break her, but he didn't care. He never wanted to let her go, he never wanted to let her out of his sight again. His precious Juan, his jewel, was safe. He felt a hand on his shoulder, his wife dropping to her knees beside them, wrapping her arms around both of them, and the three of them sat on the floor, hugging and crying, as the horror of the night's events slowly receded into the past, becoming memories that would never be forgotten.

Beijing Capital International Airport, Beijing, China

Professor James Acton watched as the Ambassador was loaded aboard the US government plane. He followed Laura up the steps, the four Bravo Team members bringing up the rear. Hundreds if not thousands of troops were in the area, throughout the airport, surrounding the tarmac, and this was one of the few flights being allowed to actually leave.

Through the night and the morning they had all been glued to the televisions at the embassy, watching the news, reading the dispatches as they arrived. Bo's forces had been defeated, the last of which, in Shanghai, had truly held out until the last man. Those participating were being summarily executed, the ensuing massacre far larger than what had happened during the actual coup.

This of course was being denied, but footage was being uploaded to the Internet at a furious pace, and the truth couldn't be held back. Already in the streets, streets filled with hundreds of thousands of troops, the cleanup had begun, and Acton had no doubt that within weeks, there would be no evidence of what had occurred, and the whitewash would begin.

The Internet was back up, the cellular networks had returned to normal, and the television networks were broadcasting again, the official stories—power outages.

It was a farce, everyone knew it. Those outside of China would discuss it in depth, non-stop, until the next global crisis came along, then it would become a footnote in a colorful Chinese history.

As Acton's mind flashed back over the events, the images, it was a horror he couldn't yet fathom. The horrors of the teenagers crushed under the treads of tanks, the indiscriminate killing of civilians, the battles waged between fellow soldiers, one side fighting for a red flag, the other for a gold, the meaning of the colors lost on their adherents.

And the heroism, the selflessness, the acts that stood out above and beyond the call of duty, that would never be known. A US vet rushing to provide first aid to a stranger, a British professor standing down a column of tanks, a Chinese police officer handing his children over to strangers, trusting the basic goodness of people, while he tried to save his country.

The memories would be there, and Acton swore that history wouldn't forget the Qing Rebellion.

Harvard University, Cambridge, Massachusetts
One week later

"Of course I was saddened to hear of my father's death. It's my feeling he was framed by those who perpetrated these events. I know my father, or rather, I knew my father. I knew him well. He loved China, he loved his Party. There is no way he would have been involved in this willingly."

"But what of the broadcast?"

"Coerced of course."

"You don't expect us to believe that, do you?"

Bo Shan smiled at the interviewer from CNN. His impudence was intolerable, but tolerate it he must, for he had to get through these coming days alive, and in the public eye of the world. He was fortunate he was attending school in America, otherwise he would be dead already. He had received word that his mother had killed herself in prison, something he wasn't sure was true or not. He didn't doubt she was dead, he just didn't believe it was by her own hand.

And his darling half-sister, killed in a car accident when she ran a red light.

Yet she didn't drive.

The regime was cleaning up the mess his father had left, but if he played his cards right, he might just survive long enough for them to decide he was too public a target to eliminate.

"Of course I do." Bo Shan stood, and removed the microphone from his collar. "Now, if you'll excuse me, I have classes to attend."

He shook hands with the interviewer, then the producer, and left the room given to them by the Harvard administration to try and minimize the impact on student life by the suddenly very public international student they found themselves hosting.

Shan returned to his dorm room and closed the door, dropping on his bed, exhausted. Six interviews, non-stop. He folded his hands behind his head and stared at the ceiling, his chest tight with the thought of his father, mother, and sister, dead.

He peered through the gold and blue of the flag pinned to his ceiling over his bed, and into the Heavens, solemnly promising to one day fulfill the legacy handed down over generations, and once again claim the throne of China in the name of the Qing Dynasty.

It isn't over, my Emperor.

ACKNOWLEDGEMENTS

The spark for this book came from a scene I had written for the end of Broken Dove. It was this great action sequence with the Order of Mary being taken out by snipers as James Acton stood by, helpless. I ended up cutting the scene for reasons that made sense at the time, and still do, but this incredible vision of bodies skidding along the pavement wouldn't leave me, and I knew I had to use it at some point.

Flags of Sin was that opportunity.

I'd like to give a special thanks to two people who helped me with this book. Li Ching and Phoebe Jiang. They provided many of the fictional names in this book saving me having to research a set of names for a culture I knew little about. Any mistakes are mine alone.

And speaking of names, this book contains many elements taken straight from the history books. Many of the names are real, the places are real, the events are real. The history is fascinating, and if you research it a little yourself, you may be surprised at how much of this novel is based upon reality.

As usual I'd like to thank my wife, daughter and parents for their help and support, as well as my friends, and you the reader. I look forward to sharing the next James Acton adventure with you soon.

ABOUT THE AUTHOR

J. Robert Kennedy is the author of eight international best sellers, including the smash hit James Acton Thrillers series, the first installment of which, The Protocol, has been on the best sellers list since its release, including a three month run at number one. In addition to the other novels from this series, Brass Monkey, Broken Dove and The Templar's Relic (also a number one best seller), he has written the international best sellers Depraved Difference, Tick Tock, The Redeemer and The Turned. Robert spends his time in Ontario, Canada with his family.

Visit Robert's website at www.jrobertkennedy.com for the latest news and contact information.

J. ROBERT KENNEDY

The Protocol

A James Acton Thriller

Book #1

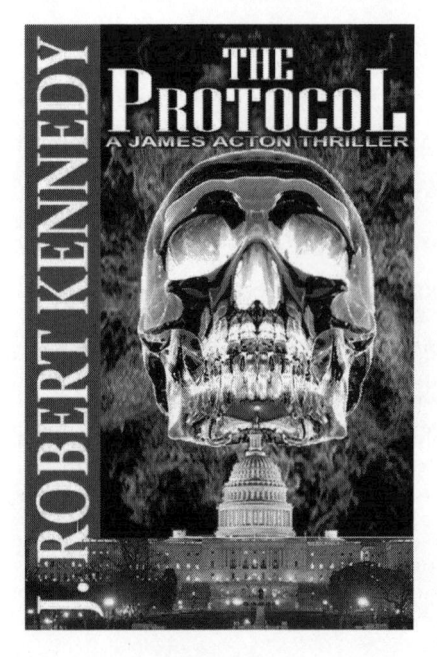

For two thousand years the Triarii have protected us, influencing history from the crusades to the discovery of America. Descendent from the Roman Empire, they pervade every level of society, and are now in a race with our own government to retrieve an ancient artifact thought to have been lost forever.

Caught in the middle is archaeology professor James Acton, relentlessly hunted by the elite Delta Force, under orders to stop at nothing to possess what he has found, and the Triarii, equally determined to prevent the discovery from falling into the wrong hands.

With his students and friends dying around him, Acton flees to find the one person who might be able to help him, but little does he know he may actually be racing directly into the hands of an organization he knows nothing about...

FLAGS OF SIN

Brass Monkey
A James Acton Thriller
Book #2

A nuclear missile, lost during the Cold War, is now in play--the most public spy swap in history, with a gorgeous agent the center of international attention, triggers the end-game of a corrupt Soviet Colonel's twenty five year plan. Pursued across the globe by the Russian authorities, including a brutal Spetsnaz unit, those involved will stop at nothing to deliver their weapon, and ensure their pay day, regardless of the terrifying consequences.

When Laura Palmer confronts a UNICEF group for trespassing on her Egyptian archaeological dig site, she unwittingly stumbles upon the ultimate weapons deal, and becomes entangled in an international conspiracy that sends her lover, archeology Professor James Acton, racing to Egypt with the most unlikely of allies, not only to rescue her, but to prevent the start of a holy war that could result in Islam and Christianity wiping each other out.

From the bestselling author of Depraved Difference and The Protocol comes Brass Monkey, a thriller international in scope, certain to offend some, and stimulate debate in others. Brass Monkey pulls no punches in confronting the conflict between two of the world's most powerful, and divergent, religions, and the terrifying possibilities the future may hold if left unchecked.

FLAGS OF SIN

Broken Dove
A James Acton Thriller
Book #3

With the Triarii in control of the Roman Catholic Church, an organization founded by Saint Peter himself takes action, murdering one of the new Pope's operatives. Detective Chaney, called in by the Pope to investigate, disappears, and, to the horror of the Papal staff sent to inform His Holiness, they find him missing too, the only clue a secret chest, presented to each new pope on the eve of their election, since the beginning of the Church.

Interpol Agent Reading, determined to find his friend, calls Professors James Acton and Laura Palmer to Rome to examine the chest and its forbidden contents, but before they can arrive, they are intercepted by an organization older than the Church, demanding the professors retrieve an item stolen in ancient Judea in exchange for the lives of their friends.

All of your favorite characters from The Protocol return to solve the most infamous kidnapping in history, against the backdrop of a two thousand year old battle pitting ancient foes with diametrically opposed agendas.

J. ROBERT KENNEDY

From the internationally bestselling author of Depraved Difference and The Protocol comes Broken Dove, the third entry in the smash hit James Acton Thrillers series, where J. Robert Kennedy reveals a secret concealed by the Church for almost 1200 years, and a fascinating interpretation of what the real reason behind the denials might be.

FLAGS OF SIN

The Templar's Relic
A James Acton Thriller
Book #4

The Church Helped Destroy the Templars. Will a twist of fate let them get their revenge 700 years later?

The Vault must be sealed, but a construction accident leads to a miraculous discovery--an ancient tomb containing four Templar Knights, long forgotten, on the grounds of the Vatican. Not knowing who they can trust, the Vatican requests Professors James Acton and Laura Palmer examine the find, but what they discover, a precious Islamic relic, lost during the Crusades, triggers a set of events that shake the entire world, pitting the two greatest religions against each other.

Join Professors James Acton and Laura Palmer, INTERPOL Agent Hugh Reading, Scotland Yard DI Martin Chaney, and the Delta Force Bravo Team as they race against time to defuse a worldwide crisis that could quickly devolve into all-out war.

At risk is nothing less than the Vatican itself, and the rock upon which it was built.

From J. Robert Kennedy, the author of six international bestsellers including Depraved Difference and The Protocol, comes The Templar's Relic, the fourth entry in the smash hit James Acton Thrillers series, where once again Kennedy takes history and twists it to his own ends, resulting in a heart pounding thrill ride filled with action, suspense, humor and heartbreak.

Flags of Sin
A James Acton Thriller
Book #5

Archaeology Professor James Acton simply wants to get away from everything, and relax. A trip to China seems just the answer, and he and his fiancée, Professor Laura Palmer, are soon on a flight to Beijing.

But while boarding, they bump into an old friend, Delta Force Command Sergeant Major Burt Dawson, who surreptitiously delivers a message that they must meet the next day, for Dawson knows something they don't.

China is about to erupt into chaos.

Foreign tourists and diplomats are being targeted by unknown forces, and if they don't get out of China in time, they could be caught up in events no one had seen coming.

J. Robert Kennedy, the author of eight international best sellers, including the smash hit James Acton Thrillers, takes history once again and turns it on its head, sending his reluctant heroes James Acton and Laura Palmer into harm's way, to not only save themselves, but to try and save a country from a century old conspiracy it knew nothing about.

J. ROBERT KENNEDY

The Turned

Zander Varga, Vampire Detective

Book #1

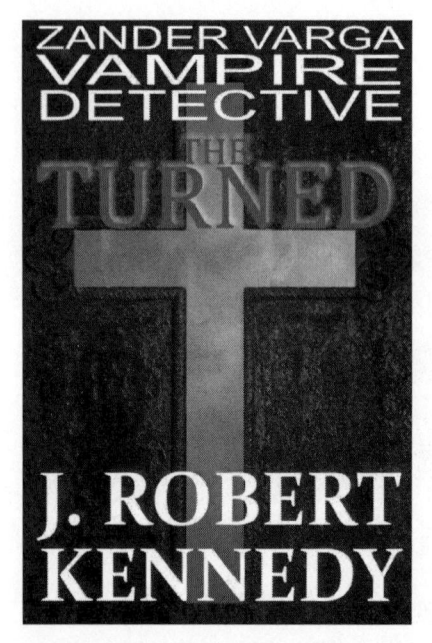

Zander has relived his wife's death at the hands of vampires every day for almost three hundred years, his perfect memory a curse of becoming one of The Turned—infecting him their final heinous act after her murder.

Nineteen year-old Sydney Winter knows Zander's secret, a secret preserved by the women in her family for four generations. But with her mother in a coma, she's thrust into the front lines, ahead of her time, to fight side-by-side with Zander.

And she wouldn't change a thing.

She loves the excitement, she loves the danger.

And she loves Zander.

But it's a love that will have to go unrequited, because Zander has only one thing on his mind. And it's been the same thing for over two hundred years.

Revenge.

But today, revenge will have to wait, because Zander Varga, Private Detective, has a new case. A woman's husband is missing. The police aren't interested. But Zander is. Something doesn't smell right, and he's determined to find out why.

FLAGS OF SIN

From J. Robert Kennedy, the internationally bestselling author of The Protocol and Depraved Difference, comes his sixth novel, The Turned, a terrifying story that in true Kennedy fashion takes a completely new twist on the origin of vampires, tying it directly to a well-known moment in history. Told from the perspective of Zander Varga and his assistant, Sydney Winter, The Turned is loaded with action, humor, terror and a centuries long love that must eventually be let go.

J. ROBERT KENNEDY

Depraved Difference
A Detective Shakespeare Mystery
Book #1

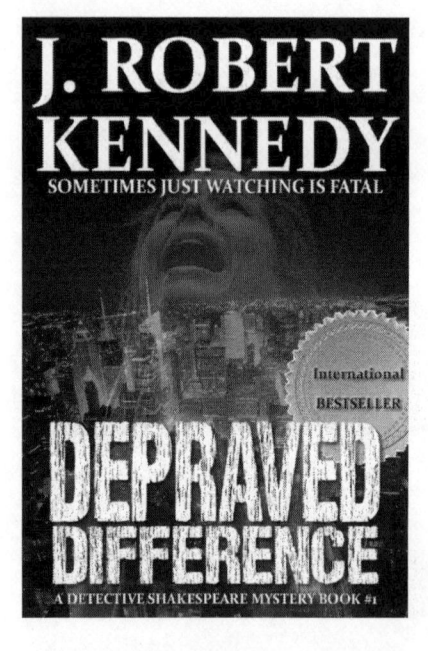

Would you help, would you run, or would you just watch?

When a young woman is brutally assaulted by two men on the subway, her cries for help fall on the deaf ears of onlookers too terrified to get involved, her misery ended with the crushing stomp of a steel-toed boot. A cellphone video of her vicious murder, callously released on the Internet, its popularity a testament to today's depraved society, serves as a trigger, pulled a year later, for a killer.

Emailed a video documenting the final moments of a woman's life, entertainment reporter Aynslee Kai, rather than ask why the killer chose her to tell the story, decides to capitalize on the opportunity to further her career. Assigned to the case is Hayden Eldridge, a detective left to learn the ropes by a disgraced partner, and as videos continue to follow victims, he discovers they were all witnesses to the vicious subway murder a year earlier, proving sometimes just watching is fatal.

From the author of The Protocol and Brass Monkey, Depraved Difference is a fast-paced murder suspense novel with enough laughs, heartbreak, terror and twists to keep you on the edge of your seat, then

FLAGS OF SIN

knock you flat on the floor with an ending so shocking, you'll read it again just to pick up the clues.

J. ROBERT KENNEDY

Tick Tock

A Detective Shakespeare Mystery

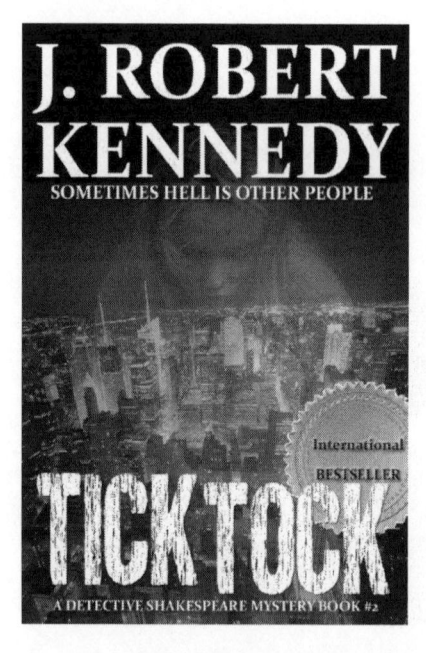

Book #2

Crime Scene tech Frank Brata digs deep and finds the courage to ask his colleague, Sarah, out for coffee after work. Their good time turns into a nightmare when Frank wakes up the next morning covered in blood, with no recollection of what happened, and Sarah's body floating in the tub. Determined not to go to prison for a crime he's horrified he may have committed, he scrubs the crime scene clean, and, tormented by text messages from the real killer, begins a race against the clock to solve the murder before his own co-workers, his own friends, solve it first, and find him guilty.

Billionaire Richard Tate is the toast of the town, loved by everyone but his wife. His plans for a romantic weekend with his mistress ends in disaster, waking the next morning to find her murdered, floating in the tub. After fleeing in a panic, he returns to find the hotel room spotless, and no sign of the body. An envelope found at the scene contains not the expected blackmail note, but something far more sinister.

Two murders, with the same MO, targeting both the average working man, and the richest of society, sets a rejuvenated Detective Shakespeare, and his new reluctant partner, Amber Trace, after a murderer whose motivations are a mystery, and who appears to be aided by the very people they would least expect—their own.

Tick Tock, Book #2 in the internationally bestselling Detective Shakespeare Mysteries series, picks up right where Depraved Difference left off, and asks a simple question: What would you do? What would you do if you couldn't prove your innocence, but knew you weren't capable of murder? Would you hide the very evidence that might clear you, or would you turn yourself in and trust the system to work?

From the internationally bestselling author of The Protocol and Brass Monkey comes the highly anticipated sequel to the smash hit Depraved Difference, Tick Tock. Filled with heart pounding terror and suspense, along with a healthy dose of humor, Tick Tock's twists will keep you guessing right up to the terrifying end.

J. ROBERT KENNEDY

The Redeemer

A Detective Shakespeare Mystery

Book #3

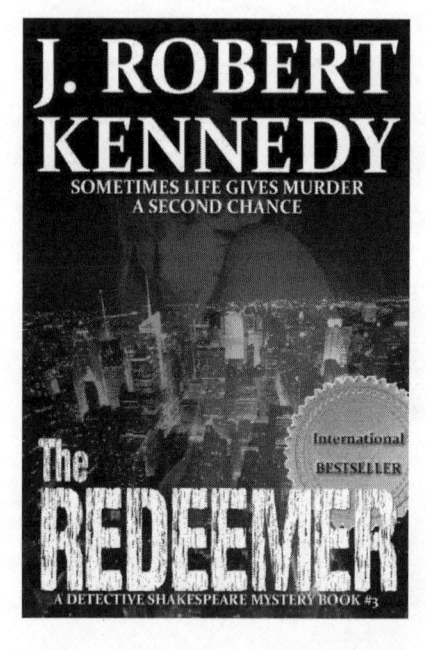

Sometimes Life Gives Murder a Second Chance

It was the case that destroyed Detective Justin Shakespeare's career, beginning a downward spiral of self-loathing and self-destruction lasting half a decade. And today things are only going to get worse. The Widow Rapist is free on a technicality, and it is up to Detective Shakespeare and his partner Amber Trace to find the evidence, five years cold, to put him back in prison before he strikes again.

But Shakespeare and Trace aren't alone in their desire for justice. The Seven are the survivors, avowed to not let the memories of their loved ones be forgotten. And with the release of the Widow Rapist, they are determined to take justice into their own hands, restoring balance to a flawed system.

At stake is a second chance, a chance at redemption, a chance to salvage a career destroyed, a reputation tarnished, and a life diminished.

A chance brought to Detective Shakespeare whether he wants it or not.

A chance brought to him by The Redeemer.

FLAGS OF SIN

From J. Robert Kennedy, the author of seven international bestsellers including Depraved Difference and The Protocol, comes the third entry in the acclaimed Detective Shakespeare Mysteries series, The Redeemer, a dark tale exploring the psyches of the serial killer, the victim, and the police, as they all try to achieve the same goals.

Balance. And redemption.

Printed in Great Britain
by Amazon.co.uk, Ltd.,
Marston Gate.